I WISH SOMEONE WERE WAITING FOR ME SOMEWHERE

Born in 1970, Anna Gavalda was a teacher whose collection of stories, *I Wish Someone Were Waiting For Me Somewhere*, shot her to fame in her native France. *Hunting and Gathering* (*Ensemble, c'est tout*) has sold over a million copies in France, has been made into a film starring Audrey Tautou and is a bestseller in several countries. Gavalda's work, including *Someone I Loved*, has been translated into thirty-six languages. The mother of two young children, she lives and writes just outside Paris.

ANNA GAVALDA

I Wish Someone Were Waiting For Me Somewhere

And

Someone I loved

TRANSLATED FROM THE FRENCH BY
Karen L. Marker and
Catherine Evans

VINTAGE BOOKS
London

Published by Vintage 2008

2 4 6 8 10 9 7 5 3 1

I Wish Someone Were Waiting For Me Somewhere was first published in France as *Je voudrais que quelqu'un m'attende quelque part* by Le Dilettante in 1999
Someone I Loved was first published in France as *Je l'aimais* by Le Dilettante in 2002

First published in Great Britain in 2008 by Vintage

Random House, 20 Vauxhall Bridge Road,
London SW1V 2SA

www.vintage-books.co.uk

Addresses for companies within The Random House Group Limited can be found at:
www.randomhouse.co.uk/offices.htm

The Random House Group Limited Reg. No. 954009

A CIP catalogue record for this book
is available from the British Library

ISBN 9780099506010

The Random House Group Limited supports The Forest Stewardship Council (FSC), the leading international forest certification organisation. All our titles that are printed on Greenpeace approved FSC certified paper carry the FSC logo. Our paper procurement policy can be found at
www.rbooks.co.uk/environment

Mixed Sources
Product group from well-managed
forests and other controlled sources
www.fsc.org Cert no. TT-COC-2139
© 1996 Forest Stewardship Council

Typeset by SX Composing DTP, Rayleigh, Essex
Printed and bound in Great Britain by
Cox & Wyman Ltd, Reading, Berkshire

Contents

I Wish Someone Were Waiting

For Me Somewhere

For my sister Marianne.

Courting Rituals of the Saint-Germain-des-Prés

Saint-Germain-des-Prés? . . . I know what you're going to say: 'God, that whole Left Bank thing is such a cliché. Françoise Sagan did it long before you – and *sooo* much better! Haven't you read *Bonjour Tristesse*!?'

I know.

But what do you expect? . . . I'm not sure any of this would've happened to me on Boulevard de Clichy or in some other part of Paris. That's just the way it is. *C'est la vie*.

So keep your thoughts to yourself and hear me out, because something tells me this story's going to amuse you.

You love this kind of sentimental fluff – having someone make your heart beat faster with these evenings full of promise, these men who want you to think they're single and a little unhappy.

I know you love it. It's perfectly normal. Still, you can't read Harlequin romances while you're sitting at Café Lipp or Deux Magots. No, of course you can't.

So, this morning, I passed a man on Boulevard Saint-Germain.

I was going up the street and he was coming down it. We were on the even-numbered side, which is more elegant.

I saw him coming from a distance. I don't know just what it was, maybe the nonchalant way he walked, or the flaps of his coat swinging casually out in front of him . . . anyhow, I was twenty metres away and I already knew I couldn't go wrong.

Sure enough, when he passes, I see him look at me. I shoot him a mischievous smile – kind of like one of Cupid's arrows, only more discreet.

He smiles back.

I keep walking, still smiling, and think of Baudelaire's *To a Passerby*. (What with that reference to Sagan earlier, by now you must have realized I'm what they call the literary type!) I slow down, trying to remember the lines of the poem . . . *Tall, slender, in deep mourning* . . . after that I don't know what . . . then . . . *A woman passed, with a sumptuous hand, raising, dangling the embroidered hem* . . . and at the end . . . *O you whom I had loved, O you who knew it.*

That gets me every time.

And during all this, pure and simple, I can sense the gaze of my Saint Sebastian (a reference to the arrow, see? stay with me, okay?!) still on my back. It warms my shoulder blades deliciously, but I'd rather die than turn around. That would ruin the poem.

I'd stopped at the curb up by rue des Saints-Pères,

watching the stream of cars for a chance to cross.

For the record: No self-respecting Parisian woman on Boulevard Saint-Germain would ever cross at the crossing when the traffic light is red. A self-respecting Parisian woman watches the stream of cars and steps out, fully aware of the risk she's taking.

To die for the window display at Paule Ka. Delicious.

I'm finally stepping out when a voice holds me back. I'm not going to say, 'a warm, virile voice' just to make you happy, because that's not how it was. Just a voice.

'Excuse me . . .'

I turn around. And who's there? . . . Why, my scrumptious prey from a minute ago.

I might as well tell you right now, from that moment on: screw Baudelaire.

'I was wondering if you'd like to have dinner with me tonight. . . .'

In my head, I think, 'How romantic . . .' But I answer:

'That's a little fast, don't you think?'

Without missing a beat, he says (and I swear this is the truth):

'Well, yes, I'll grant you that. But when I saw you walking away, I said to myself, "This is ridiculous. Here's this woman I pass in the street. I smile at her, she smiles at me, we brush past one another, and we're about to lose each other. . . . It's ridiculous – no, really, it's absurd." '

'. . .'

'What do you think? Does that seem like total nonsense to you, what I just said?'

'No, no, not at all.'

I was beginning to feel a little uneasy. . . .

'Well, then? . . . What do you say? Let's say we meet here, tonight, at nine o'clock? Right at this spot.'

Get hold of yourself, girl. If you're going to have dinner with every man you smile at, you'll never get out of the starting gate. . . .

'Give me one good reason to say yes.'

'One good reason . . . God . . . that's hard. . . .'

I watch him, amused.

And then, without warning, he takes my hand. 'I think I've found a more or less suitable reason. . . .'

He passes my hand over his scruffy cheek.

'One good reason. There: Say yes so I'll have a reason to shave. . . . You know, I think I look a lot better when I've shaved.'

And he gives me back my arm.

'Yes,' I say.

'Good, then we're on! Can I walk you across the street? I don't want to lose you now.'

This time I'm the one watching him walk off. He must be stroking his cheeks like a guy who's struck a good deal. . . .

I'm sure he's enormously pleased with himself. He should be.

Late afternoon and a little nervous, I have to admit.

Beaten at my own game. Should've read the rule book.

A little nervous, like a debutante having a bad-hair day.

A little nervous, like someone on the threshold of a love story.

At work, I answer the phone, I send faxes, I finish a mock-up for the photo researcher (what did you expect . . . a pretty, vivacious girl who sends faxes from Saint-Germain-des-Prés works in publishing, naturally . . .).

The tips of my fingers are ice-cold and everyone has to tell me everything twice.

Breathe, girl, breathe. . . .

At dusk, the street is quieter and the cars all have their headlights on.

The café tables are being brought in from the pavements. There are people on the church square waiting to meet up with friends, and at the Beauregard people are lining up to see the latest Woody Allen film.

I don't want to be the first one there. It wouldn't be

right. In fact, I decide to go a little late. Better to make him want me a little.

So I go and have a little pick-me-up to get the blood flowing back to my fingers.

Not at the Deux Magots, it's a little uncouth in the evenings — no one but fat American women on the lookout for the ghost of Simone de Beauvoir. I take rue Saint-Benoît. The Chiquito will do just fine.

I push the door open, and right away there's the smell of beer and stale tobacco . . . the ding ding of the pinball machine . . . the hieratic bar owner with her dyed hair and nylon blouse, support bra showing . . . the sound of the Vincennes night race playing in the background . . . some builders in stained overalls, putting off the hour of solitude or the old ball and chain . . . and the old regulars, with yellowed fingers, annoying everyone with their rents that have been fixed since '48. Bliss.

The men at the bar turn around from time to time and giggle among themselves like a bunch of schoolboys. My legs are in the aisle. They're very long. The aisle is kind of narrow and my skirt is very short. I see their stooped backs jiggling in fits and jerks.

I smoke a cigarette, sending the smoke out far in front of me. I stare off into space. Beautiful Day has won in the final straight, ten-to-one odds, I learn.

I remember I've got *Kennedy and Me* in my bag, and

I wonder if I wouldn't be better off staying here.

Salt pork with lentils and a half pitcher of rosé . . . wouldn't that be nice. . . .

But I pull myself together. You're there, over my shoulder, hoping for love (or less? or more? or not exactly?) with me, and I'm not going to leave you stranded with the owner of the Chiquito. That would be a little harsh.

I go out, cheeks rosy, and the cold whips my legs.

He's there, at the corner of rue des Saint-Pères, waiting for me. He sees me and walks over.

'I was worried – I was afraid you wouldn't come. I saw my reflection in a window, and I couldn't help but admire my cheeks, all nice and smooth. So I was worried.'

'I'm sorry. I was waiting for the end of the Vincennes race and I lost track of time.'

'Who won?'

'Do you bet?'

'No.'

'Beautiful Day.'

'Of course. I should've known.' He smiles, taking my arm.

We walk in silence as far as rue Saint-Jacques. From time to time, he steals a look at me, examining my profile, but I know what he's really wondering just then is whether I'm wearing tights or stockings.

Patience, my good man, patience. . . .

★

'I'm going to take you to a place I really like.'

I can picture it now . . . the kind of place where the waiters are relaxed but obsequious, smiling at him with a knowing air: 'Good eeevening, monsieur . . . (*there she is then, the latest . . . you know, I liked the brunette from last time better . . .*) . . . the little table in the back as usual, monsieur?' . . . bowing as he shows the way (. . . *but where does he dig up all these babes? . . .*), '. . . May I take your coats? Veeery well.'

He digs them up in the street, stupid.

But it's nothing like that.

He holds the door, letting me lead the way into a little wine bistro, and a bored-looking waiter asks us if we smoke. That's all.

He hung our things on a coat rack. In the half second he paused when he caught sight of the round softness of my cleavage, I knew he didn't regret the little nick he'd given himself under the chin earlier, when his hands betrayed him while he was shaving.

We drank extraordinary wine out of fat wine glasses. We ate relatively subtle things, conceived precisely so as not to spoil the aroma of our nectars.

A bottle of Côte de Nuits, Gevrey-Chambertin 1986. Baby Jesus in velvet britches.

The man sitting across from me crinkles his eyes as he drinks.

I'm getting to know him better now.

He's wearing a grey cashmere turtleneck sweater. An old one. It's got elbow patches and a small tear near the right wrist. His twentieth birthday present, maybe . . . I can just see his mother, troubled by his disappointed pout, telling him, 'You won't be sorry, go ahead, try it on . . .' as she kisses him and strokes his back.

His jacket is unpretentious – it looks like any old tweed – but, as it's me and my lynx eyes, I can tell it's tailor-made. At Old England, the labels are bigger when the merchandise goes out straight from the Capucines workshops, and I saw the label when he leaned down to pick up his napkin.

His napkin that he'd dropped on purpose in order to settle once and for all this question of stockings, or not, I imagine.

He talks to me about a lot of things but never about himself. He always has a little trouble holding on to his train of thought when I let my fingers trail across my neck. He says, 'And you?' and I don't ever talk about myself, either.

As we wait for dessert, my foot touches his ankle.

He puts his hand on mine and pulls it back suddenly because the sorbets have arrived.

He says something, but his words don't make a sound and I don't hear anything.

We're all worked up.

★

Horrors. His mobile phone just rang.

As though they were one, all eyes in the restaurant fix on him as he deftly switches it off. He's certainly just wasted a lot of very good wine. Half-gulped mouthfuls caught in rasping throats. People choking, their fingers clenching knife handles or the creases of starched napkins.

Those damn things. There always has to be one, no matter where, no matter when.

The boor.

He's embarrassed. He's suddenly a little warm in his mummy's cashmere.

He nods his head at this group and that, as though to express his dismay. He looks at me and his shoulders have slumped a little.

'I'm sorry. . . .' He smiles at me again, but it's less self-assured, you could say.

I tell him, 'It's no big deal. It's not like we're at the cinema. Someday I'm going to kill someone. Some man or woman who answers the phone in the middle of the show. When you read it in the news reports, you'll know it was me. . . .'

'I will.'

'You read the news reports?'

'No. But I'm going to start, now that I have a chance of finding you there.'

★

The sorbets were, how should I put it . . . delicious.

Reinvigorated, my prince charming came to sit next to me when the coffee was served.

So close that now he's sure: I'm wearing stockings. He felt the little hook at the top of my thigh.

I know that at that moment, he doesn't know where he lives anymore.

He lifts my hair and kisses my neck, in the little hollow spot at the nape.

He whispers into my ear that he loves Boulevard Saint-Germain, he loves burgundy and blackcurrant sorbets.

I kiss his little cut. After all the time I've waited for this moment, I really get into it.

The coffee, the bill, the tip, our coats, all that is just details, details, details. Details that get in our way.

Our hearts are slamming against our chests.

He hands me my black coat and then . . .

I admire the work of the artist, hats off, it's very discreet, barely noticeable, it's very well calculated and perfectly executed: in placing the coat on my bare shoulders, proffered to him and soft as silk, he finds the half second necessary and the perfect tilt toward the inside pocket of his jacket to glance at the message screen on his mobile.

★

I come to my senses. All at once.

Traitor.

Ingrate.

What in heaven's name were you thinking?!

What could possibly have distracted you when my shoulders were so round and warm and your hand was so close!?

What business was more important than my breasts offered to your view?

How could you let yourself be sidetracked while I was waiting for your breath on my back?

Couldn't you have waited to mess with the damn thing later, after you'd made love to me?

I button my coat all the way up.

In the street, I'm cold, I'm tired, and I feel sick.

I ask him to walk me to the nearest taxi stand.

He's in a panic.

Call 999, buddy, you've got what you need.

But no. He's a stoic.

As if nothing has happened. As in, I'm walking a good friend to her taxi, I'm rubbing her sleeves to warm her, and I'm chatting about the Paris night.

Classy almost to the end, I have to grant him that.

Before I climb into a black Mercedes taxi with Val-de-Marne plates, he says:

'But . . . we'll see each other again, won't we? I

don't even know where you live. . . . Give me something, an address, a phone number. . . .'

He tears a scrap of paper out of his diary and scribbles
some numbers.

'Take this. The first number, that's home, the
second, that's my mobile, you can reach me there
anytime. . . .'

That much I'd figured out.

'Don't hesitate, no matter when, okay? . . . I'll be
waiting to hear from you.'

I ask the driver to let me out at the top of the
boulevard. I need to walk.

I kick some imaginary tin cans.

I hate mobile phones, I hate Sagan, I hate
Baudelaire and all those charlatans.   ·

I hate my pride.

Pregnant

They're nuts, these women who want a baby. Nuts.

They barely even find out they're pregnant before they open wide the floodgates: of love, love, love.

They never close them again afterwards.

They're nuts.

She's like the rest of them. She thinks she's pregnant. She supposes. She imagines. She isn't sure-sure yet but almost.

She waits a few more days. To see.

She knows that a Predictor pharmacy test costs nine euros. She remembers from the first baby.

She says to herself: I'll wait two more days and I'll do the test.

Of course she doesn't wait. She says to herself: What's nine euros when maybe, just maybe, I'm pregnant? What's nine euros when in two minutes I could know?

Nine euros finally to throw open the floodgates because back there it's beginning to cave, it's boiling, it's swirling and it's making her a little sick to her stomach.

She runs to the pharmacy. Not her usual pharmacy, one more discreet where no one knows her. She assumes a detached air, a pregnancy test please, but her heart's already thumping.

She goes back to the house. She waits. She prolongs the exquisite agony. The test is there, in her bag on the table in the entryway, and as for her, she's a bit restless. She remains master of the situation. She folds laundry. She goes to the nursery to pick up her child. She chats with the other mothers. She laughs. She's in a good mood.

She makes the tea. She butters slices of bread. She really gets into it. She licks the spoon from the jam. She can't stop kissing her child. Everywhere. On the neck. On the cheeks. On the head.

He says stop, Mum, you're annoying me.

She gets him settled in front of a box of LEGO and she lingers a little while, still getting in his way.

She goes downstairs. She tries to ignore her bag but she can't. She stops. She picks up the test.

She loses patience with the packaging. She tears off the wrapper with her teeth. She'll read the instructions in a minute. She pees on the gadget. She puts its top back on, the way you cap a ballpoint pen. She holds it in her hand and it's all warm.

She sets it down somewhere.

She reads the instructions. You must wait four minutes and check the test windows. If both windows are pink, madame, your urine is full of hCG (human chorionic gonadotropin); if the two windows are pink, madame, you are pregnant.

Four minutes is such a long time. She drinks a cup of tea while she waits.

She sets the kitchen timer for a soft-boiled egg. Four minutes . . . there.

She doesn't fiddle with the test. She burns her lips on her tea.

She looks at the cracks in the kitchen and she wonders what on earth she's going to manage to make for dinner.

She doesn't wait the four minutes, anyway there's no reason to. You can already read the result. She's pregnant.

She knew it.

She flings the test to the very bottom of the rubbish bin. She arranges other empty packages on top to cover it completely. For the moment, it's her secret.

She feels better.

She breathes in deeply, she takes in air. She knew it.

It was just to be sure. That's that, the floodgates are open. Now she can think about other things.

She'll never think about anything else again.

Look at any pregnant woman: You think that she's crossing the street or that she's working or even that she's talking to you. Wrong. She's thinking about her baby.

She'll never admit it but not one minute goes by in

those nine months that she's not thinking about her baby.

Okay so she listens to you, but she doesn't really hear you. She nods her head but in truth, she couldn't care less.

She imagines it. Five millimetres: a grain of wheat. A centimetre: a pasta shell. Five centimetres: this rubber sitting on the desk. Twenty centimetres and four and a half months: her hand wide open.

There's nothing there. You can't see anything and yet she touches her belly often.

But no, it's not her belly that she touches, it's him. Exactly as she runs her fingers through the hair of the older one. Just the same.

She told her husband. She'd dreamed up a whole host of imaginative ways to announce the news.

Various settings, tones of voice, sound-the-trumpets . . . or then again not.

She told him one evening, in the dark, when their legs were intertwined but just for sleeping. She told him: I'm pregnant, and he kissed her ear. So much the better, he answered.

She told her other child too. You know there's a baby in Mummy's tummy. A little brother or a little sister like Pierre's mummy. And you'll be able to push the baby's pushchair, like Pierre.

He lifted her sweater and he said: Where is he? He's not there, the baby?

She scoured her bookshelves to find *Nine Months to Motherhood* by Laurence Pernoud. The book's a little worn – it served her sister-in-law and a girlfriend in the meantime.

Right away, she goes to the photos in the middle to look at them all over again.

The chapter is called 'Images of life before birth', from 'The ovum surrounded by spermatozoids' to 'Six months: he sucks his thumb.'

She scrutinises the itty-bitty hands, so transparent that you can see the blood vessels, and then the eyebrows – in some shots, you can already see the eyebrows.

Next she goes straight to the chapter 'When will I give birth?' There's a table that gives the estimated date of birth. ('Numbers in black: date of the first day of period. Numbers in colour: probable date of delivery.')

That gives us a baby on 29 November. What's 29 November? She raises her eyes and grabs hold of the post office calendar hanging next to the microwave . . . 29 November . . . Saint Saturninus.

Saturninus, now there's a name for you! she says to herself, smiling.

She sets the book down haphazardly. It's not likely she'll open it again. Because for the rest (how should you eat? backache, pregnancy-related breakouts, stretch marks, sexual relations, will your child be normal? how should you prepare for delivery? the truth about the pain, etc.), all that, she scoffs at a little, or rather, it doesn't interest her. She's confident.

In the afternoons she's asleep on her feet, and she eats huge Russian pickles at every meal.

Before the end of the third month comes the first compulsory visit to the gynaecologist. For the blood tests, the social security papers, the declaration of pregnancy to send to her employer.

She goes during her lunch hour. She's more emotional than she seems.

She sees the same doctor who brought her first child into the world.

They talk a little about this and that: and your husband, the job? and your work, it's coming along? and your children, school? and that other school, do you think?

Next to the examining table is the ultrasound. She settles in. The screen is still dark but she can't stop looking at it.

First and foremost, he has her listen to the beating of the invisible heart.

The sound is set fairly loud, and it resonates throughout the whole room:

boom-boom-boom-boom-boom-boom

What an idiot, she already has tears in her eyes.

And then he shows her the baby.

A tiny little fellow who moves his arms and his legs. Ten centimetres and forty-five grams. His spinal column is clearly visible, you could even count the vertebrae.

Her mouth must be wide open, but she doesn't say a thing.

The doctor makes jokes. He says: ha, I was sure of it, that shuts up even the biggest chatterboxes.

While she gets dressed, he puts together a little file with photos that came out of the machine. And a little later, when she's in her car, before she starts the engine, she'll spend a long time looking at these photos and while she's learning them by heart, you won't hear the sound of her breathing.

Weeks have passed and her belly has got bigger. Her breasts, too. Now, she wears a 36C. Unthinkable.

She went to a maternity shop to buy clothes that fit. She splurged. She chose a very pretty and rather expensive dress for her cousin's wedding in late August. A linen dress with little mother-of-pearl buttons all the way down. She hesitated for a long time because she's not sure she'll ever have another child. And then, obviously, it's a bit pricey. . . .

She mulls it over in the fitting room, she gets bogged down in calculations. When she comes back out, with the dress in her arms and hesitation on her face, the saleswoman says: go ahead, treat yourself! Okay, so you won't be able to wear it for long, but what a pleasure! . . . Besides, a pregnant woman should always have her way. She says it in a joking tone but all the same, she's a good saleswoman.

She thinks of that once she's in the street with the big impractical bag in her hand. She really has to pee. As usual.

Plus, it's an important wedding for her because her son is the ring bearer. It's stupid but it makes her really happy.

Another topic of infinite deliberations is the sex of the baby.

Should they, yes or no, ask whether it's a girl or a boy?

The fifth month is coming up and with it the second ultrasound, the one that tells all.

At work, she has a lot of irritating problems to solve and decisions to make every other minute.

She makes them. That's what she's paid for.

But this . . . she doesn't know.

For the first one, she'd wanted to know, it's true. But this time, she really couldn't care less if it's a girl or a boy. Really.

All right, she won't ask.

'You're sure?' said the doctor. She doesn't know anymore. 'Listen, I won't say anything and we'll see if you can see anything for yourself.'

He moves the transducer slowly over her gel-covered belly. Sometimes he stops, he takes measurements, he comments, sometimes he moves it quickly, smiling. Finally he says: okay, you can get back up.

'Well?' he asks.

She says that she has an inkling but she isn't sure. 'And what's your inkling?' Well . . . she thought she saw evidence of a little boy, didn't she? . . .

'Ah, I don't know,' he answers, making a teasing face. She wants to grab him by the shirt and shake him so that he'll tell, but no. It's a surprise.

In summer, a huge belly, it keeps you warm. Not to mention the nights. You sleep so badly, no position is comfortable. But fine.

The date of the wedding is approaching. Tension mounts in the family. She offers to take care of the bouquets. It's the perfect job for a cetaceous creature like her. They'll put her right in the middle of things, the boys will bring her whatever she needs and she'll make it all as beautiful as can be.

While she waits she runs to shoe shops looking for closed-toe white sandals. The bride wants to see them all wearing the same shoes. How practical. Impossible to find white sandals at the end of August. 'But madame, we're getting ready for back-to-school now.' Finally she finds something not very attractive and one size too big.

She looks at her big little boy posing proudly in front of the mirrors at the shop, with his wooden sword jammed into one of the belt loops of his Bermuda shorts, and his new shoes. For him they're intergalactic boots with laser buckles, beyond a shadow of a doubt. She thinks he's adorable with his hideous sandals.

Suddenly, she receives a good kick in the stomach. A kick from the inside.

She's felt jerks, jolts, and things inside but there, for the first time, it's plain and clear.

'. . . Madame? Madame? . . . Will that be all? . . .'

'Yes, yes of course, excuse me.'

'It's no problem, madame. You want a balloon, sweetie?'

On Sundays her husband potters around the house. He's fixing up a little bedroom in the space they used for a laundry room. Often, he asks his brother to lend him a hand. She's bought some beer and she's always scolding the little one so that he doesn't get underfoot.

Before going to bed she sometimes flips through decorating magazines to find ideas. Anyway, there's no rush.

They don't talk about the name because they don't really agree, and since they know very well that she'll have the last word . . . what's the point?

★

On Thursday, 20 August, she has to go to the six-monthly check-up. What a drag.

It's not very good timing, what with the wedding preparations. Especially since the bridal couple went to Rungis that same morning and brought back mountains of flowers. They requisitioned both bathtubs and the plastic kiddie pool for the occasion.

About two in the afternoon, she puts down her shears, she takes off her apron, and she tells them that the little one's sleeping in the yellow bedroom. If he wakes up before she gets back, could you give him a snack? No, no, she won't forget to pick up bread, superglue, and raffia.

After taking a shower, she slides her big belly behind the wheel of her car.

She clicks on the radio and tells herself that in the end, it's not so bad, this break, because a bunch of women sitting around a table with their hands busy, they'll soon be telling a lot of stories. Big ones and little ones, too.

In the waiting room, there are already two other ladies. The big game in these cases is always to try to guess by the shape of their bellies what month they're in.

She reads a *Paris Match* from the time of Moses, when Johnny Hallyday was still with Adeline.

When she goes in, it's a handshake, you're doing all right? Yes, thanks, and you? She puts down her bag and sits. He plunks her name into the computer. He knows now how many weeks of gestation she's at and everything that follows.

Then she gets undressed. He rolls out some paper on the table while she weighs herself and then he's going to take her blood pressure. He's going to do a quick 'check-up' ultrasound to see the heart. Once the examination's over, he'll go back to his computer to add a few things.

Gynaecologists have a trick of their own. When the woman has propped her heels in the stirrups, they ask a multitude of questions out of the blue so that she'll forget, if only for a moment, about being in such an immodest position.

Sometimes it works, a little bit, more often not.

In this case, he asks her if she's felt it move; she begins to answer that before yes but now less often, but she doesn't finish her sentence because she sees clearly that he's not listening. Apparently he's already understood. He fiddles with the buttons of the machine to put her off the scent but he's already understood.

He places the monitor in another position but his movements are so brusque and his face is so old all of a sudden. She lifts herself on her forearms and she's understood too but she says: What's going on?

He tells her 'Go and get dressed' as if he hadn't heard her and she asks again: What's going on? He answers: there's a problem, the foetus is no longer alive.

She gets dressed.

When she comes back to sit down, she's silent and her face doesn't show anything. He types a bunch of stuff on his keyboard and at the same time he makes some phone calls.

He tells her: 'We're about to spend some not-much-fun moments together.'

At the moment, she doesn't know what to make of a statement like that.

By 'some not-much-fun moments', maybe he meant the thousands of blood tests that would leave her arm a mess, or the ultrasound the next day, the images on the screen and all the measurements to understand what he would never understand. Unless 'not-much-fun' was the emergency delivery on Sunday night with the on-call doctor mildly annoyed to be woken up *again*.

Yes, that must be it, 'some not-much-fun moments', that must be giving birth in pain and without anaesthetic because it's too late. To be in so much pain that you throw up all over yourself instead of pushing like they tell you to. To see your husband powerless and so awkward as he caresses your hand and finally to push it out, this dead thing.

Then again, 'some not-very-fun moments' is to be stretched out the next day in the maternity ward with an empty belly and the sound of a crying baby in the room next door.

The only thing that she won't be able to figure out is why he said '*we* are about to spend some not-very-fun moments . . .'

For now, he continues to fill out her file, and in between clicks he talks about having the foetus dissected and analysed in Paris at the I-don't-know-what centre but she stopped listening to him some time ago.

He tells her, 'I admire your composure.' She doesn't answer.

She goes out by the little door at the back because she doesn't want to walk through the waiting room again.

She'll cry for a long time in her car but there's one thing she's sure of, she won't spoil the wedding. For the sake of the others, her grief can surely wait two days.

And that Saturday, she put on her linen dress with the little mother-of-pearl buttons.

She dressed her little boy and took his picture because she knows all too well that a Little Lord Fauntleroy outfit like that won't last long.

Before going to the church they stopped at the clinic so that she could take, under close supervision, one of those awful pills that force all babies out, wanted or not.

*

Anna Gavalda

She threw rice at the newlyweds and she walked down the well-raked gravel paths with a glass of champagne in her hand.

She raised her eyebrows when she saw her Little Lord Fauntleroy drinking cola straight from the bottle and she worried about the bouquets. She made small talk since this was the time and the place for it.

And the other woman came up just like that, out of nowhere, a ravishing young woman she didn't know, from the groom's side, no doubt.

In an act of total spontaneity, she placed her hands flat on her belly and said: 'May I? . . . They say it brings luck. . . .'

What did you want her to do? She tried to smile at her, of course.

This Man and This Woman

This man and this woman are in a foreign car. The car cost forty-nine thousand euros, but, strangely enough, what made the man hesitate at the dealership was mainly the cost of the registration and taxes.

The windscreen washer on the passenger side isn't working properly, and it's driving him crazy.

On Monday, he'll ask his secretary to call Salomon. For just a second he thinks about his secretary's breasts, which are very small. He's never slept with his secretaries. It's vulgar, and these days it could cost you some serious money. Anyway, he doesn't cheat on his wife anymore, not since the day he and Antoine Say entertained themselves during a round of golf by calculating just how much each of them would have to pay in alimony.

They're headed to their place in the country – a very pretty farmhouse, out near Angers. Lovely proportions.

They bought it for next to nothing. The renovations, on the other hand . . .

There's panelling in every room, and a fireplace they'd had dismantled and then put back together, stone by stone, after they fell in love with it at an English antique shop. Every window's draped in heavy fabric, held in place with tiebacks. There's a totally modern kitchen, with damask dish towels and grey marble countertops . . . as many bathrooms as bedrooms . . . not much furniture, but all period pieces. On the walls are huge, gilded frames that overwhelm the nineteenth-century engravings they hold – mostly hunting scenes.

It's all kind of nouveau riche, but fortunately they don't realise it.

The man's in his weekend gear, old tweed trousers and a sky-blue cashmere turtleneck (a gift from his wife for his fiftieth birthday). His shoes are John Lobbs – nothing in the world would persuade him to change to another make. Obviously, his socks are made of lisle yarn and come up to his knees. Obviously.

He drives rather fast, lost in thought. When he gets there, he'll have to talk to the caretakers about the property, the housework, pruning the beeches, poaching . . . and he hates all that.

He hates it when he feels someone's taking him for a ride, and that's exactly what happens with those two, who start work Friday morning, dragging their feet, because they know the boss will be showing up that

night, and they have to give the impression they've
done something.

He ought to just get rid of them, but he really
doesn't have the time to deal with it at the moment.

He's tired. His partners annoy the crap out of him,
he almost never makes love to his wife anymore, his
windscreen is riddled with mosquitoes, and the washer
doesn't work properly on the passenger side.

The woman's name is Mathilde. She's pretty, but in
her face you can see all the things she's given up on in
life.

She's always known when her husband was cheating
on her, and she also knows that, if he doesn't do it
anymore, it's the same old story – money.

She's in the death seat. She's always very melan-
choly during these endless weekend drives to the
country and back.

She thinks about how she's never been loved, she
thinks about how she never had any children, she
thinks about the caretaker's little boy, Kevin, who's
going to be three in January. . . . Kevin, what a horrible
name. If she'd had a son, she'd have named him Pierre,
like her father. She remembers that awful scene when
she mentioned adoption. . . . But she also thinks about
the nice little green tailored suit she saw the other day
in the window at Cerruti's.

They're listening to the radio station FIP. It's good,

FIP: classical music that you can be proud of being able to appreciate, music from around the world that makes you feel you're open-minded, and short little news flashes that barely leave enough time for the misery to come rushing into the car.

They've just passed the motorway toll. They haven't exchanged a single word, and they still have a long way to go.

The Opel Touch

Just as you see me now, I'm walking down the rue Eugène-Gonon.

The whole deal.

What, no kidding? You don't know the rue Eugène-Gonon? Hold on, are you having me on?

The whole street's lined with these classic little stone-clad houses, with their little gardens and wrought-iron canopies. The famous rue Eugène-Gonon in Melun.

Oh, come on! You know, *Melun* . . . the place with the prison, the brie – its brie deserves to be better known – and the train crashes.

Melun.

Sixth zone on the Paris-area train network.

I take the rue Eugène-Gonon several times a day. Four in all.

I go to classes, I come back from classes, I eat, I go to classes, I come back from classes.

At the end of the day, I'm wiped out.

I know it doesn't seem that bad, but *you* try it. Take the rue Eugène-Gonon in Melun four times a day to go to law school so you can take exams for ten years in order to have a career you don't even want. . . . Years and years of civil law, penal law, course packs, articles, paragraphs, legal texts, you name it. And mind you, all for a career that already bores me.

Be honest. Admit that I've got good reason to be wiped out at the end of the day.

So anyway, as I was saying, I'm on trip number three. I've had lunch and once again I'm setting off with a determined step towards the law school, yippee. I light a cigarette. All right, I say to myself, last one.

I start to snigger under my breath. If that's not the thousandth last one this year . . .

I walk along past the little stone-clad houses. *Villa Marie-Thérèse, My Felicity, Sweet Nest.* It's spring and I'm starting to get seriously depressed. Not the big guns: crocodile tears, medication, loss of appetite and all that crap. Nothing like that.

It's just . . . this trek down the rue Eugène-Gonon four times a day. It wipes me out. Let those who are able to understand.

I don't see what that has to do with the springtime. . . .

Yeah, well. In the spring, you've got little birds squabbling among the poplar buds. At night, tomcats making an infernal racket, drakes chasing after ducks on the Seine, plus all the lovers. Don't tell me you don't see them, the lovers, they're everywhere. Never-ending kisses with lots of saliva, hard-ons under jeans, roaming hands and every bench occupied. It drives me crazy.

It drives me crazy. That's all.

You're jealous? You want some of it?

Me? Jealous? Want some of it? Nononono, come on . . . you've gotta be kidding.

(. . .)

Hmpphh, whatever. That's all I need is to be jealous of these little jerks who grate on everybody's nerves with their lust. Whatever.

(. . .)

Hell, yes, I'm jealous!!! What, like it's not obvious? You need glasses? You don't see that I'm so jealous it's killing me, you don't see that I need loooovvve.

You can't see that? Yeah, well, I wonder what's wrong with you. . . .

I'm like a character out of a Bretécher comic strip: a girl seated on a bench with a sign round her neck: 'I want love', and tears spouting like two fountains from either side of her eyes. I can see it now. What a sight.

Well, no, only now I'm not on rue Eugène-Gonon anymore (I have my dignity, after all), now I'm at Pramod.

Pramod's not hard to picture – they're everywhere. A department store, full of inexpensive clothes, mediocre quality . . . let's say passable, otherwise I might get fired.

It's my daily grind, my moola, my smokes, my espressos, my nights on the town, my silky lingerie, my Guerlain, my blusher splurges, my paperbacks, my flicks. Everything.

I hate working at Pramod, but without it? What would I do, wear stinking Gemey for ninety-five cents, rent movies at the Melun Video Club, and add the latest Jim Harrison to the suggestion book at the municipal library? No, thanks, I'd rather die. I'd rather work at Pramod.

And anyway, when I stop to think about it, I'd rather take on a bunch of pudgy women than the stench of deep-fat frying at McDonald's.

The problem is my co-workers. I know what you're going to say: Girl, the problem is always the co-workers.

Okay, but do you know Marilyne Merchandise? (No kidding, she's the manager of the Pramod in central Melun and her name's Merchandise. . . . Oh, destiny.)

No, of course you don't know her, and yet she's the most, she's the most . . . managerial of managers of all the Pramods in France. And vulgar too, really vulgar.

I can't begin to tell you. It's not so much her looks, although . . . her dark roots and the mobile on her hip kill me. . . . No, it's more a problem of the heart.

The vulgarity of the heart, that's an inexpressible thing.

Look there, how she speaks to her employees. It's the pits. Her upper lip is curling, she must think we're sooo, sooo stupid. For me, it's worse, I'm the brain. The one who makes fewer spelling errors than she does, and that really pisses her off.

'Your going to love our new summer fashions!'

Hold on, big girl . . . there's a problem.

No one ever taught you how to tell the difference between a possessive pronoun and a contraction? In your bleached little head you say to yourself, 'I'm or he's or she's going to love our new summer fashions.' See, it's not hard, you just put the noun and the verb together! Isn't that something!?

My, oh my, how she looks at me. Then she goes and redoes her sign:

'*You will* love our new summer fashions!' I gloat.

When she talks to me her lip stays in place, but it's killing her.

Note that aside from the energy spent managing my manager, I do all right.

I don't care what customer you give me, I'll dress her head to toe. Accessories included. Why? Because I look at her. Before I give her any advice, I look at her. I like looking at people. Especially women.

Even the ugliest ones, there's always something. At least the desire to be pretty.

'Marianne, I can't believe it, the summer bodysuits are still in the storeroom. You'd better go. . . .' You have to tell them everything, it's unbelievable. . . .

I'm going, I'm going. All the same.

I want love.

Saturday night, *zee Saturday night fever.*

The Milton is Melun's cowboy saloon; I'm with my girlfriends.

I'm glad they're here. They're pretty, they laugh a lot, and they know how to handle themselves.

I hear the screech of GTIs in the car park, the putt–ut–uh putt–ut–uh of undersized Harleys, and the click of Zippo lighters. Someone hands us cocktails on the house, but they're too sweet – they must have put in a ton of grenadine to keep down the costs on the good stuff. Plus, everyone knows, girls like grenadine. . . . But what the hell am I doing here? I'm a bundle of nerves. My eyes are stinging. Lucky me, I wear contacts, so with the smoke, go figure.

'Hi, Marianne, how are you?' asks a girl I knew in high school.

'Hi!' . . . *leaning forward for the four kisses* . . . 'All right.

Good to see you, it's been a while. . . . Where've you been?'

'You didn't hear? I was in the *States*. Get this, you'll never believe it, it was a hell of a deal. L.A., a mansion, you can't imagine. Swimming pool, Jacuzzi, a stunning view of the ocean. And get this, the best part, it was with hyper-cool people, not the usual uptight Americans you see. God, no, it was too much.'

She shakes her California highlights to show her immense nostalgia.

'You didn't run into George Clooney?'

'What . . . why do you ask?'

'No, no, never mind. I thought, to top it all off, you'd have met George Clooney, that's all.'

'You've got a problem you know,' she finishes, going off to romanticise her little au pair stint for the benefit of other, less candid souls.

Hey, look who's there . . . it's Buffalo Bill.

A skinny kid with a prominent Adam's apple and a little, meticulously maintained goatee – everything I go for – comes up to my breasts and tries to brush up against them.

The guy: 'Don't we know each other from somewhere?'

My breasts: '. . .'

The guy: 'Yes, of course! I remember now, weren't you at the Garage on Halloween?'

My breasts: '. . .'

The guy, not giving up: 'Are you French?' And, in English, *'Do you understand me?'*

My breasts: '. . .'

Eventually, Buffalo raises his head. Oh, look, what do you know? . . . I have a face.

He scratches his goatee in defeat (scritch scritch scritch) and seems plunged in deep thought.

'From where are you from?'

Wooowww, Buffalo! Vous parlez cowboy!

'From Melun, 4 Place de la Gare, and I might as well tell you right now, I haven't got a walkie-talkie stashed in my bra.'

Scritch scritch . . .

I have to go. I can't see a thing anymore. Fuck these contacts.

Plus, you're crude, girl.

I'm in front of the Milton, I'm cold, I'm crying like a baby, I wish I were anywhere but here, I wonder how the hell I'm going to get home. I look at the stars, and there aren't even any. So I cry harder.

In cases like this, when the situation is desperate, the smartest thing I can do . . . is call my sister.

Dring driiiinng driiinng . . .

'Hello . . .' (husky voice)

'Hey, it's Marianne.'

'What time is it? Where are you?' (irritated voice)

'I'm at the Milton, can you come and get me?'

'What happened? What's the matter?' (worried voice)

I repeat:

'Can you come and get me?'

Headlights flash at the far end of the car park.

'Come on, hon, get in,' says my sister.

'What are you doing in that old-lady night-gown?!!'

'I came as fast as I could, I'll have you know.'

'You came to the Milton in a see-through granny nightie!' I say, laughing my head off.

'First, I'm not getting out of the car like this, second, it's not see-through, it's lacework, didn't they teach you that at Pramod?'

'What if you run out of petrol? Not to mention, some of your old admirers are here. . . .'

'No way . . . where?' (interested)

'Look, is that "Teflon Pete" by any chance?'

'Move over a little. . . . Oh, yeah! You're right. . . . God, he's ugly, he's even uglier than before. What's he driving these days?'

'An Opel.'

'Oh! I see, "The Opel Touch", it's on the rear window.'

She looks at me, and we laugh like maniacs. We're together and we laugh:

1) at the good old days

2) at 'Teflon Pete' (because whatever else he didn't want to get attached)

3) at his customised Opel

4) at his fleece-covered steering wheel

5) at the Perfecto motorcycle jacket that he only wears at weekends, and at the impeccable crease in his 501 jeans that his mum achieves by bearing down really hard on the iron.

I feel better.

My sister, with her big yuppie car, leaves the Milton car park in a screech of tyres. Heads turn. She says, 'Jojo's going to have a fit, that ruins them. . . .'

She laughs.

I take out my contacts and tilt the seat back.

We go in on tiptoe because Jojo and the kids are sleeping.

My sister pours me a gin and tonic, without the Schweppes, and says:

'So what's up?'

So I tell her. But without getting my hopes up because my sister's not much of a psychologist.

I tell her that my heart is like a big empty sack. The sack's sturdy, it could hold a whole souk, and yet, there's nothing inside.

46

★

I say a sack, but I'm not talking about those pathetic little bags they have at the supermarket that always split open. My sack . . . at least the way I picture it . . . it looks more like one of those big square white-and-blue-striped contraptions that the big black mamas carry on top of their heads in Paris in the Barbès district.

'Oh well . . . we're in deep now,' my sister says as she pours us each another glass.

Amber

I've fucked thousands of girls and most of them, I don't even remember their faces.

I'm not saying that to be a smart-arse. The point where I'm at, with all the cash I'm making and all the arse-lickers I've got hanging around, you really think I need to run off at the mouth just for the hell of it?

I'm saying it because it's true. I'm thirty-eight years old and I've forgotten just about everything that's happened in my life. It's true of the girls and it's true of everything else.

I happened to come across an old magazine the other day, the kind fit to wipe your arse with, and I saw a picture of me with some bimbo on my arm.

So I read the caption and I learn that the girl in question is named Laetitia or Sonia or whatever, and I look at the picture again as if that's going to help, like I'll be able to say: 'Oh, yeah, of course, Sonia, the little brunette from the Villa Barclay, the one with all the piercings and the vanilla-scented perfume. . . .'

But no. I can't remember any of it.

In my head I keep repeating 'Sonia' like an idiot,

and I put down the magazine to look for a cigarette.

I'm thirty-eight years old and I'm well aware that my life is going up in fucking smoke. The ceiling is flaking off oh-so-gently. One scratch of the fingernail and entire weeks are gone. Seriously, the other day I heard someone talking about the Gulf War. I turned around and said:

'When was that, the Gulf War?'

'In 'ninety-one,' they answered, like I needed the *Britannica* for the details. . . . But the truth is, fuck it, that was the first time I'd heard anybody mention it.

The whole Gulf War, gone.

Never saw it. Never heard about it. A whole year that's now useless to me.

In 1991, I wasn't there.

In 1991, I was probably busy trying to find my veins and didn't notice there was a war. What the fuck, it doesn't matter. I'm talking about the Gulf War because it's a good example.

I forget just about everything.

Sorry, Sonia, but it's true. I don't remember you.

And then I met Amber.

All I have to do is say her name, and I feel good.

Amber.

The first time I saw her was at the recording studio on rue Guillaume Tell. We'd been in a bind all week and everyone was doing our heads in over money all because we were late.

You can't plan for everything. It just can't be done. Take us: When we paid a small fortune to bring that hotshot mixer over from the *States* to make all the fat cats at the record company happy, there's no way we could've known he would croak on us on the first track.

'The strain and the jet lag must not have agreed with him,' said the medic.

Obviously, that was a load of bullshit, jet lag had nothing to do with it.

The jerk just had eyes that were bigger than his stomach, and so much the worse for him. Now he looked like an arsehole with his contract 'to make the little *Frenchies* dance' . . .

That was a hellish time. I hadn't seen the light of day for weeks and I didn't dare touch my hands to my face because it felt like my skin was going to crack or split open or something.

In the end I couldn't even smoke anymore because my throat was too sore.

Fred was annoying the shit out of me going on about some friend of his sister's. Some chick photographer who wanted to go along on tour with me – as a freelancer, but not to sell the photos. Just for herself.

'Hey, Fred, give me a break about that. . . .'

'Wait, why would you give a fuck if I brought her

here one night, huh? Why would you give a fuck?'

'I don't like photographers, or artistic directors, or journalists – I don't like people getting in my way, and I don't like people looking at me. You can understand that, can't you?'

'Shit, chill out. Just one night, two minutes. You won't even have to talk to her, chances are you won't even see her. Shit, do it for me. Obviously you don't know my sister.'

Earlier I was telling you how I forget everything, but that, you see, no.

She came in through the little door that's on the right when you're looking at the mixing station. She looked apologetic, walking on tiptoe, and she was wearing a white tank top with narrow straps. From where I was, behind the glass, I didn't see her face right away but when she sat down, I caught a glimpse of her small little breasts, and already I wanted to touch them.

Later she smiled at me. Not like the girls who usually smile at me, because they're happy to see that I'm looking at them.

She just smiled at me, to make me happy. And the take that day seemed to last forever.

When I finally got out of my glass cage, she was gone.

I asked Fred:

'That your sister's friend?'

'Yeah.'

'What's her name?'

'Amber.'

'She leave?'

'I dunno.'

'Shit.'

'What?'

'Nothing.'

She came back on the last day. Paul Ackermann had arranged a little party at the studio – 'to celebrate your next gold disk,' he'd said, that arsehole. I had just come out of the shower – I was still bare-chested, rubbing my head with an oversized towel, when Fred introduced us.

I couldn't get a word out. It was like I was fifteen, and I let the towel drop to the floor.

She smiled at me again, just like before.

Pointing at a bass, she asked politely:

'So, is this your favourite guitar?'

And I couldn't figure out if the reason I wanted to kiss her was because she was so entirely clueless or because she asked nicely.

Everyone else just says 'hey, you' while cuffing me in the stomach. . . . From the president of the Republic down to the last arsehole, all of them, they all act as if we'd raised pigs together.

It's the scene that does it.

'Yes,' I told her, 'that's my favourite.'

And I looked around for something to wear.

We talked for a while but it was hard because Ackermann had invited some journalists. I should have known.

She asked me about the tour and I said 'yes' to everything she asked, looking at her breasts on the sly. Then she said good-bye and I looked everywhere for Fred, or Ackermann, or somebody, anybody. . . . I wanted to break somebody's neck because it was all boiling over inside.

There were ten dates to the tour, almost all of them outside France. We did two nights in Paris at the Cigale, and I get the rest all mixed up. We played Belgium, Germany, Canada, and Switzerland – but don't ask me in what order. I won't be able to give it to you.

Touring wears me out. I play my music, I sing, I try to stay *clean* (as much as I can), and I sleep in a Pullman.

Even if I start shitting gold I'll still go on the road with my band in an air-conditioned Pullman car. The day you see me take a plane without them and then shake their hands just before we go onstage, you let me know because when that day comes, it means I don't give a shit about anything here anymore and it's time for me to move on.

Amber came with us but I didn't know it at first.

She took her photos without anyone even noticing. She shared a room with the backup singers. You could hear them giggling in the hotel corridors sometimes when Jenny read their cards. Whenever I caught sight of her, I raised my head and tried to stand up straight. But in all those weeks, I never once went up to her.

I can't mix work and sex anymore. I'm too old.

The last night was a Sunday. We wanted to go out with a bang, so we were at Belfort doing a special concert for the tenth anniversary of Eurock Festival.

I sat down next to her at the farewell dinner.

It's like some kind of sacred thing . . . everyone respects it and keeps it just for us – the stage hands, the techies, the musicians, and everyone who helped us during the tour. It's not the time to let some starlet or small-time reporter give us shit, you know . . . even Ackermann wouldn't dare call Fred on his mobile to get the latest update or to ask about the takings.

I should probably also mention that, in general, it's pretty bad for our image.

Among ourselves, we refer to these little parties as shroom fests, and that about says it all.

Tons of stress melting away, the satisfaction of a job well done, all those reels snug in their cases, and my manager just beginning to smile for the first time in months . . . it's too much all at once, and it doesn't take much for it to get out of hand. . . .

★

At first I tried to get chatty with Amber, but then when I realised I was too far gone to fuck her decently, I let it go.

She didn't say a thing, but I know she knew exactly what was going on.

At one point, when I was in the bog at the restaurant, I stood in front of the mirror by the sinks and said her name slowly. Instead of taking a good deep breath and splashing some cold water on my face and going to tell her to her face: 'When I look at you, my gut aches like I'm in front of ten thousand people. . . . Please, make it stop . . . and just take me in your arms. . . .' No, instead of doing that, I turned around and got some from the dealer on duty, three hundred euros and I was gone.

Months went by, the album came out . . . I won't tell you any more about it. It's a period I handle worse and worse . . . when I can't be alone anymore with my pointless questions and music.

As usual, Fred was the one who took me to her. He picked me up on his black Vmax.

She wanted to show us her work from the tour.

I was feeling good. I was glad to see Vickie, Nat, and Francesca again – they all used to sing live with me. They were all going their separate ways now, every one of them. Francesca wanted to do a solo album, so

I got down on my knees and promised her, one more time, to write her something unforgettable.

Her apartment was minuscule and we were all tripping over each other. We drank some sort of pink tequila that the neighbour down the hall had scrounged up. He was Argentinean, at least six foot six, and he smiled all the time.

I was dumbfounded by his tattoos.

I got up. I knew she was in the kitchen. She asked:

'You've come to help me?'

I said no.

She asked:

'You want to see my photos?'

I wanted to say no again, but I said:

'Yeah, I'd like that.'

She went into her room. When she came back, she locked the door and cleared everything off the table with a sweep of her arm. It made quite a racket, thanks to some aluminium trays.

She set her box of pictures down flat, and she sat down across from me.

I opened it. All I saw were my hands.

Hundreds of black-and-white photos of nothing but my hands.

My hands on guitar strings, my hands around the mike, my hands beside my body, my hands caressing the crowd, my hands shaking other hands backstage, my hands holding a cigarette, my hands touching my face, my hands signing autographs, my hands feverish, my hands beseeching, my hands throwing kisses, and my hands shooting up, too.

Big, thin hands with veins like little rivers.

Amber was toying with a bottle cap, crushing crumbs.

'That's it?' I said.

For the first time, I looked her in the eyes for more than a second.

'You disappointed?'

'I don't know.'

'I took your hands because that's the only thing about you that's not falling apart.'

'You think so?'

She nodded her head yes and I caught the scent of her hair.

'What about my heart?'

She smiled at me and leaned across the table.

'You're telling me your heart's not falling apart?' she answered with a doubting little pout.

We heard laughter and tapping on the other side of the door. I recognised Luis's voice shrieking: *'We need i-eece!'*

I said:

'I don't know, have to see. . . .'

I thought they were going to break down the door with the shit they were pulling.

She put her hands on mine and looked at them as if she were seeing them for the first time. She said:

'That's exactly what we're going to do.'

Leave

Whenever I do anything, I think of my brother, and whenever I think of my brother, I realise he'd have done it better than me.

Twenty-three years this has been going on.

You can't really say that makes me bitter; no, it just makes me lucid.

Now, for instance, I'm on train 1458 from Nancy, in north-eastern France. I'm on leave – my first in three months.

Okay, for starters, I'm doing my military service like some measly errand boy, whereas my brother went through officer training. He always ate at the officers' table, and he got to come home every weekend. Let's move on.

I'm coming back by train. I've reserved a seat facing forward, but when I get to it, there's some woman sitting in my place with a whole jumble of embroidery spread out over her knees. I don't dare say anything. I swing my huge canvas bag up onto the luggage rack and sit down across from her. There's a girl in the same carriage who's kind of pretty, reading a bestselling novel about ants. She has a spot at the corner of her lip. Pity; otherwise she's not bad.

I go and buy myself a sandwich from the buffet car.

And here's how that would have worked if it had been my brother: He'd have flashed the lady a big charming smile and shown her his ticket with an *excuse me, madame, listen, I may have made a mistake but it seems to me* . . . And she'd have apologised like crazy, stuffing all her pieces of thread in her bag and getting up in a hurry.

For the sandwich, he'd have made some kind of scene with the guy, saying that for four euros, really, they could at least give him a little thicker slice of ham. And the waiter, with his ridiculous black waistcoat, would've changed the sandwich pronto. I should know, I've seen my brother in action.

As for the girl, it's even more perverse. He would have given her one of those looks so she'd have known right away he was interested.

But she'd have known at exactly the same time that he had also noticed her little pimple. And then she'd have had a hard time concentrating on her novel, and she'd try to play it cool just in case.

That is, if he intended to take an interest in her.

Because, anyway, junior officers travel first class, and how many girls in first have spots?

As for me, I never even found out if this chick was impressed with my crew cut and ranger boots, because

I fell asleep almost right away. They had dragged us out of bed at four again this morning to make us do some boneheaded drill.

Marc, my brother, did his military service after three years of college, before he started his engineering studies. He was twenty.

Me, I'm doing it after two years of vocational training, and when I finish I'll be looking for a job in electronics. I'm twenty-three.

What's more, tomorrow's my birthday.

My mother insisted that I come home. I'm not big on birthdays – I'm too old for that. But whatever. I'm doing it for her.

She's lived alone ever since my father ran off with the lady next door on their nineteenth anniversary. Symbolically, you could say, that was rich.

I don't really understand why she hasn't started again with someone else. She could have – actually, she still could, but . . . I don't know. Marc and I only talked about it just one time and we agreed: we think she's afraid now. She doesn't want to risk being abandoned all over again. At one point, we tried to coax her into signing up for one of those dating things, but she never wanted to.

Since then, she's taken in two dogs and a cat, so you can imagine . . . with a menagerie like that, finding a nice guy is pretty much Mission Impossible.

*

Anna Gavalda

We live just south of Paris, near the suburb of Corbeil, in a little villa on Highway 7. It's okay. It's quiet.

My brother never says *villa*, he says *house*. He thinks the word *villa* is naff.

My brother will never get over the fact that he wasn't born in Paris.

Paris. It's all he ever talks about. I think the best day of his life was when he bought his first Paris network season pass so he could go into the city. For me – Paris, Corbeil – it's all the same.

One of the few things I remember from school is a theory by one of those ancient philosophers, who said the important thing isn't where you are, it's the state of mind you're in.

I remember he wrote that to one of his friends who had the hump and wanted to travel. He basically told him, in so many words, that it wasn't worth the trouble since he was bound to lug his load of problems around wherever he went. The day the teacher told us that, my life changed.

That's one of the reasons I chose a career in manual labour.

I'd rather let my hands do the thinking. It's easier.

In the army, you meet your fair share of morons. I live with guys I never could have imagined. I bunk with them, get dressed with them, eat with them, clown around with them, sometimes even play cards with them . . . but still, it's like everything about them makes me sick. I'm not a snob or anything, it's just that these guys have zilch. And I'm not talking about being deep or whatever – that's like some kind of insult. I'm talking about weighing something.

I know I'm not doing a very good job explaining myself, but I know what I mean. If you took one of these guys and put him on a scale, obviously you'd have his weight, but really, he doesn't weigh anything. . . .

It's like there's nothing in these guys that has any real substance. They're like ghosts – you can stick your arm right through them and all you'll touch is a big, noisy void. Of course, if you tell them that, they'll say if you try to stick your arm through, you're asking for it. Har har.

At first, I couldn't sleep at night because of all the stuff they did and all the crazy things they'd say. But now I'm used to it. They say the army makes a man of you, but in my case it's only made me even more pessimistic.

I'm not inclined to believe in God or some Superior Thing, because it's hard to imagine that anyone could have purposely created what I see every day in the barracks at Nancy-Bellefond.

It's funny, I do more thinking when I'm on the train . . . like why the army's not all bad. . . .

When I get to the Paris station, Gare de l'Est, I

always secretly hope there'll be someone waiting for me. It's stupid. I already know my mum's at work, and Marc's not the kind of guy to come slogging across the suburbs just so he can carry my bag. But still, I always have this idiotic hope.

This time's no different. Before I take the escalator down to the metro, I take a quick look around, just in case there's anyone there. . . . And when I get on the escalator, my bag seems a little heavier, same as always.

I wish someone were waiting for me somewhere. . . . Is that so much to ask?

Fine, whatever. It's time for me to get to the house. I could use a good scuffle with Marc – I'm starting to think too much and I'm about to blow a gasket. While I'm waiting for the train, I'm going to light up on the platform. I know it's forbidden, but just let them mess with me – I'll pull the military card.

I work for Peace, monsieur! I get up at four in the morning for France, madame.

No one at the station in Corbeil . . . that's a little harder to take. Maybe they forgot I was coming tonight. . . .

I'll walk the rest of the way. I'm sick of communal transportation. In fact, I think I'm sick of everything communal.

I run into some guys I went to school with. They're in no big hurry to shake my hand. Face it, the army sucks.

I stop in at the café on the corner of my street. If I'd spent less time in this café growing up, maybe now I wouldn't be in danger of having to go down to the unemployment agency in another six months. There was a time when I used to spend more hours behind this pinball machine than in the classroom . . . I'd play until five o'clock, and then when the other kids showed up, the ones who'd had to listen to the teachers blabbering all day, I'd sell them my bonus rounds. It was a good deal for them: they paid half price and had a chance to get their initials on the high score list.

Everyone was happy, and I bought myself my first packet of fags. I swear, back then, I thought I was king. The king of jerks, maybe.

The owner says:

'So? . . . Still in the army?'

'Yeah.'

'Good for you!'

'Yeah . . .'

'So come and see me some night after I close, so we can chat. . . . You know, I was in the Legion myself, and that was really somethin' else. . . . They'd never have let us take a weekend off just like that, I can tell you.'

And he goes back to the counter to relive the war with his drunken cronies.

The Foreign Legion . . .

I'm tired. I'm fed up with this bag cutting into my

shoulder and the street just keeps on going. When I get to my house, the gate is locked. Fuck, that does it. I could just about cry right there.

I've been on my feet since four a.m., I've just come halfway across the country in stinking carriages, and now it's about time to cut me some slack, don't you think?

The dogs are waiting for me. Between Bozo howling himself to death for joy and Micmac jumping ten feet in the air . . . it's a party. Now *that's* a welcome.

I throw my bag over the top and go over the wall like I used to back in my moped-riding days. The dogs pounce on me, and for the first time in weeks, I feel better. So there, there are still living creatures on this little planet who love me and are happy to see me. Come here, my sweet things. Oh, yes, you're beautiful, you, oh, yes, you're beautiful!

The house is dark.

I put my bag down on the doormat by my feet. I open it and start hunting for my keys, which are all the way at the bottom under kilos of dirty socks.

The dogs go in ahead of me and I go to turn on the hall light . . . no power.

Well, shiiiiiit. Well, shit.

Just then I hear Marc, that fuckwit, saying:

'Hey, show some manners in front of your guests.'

It's still dark. I answer:

'What is this shit?'

'Aren't you a delinquent second-class squaddie. Enough of the four-letter words. We're not in the Hicksville barracks here, so watch your mouth or I won't turn on the lights.'

He turns the lights on.

That's all I need: All my friends and my whole family are there in the living room, holding on to their drinks and standing around under paper streamers, singing 'Happy Birthday.'

My mother says:

'Well, kiddo, put down your bag.'

And she hands me a drink.

No one's ever done anything like this for me before. I can't be looking all that great, standing there with a stupid expression on my face.

I go and shake everyone's hand and kiss my grandmother and my aunts.

When I get to Marc, I mean to give him a slap round the ear, but he's with a girl. He's got his arm round her waist. And from the minute I see her, I already know I'm in love.

I give my brother a punch on the shoulder, and, jerking my chin at the girl, I ask:

'That my present?'

'Dream on, moron,' he answers.

I'm still looking at her. It's like there's something

playing the clown in my stomach. I feel sick, and she's beautiful.

'You don't recognise her?'

'No.'

'Of course you do, it's Marie, Rebecca's friend. . . .'

'???'

She says:

'We went to summer camp together. At Glénans, don't you remember? . . .'

'Nope, sorry.' I shake my head and ditch them. I go and get myself something to drink.

Damn right, I remember her. I still have nightmares about that sailing course. My brother, always first. He was the counsellors' pet: tanned, muscular, laid-back. He read an instruction manual at night, and he understood everything as soon as he got on board. I can still see him going out on the trapeze and sending up a spray of water, yelling over the waves. He never capsized once.

All those girls with their little breasts and their vacant eyes staring like fish on a platter, thinking of nothing but the party on the last night.

All those girls who'd written their addresses on his arm with a felt-tip pen while he was pretending to sleep on the bus. And the ones who cried in front of their parents when they saw him heading toward our family Renault.

And me . . . getting seasick.

Yes, I remember Marie, all right. One night, she was telling some of the other kids that she'd surprised a couple of lovers kissing on the beach, and that she'd heard the sound of the girl's pants snapping.

'What did it sound like?' I asked, just to put her on the spot.

She looked me straight in the eye. She pinched her underwear through the cloth of her dress, pulled it back, and let it go.

Snap.

'Like that,' she answered, still looking at me.

I was eleven.

Marie.

Damn right, I remember. Snap.

The later it got, the less I felt like talking about the army. The less I looked at Marie, the more I wanted to touch her.

I drank too much. My mother shot me a dirty look.

I went out in the garden with a couple of friends from technical school. We were talking about videos we wanted to rent and cars we'd never be able to buy. Michael had put a souped-up sound system in his Peugeot.

Almost two thousand francs to listen to techno. . . .

I sat down on the iron bench – the one my mother asks me to repaint every year. She says it reminds her of the Tuileries garden in Paris.

I smoked a cigarette, looking at the stars. I don't know many by name. So whenever I have a chance, I look for them. I know four.

Another lesson from Glénans that didn't quite take.

I saw her coming while she was still a way off. She smiled at me. I looked at her teeth and the shape of her earrings.

She sat down next to me and said:

'May I?'

I didn't answer because my stomach was hurting again.

'So, is it true you don't remember me?'

'No, it's not.'

'You do remember?'

'Yes.'

'What do you remember?'

'I remember that you were ten, that you were four foot three, that you weighed twenty-six kilos and that you'd had mumps the year before. I remember the medical. I remember that you lived at Choisy-le-Roi and at the time it would have cost me forty-two francs to go and see you by train. I remember that your mother's name was Catherine and your father's name was Jacques. I remember that you had a water turtle named Candy, and your best friend had a guinea pig named Anthony. I remember that you had a green bathing suit with white stars, and your mother had even made you a bathrobe with your name embroidered on it. I remember that you cried one morning because there were no letters for you. I remember that you stuck some sequins on your cheeks the night of the party, and you and Rebecca put on a show to the music from *Grease*. . . .'

'Oh my God – it's incredible that you remember those things!!'

She's even more beautiful when she laughs. She leans back and rubs her hands on her arms to warm them up.

'Here,' I say, pulling off my sweater.

'Thanks . . . but what about you? Won't you be cold?!'

'Don't worry about me – go ahead.'

She looks at me differently. Any girl would have understood what she understood just then.

'What else do you remember?'

'I remember that one night in front of the Optimists' shed you told me you thought my brother was a show-off. . . .'

'Yes, that's right! I said that, and you told me it wasn't true.'

'Because it's not. Marc does a million things like it's nothing, but he doesn't show off. He just does them, that's all.'

'You always stuck up for your brother.'

'Yeah, he's my brother. Besides, you don't think he's got all that many faults right now, either, do you?'

She got up. She asked if she could keep my sweater.

I smiled at her. Despite the bog of muck and misery I was flailing around in, I was happy as ever.

My mother came up while I was still smiling like a big, fat fool. She said she was going to sleep at my grandmother's. The girls should sleep on the first floor and the boys on the second. . . .

'All right, Mum, we're not kids anymore, it's okay. . . .'

'And make sure the dogs are in before you lock up, and . . .'

'All right, Mum. . . .'

'I have a right to worry, you all drink like fish and you, you must be completely drunk. . . .'

'You don't say drunk in this case, Mum, you say "wasted". See, I'm wasted. . . .'

She backed off, shrugging her shoulders.

'At least put something on – you'll catch your death.'

I smoked three more cigarettes, to give myself time to think, and then I went to find Marc.

'Hey . . .'

'What?'

'It's about Marie. . . .'

'What?'

'Let me have her.'

'No.'

'I'm going to smash your face.'

'No.'

'Why not?'

'Because you've had too much to drink tonight, and because I need to have my little angel face for work on Monday.'

'Why?'

'Because I'm giving a talk on the incidence of fluids in an established area.'

'Oh?'

'Yeah.'

'Sorry.'

'Don't mention it.'

'And about Marie?'

'Marie? She's mine.'

'Don't be so sure.'

'What do you know about it?'

'Oh! It . . . Call it an artillery soldier's sixth sense.'

'My arse it is.'

'Listen, I'm up against it here – there's nothing I can do. That's just the way it is. I know, I'm an idiot. So let's find a solution at least for tonight, okay?'

'Let me think. . . .'

'Hurry up. Later I'll be too far gone.'

'Foosball.'

'What?'

'We'll play foosball for her.'

'That's not very chivalrous.'

'It'll be just between us, mister gentleman-wipe-my-arse who tries to steal other guys' girls.'

'Okay. When?'

'Now. In the basement.'

'Now??!'

'Yes, sir.'

'I'll be right there. I'm going to make myself a mug of coffee.'

'Make me one, too, please.'

'No problem. I'll even piss in it.'

'Military moron.'

'Go and warm up. Go and say good-bye to her.'

'Die.'

'It's no big deal, go ahead. I'll console her.'

'Count on it.'

We drank our burning-hot coffees over the sink. Marc went downstairs first. Meanwhile, I stuck both my hands in a sack of flour. I thought about my mum making us breaded chicken.

Only now I had to piss. Wasn't that brilliant. Holding on to it with two chicken cordon bleus . . . it's not the most practical thing. . . .

Before I went down, I looked around for Marie. I needed to buck up my resolve, because if I'm a pinball-playing fiend, foosball's more my brother's thing.

I played like shit. The flour was supposed to keep me from sweating, but instead it just turned the tips of my fingers into little white meatballs.

Plus, Marie and the others came down when we were 6 all, and from then on, I lost it. I could feel her moving behind me, and my hands slipped on the handles. I smelled her perfume and forgot my attackers. I heard the sound of her voice, and I got slammed, goal after goal.

When my brother had moved the marker to 10 on his side, finally I could wipe my hands on my thighs. My jeans were all white.

Marc, the bastard, looked at me like he was really sorry.

Happy birthday, I thought.

The girls said they wanted to go to bed and asked to be shown to their room. I said I was going to sleep on the couch in the living room so I could finish off the dregs of the bottle in peace, without anyone bothering me.

Marie looked at me. I thought that if only she were still four foot three inches tall and twenty-six kilos right then, I could've tucked her inside my shirt and taken her with me everywhere.

And then the house got quiet. The lights went out, one after another, and I didn't hear anything except a few chuckles here and there.

I supposed Marc and his friends were acting like imbeciles, scratching at the girls' door.

I whistled for the dogs and locked the front door.

I couldn't fall asleep. Of course.

I smoked a cigarette in the dark. The only thing

visible in the room was the little red point, moving a
little from time to time. And then I heard a noise –
like paper rustling. At first, I thought it was one of the
dogs getting into trouble. I called:

'Bozo? . . . Micmac? . . .'

No response, and the noise was getting louder – now
also with a scritch, scritch, like Sellotape being pulled off.

I sat up and reached out to switch on the light.

I'm dreaming. Marie is standing in the middle of the
room, naked, in the process of covering her body with
pieces of wrapping paper. She has blue paper on her
left breast, silver on the right, and ribbon twisted
around her arms. There's some heavy paper that my
grandmother had used to wrap the motorcycle helmet
she gave me – she's got that wrapped around her like
some kind of loincloth.

She's walking around half naked in the middle of all
the thrown-away wrappers, among the full ashtrays
and the dirty glasses.

'What are you doing?'

'It's not obvious?'

'Well, no . . . not really. . . .'

'Didn't you say earlier, when you first got here, you
wanted a present?'

She kept smiling and tied some red ribbon around her
waist.

I got up right away.

'Hey, don't get too wrapped up,' I said.

Even as I said it, I wondered if 'don't get too wrapped up' meant: don't cover your skin like that – leave it for me, I beg you.

Or if 'don't get too wrapped up' meant: don't invest too much too fast, you know . . . not only do I still get seasick, but on top of that, I have to go back to Nancy tomorrow, to the base, so, you see . . .

Lead Story

I'd be better off just going to bed, but I can't.

My hands are shaking.

Maybe I should write some sort of report.

I'm used to it. I write one every Friday afternoon for my boss, Guillemin.

This time I'll do it for myself.

I tell myself: 'If you retell the whole thing just the way it happened, if you really apply yourself, then afterwards when you read it back, maybe, just maybe, for two seconds you'll be able to believe that fucking idiot in the story is someone else. And then maybe you'll be able to judge yourself objectively. Maybe.'

So here I am. I'm sitting in front of the little laptop I usually use for work. I hear the noise of the dishwasher downstairs.

My wife and kids went to bed a long time ago. I know the kids must be asleep, but I'm sure my wife's not. She's waiting up for me, trying to make sense of it all. I think she's afraid because she already knows she's lost me. Women can sense those things. But I can't just go and curl up with her and fall asleep – and she knows that as well as I do. I need to write it all down for the sake of the two seconds that could be so important if I can just pull it off.

I'll start at the beginning.

I was hired at Paul Pridault on 1 September, 1995. Before that I was with a competitor, but there were too many little things getting under my skin – like, for example, expense claims being paid six months late. So I packed it all in on a sudden whim.

I was out of work for almost a year.

Everyone thought I'd go nuts, sitting at home twiddling my thumbs and waiting for a call from the temp agency I'd signed up with.

But actually, I have a lot of good memories from that time. I was finally able to finish the house – all those things that Florence had been after me forever to get done. I hung all the curtain rods and fixed up a shower in the back storage room. I rented a rototiller, turned over the whole garden, and put down fresh turf.

In the afternoons, I'd pick up Lucas from the sitter's, and then when school got out we'd collect his big sister. I'd make them huge snacks and hot chocolate. Not Nesquik – real stirred cocoa that gave them great big moustaches. Afterwards, we'd go and look at them in the bathroom mirror before they licked them off.

In June, it dawned on me that Lucas wouldn't be going to Madame Ledoux's much longer, now that he was old enough for nursery school. I started getting serious again about looking for work, and in August, I found it.

At Paul Pridault, I'm the sales rep for the whole western part of France. The company's a major pork producer – like a butcher, sort of, but on an industrial scale.

Old man Pridault's stroke of genius is his *jambon au torchon,* country ham wrapped in a real red-and-white-checked cloth. Of course, it's a factory ham made from factory pigs, and the famous country cloth is made in China, but whatever – it's what he's famous for. Just ask any housewife behind her shopping trolley what the name Paul Pridault means to her, and she'll tell you *'jambon au torchon'* – all the market surveys prove it. And if you press the point, you'll learn that our *jambon au torchon* is miles better than anybody else's because it tastes more authentic.

Hats off to the *artiste.*

We have a net annual revenue of five million euros.

I spend the better part of the week behind the wheel of my company car. A black Peugeot 306 with a transfer of a grinning pig's head on the sides.

People have no concept of what life's like for these guys on the road, all the truck drivers and sales reps.

It's like there are two worlds on the highway: those out for a drive, and us.

★

It's a bunch of things. First, there's the way we feel about our cars.

From the little Renault Clio to the huge German trailer trucks, when we climb in, we're at home. It's our smell, our mess, our seats taking the form of our arses – and believe me, we get enough shit about that. Then there's the CB, which is a whole mysterious world of its own, with codes most people can't even understand. I don't use it much. I put it on mute from time to time when I smell something burning, but that's all.

Then there's the whole food thing. The Cheval Blanc hotel-restaurants, the roadside diners, the ads for the golden arches. . . . Daily specials, pitchers, paper napkins. . . . All those faces that you pass and never see again. . . .

And the waitresses' arses – which are catalogued, rated, and updated better than the Michelin Guide. They call it the Micheline Guide.

There's the tiredness, the itineraries, the loneliness, the thoughts – always the same ones turning over and over.

Potbellies have a way of sneaking up on you. Hookers, too.

There's a whole universe that's like a big, insurmountable barrier between those who live on the road and those who don't.

Roughly speaking, my job consists of making the rounds to all our distribution outlets.

I work with mid– to large-scale grocery managers. We define launching strategies together, do sales projections, and conduct informational meetings about our products.

For me, it's a little like going for a walk with a pretty girl, showing everyone how sweet and charming she is. As though I'm trying to find her a good match.

But it doesn't end with finding her a husband – I still have to look out for her. When I get a chance, I test the vendors to see if they're putting our merchandise up front, if they're trying to sell generic stuff, if they've got the *torchon* cloth unfolded just like on TV, if the *andouillettes* are bathing in their jelly, if the pâtés are in real old-fashioned terrines, if the sausages are hung up as though they're drying, and if and if and if . . .

No one notices all these little details, but they're what make the Paul Pridault difference.

I know I'm talking too much about my work, and that has nothing to do with what I need to write.

Right now it's pork, but I could sell lipstick or shoelaces just as well. What I love is making contacts, talking to people, and getting to see the country. Most of all, I love not being closed up in some office with a boss on my back all day. Just thinking about it gives me grief.

On Monday, 29 September, 1997, I got up at a quarter

to six. I got my stuff together without making a sound so my wife wouldn't grump at me. Then I barely had time to shower, because the car was almost out of fuel and I wanted to use the chance to check the tyre pressure.

I drank my coffee at the Shell station. I hate when I have to do that. The smell of diesel and sweetened coffee mixing together always makes me sort of want to throw up.

My first appointment was at eight-thirty at Pont-Audemer. I helped the shelf stackers at Carrefour put together a new display shelf for our vacuum-packed meals. It's a new thing that we just brought out in conjunction with a big-name chef. (You should see the profits he rakes in just for showing his pretty face and toque on the package, jeez.)

The second appointment was set for ten o'clock in the Bourg-Achard industrial zone.

I was running a little late, mostly due to fog on the motorway.

I turned off the radio because I needed to think.

I was worried about this interview. I knew we were up against an important competitor, and it was a major challenge for me. Besides, I nearly missed my exit.

At one in the afternoon, I got a panicked phone call from my wife:

'Jean-Pierre, is that you?'

'What, who did you expect?'

'. . . My God. . . . Are you okay?'

'Why are you asking me that?'

'Because of the accident, of course! For two hours I've been trying to reach you on your mobile, but they said all the lines were overloaded! For two hours I've been sick with worry! I must've called your office at least ten times! Shit! You could at least have called, you know. You really suck. . . .'

'Wait, what are you talking about . . . what's this all about?'

'The accident this morning on the A13. Weren't you supposed to take the A13 today?'

'What accident?'

'You can't be serious!!! *You're* the one who listens to France Info all day!!! It's all anybody's talking about. Even on TV! There was a terrible accident this morning near Rouen.'

'. . .'

'Well, okay, I'll let you go, I've got a mass of work. . . . I haven't done a thing since this morning. I was sure I must be a widow. I could already see myself throwing a handful of dirt on your coffin. Your mother called, my mother called. . . . Talk about a morning.'

'Nope! Sorry . . . not this time! You'll have to wait a little longer to get rid of my mother.'

'Idiot.'

'. . .'

'. . .'

'Hey, Flo . . .'

'What?'

'I love you.'

'You never say it.'

'And just now? What did I just do?'

'. . . All right. . . . See you tonight. Call your mother or else she's the one who's going to kick the bucket.'

At seven o'clock I watched the local news. Awful.

Eight dead and sixty injured.

Cars crushed like cans.

How many?

Fifty? A hundred?

Trucks flattened and completely burned. Dozens and dozens of ambulances. A policeman talking about carelessness, about excessive speeding, about the fog that had been forecasted the night before, and about some bodies they still hadn't been able to identify. Haggard, silent people in tears.

At eight I listened to the news highlights on TV. Nine deaths this time.

Florence shouted from the kitchen:

'Enough already! Turn that off! Come in here.'

We clinked glasses in the kitchen. But it was just to make her happy – my heart wasn't in it.

Right then, at that moment, I felt afraid. I couldn't eat anything, and I was stunned like a boxer who's been hit once too often.

Since I couldn't sleep, my wife made love to me, very gently.

At midnight I was back in the living room. I turned on the TV and put it on mute, and I looked all over for a cigarette.

At twelve-thirty, I turned the volume back up a little to watch the last newscast. I couldn't tear my eyes from the mass of sheet metal scattered across the lanes in both directions.

What a fuck-up.

I said to myself: people are just too stupid.

And then a truck driver came on the screen. He was wearing a T-shirt that said Le Castellet. I'll never forget his face.

That night, in my living room, this guy said:

'Okay, yeah, so it was foggy, and yeah, people drive too fast, but none of this shit ever would've happened if that arsehole hadn't backed up to make the Bourg-Achard exit. From the cab, I could see the whole thing. The two cars next to me slowed down, and then after that I could hear the others embedding themselves like cutting through butter. Believe it or not, I couldn't see a thing in my mirrors. Nothing. It was all just white. I hope it doesn't keep you up at night, you bastard.'

That's what he said. To me.

To me, Jean-Pierre Faret, naked in my living room.

That was yesterday.

Today, I bought all the papers. On page 3 of the *Figaro* dated Tuesday, 30 September:

DRIVER ERROR SUSPECTED

'An illegal manoeuvre by a driver, who is thought to have backed up at the Bourg-Achard interchange in Eure, may have triggered the pile-up that caused the deaths of nine persons yesterday morning in a series of collisions on the A13 motorway. The error is thought to have provoked the first collision, in the Paris-bound lanes, whereupon a tanker immediately caught fire. The flames attracted the attention of . . .'

And on page 3 of the *Parisien*:

THE SHOCKING THEORY OF DRIVER ERROR

'The carelessness, indeed the recklessness, of a motorist may have been the source of the tragedy that manifested itself in the indescribable heap of crushed metal from which at least nine bodies were removed yesterday morning on the A13 motorway. Indeed, according to the shocking statement taken down by police, a car backed up to make the Bourg-Achard exit, roughly twenty kilometres from Rouen. It was in an attempt to avoid this car that the . . .'

And as if that weren't enough:

'In trying to cross the motorway in order to aid the injured, two other persons were killed, mowed down by a car. In less than two minutes, roughly a hundred cars, three heavy goods . . .' (*Libération*, same day.)

Not even twenty metres, hardly – just a little short cut across the white stripes.

It took a matter of seconds. I'd already forgotten.

My God . . .

I don't cry.

Florence came looking for me in the living room at five in the morning.

I told her everything, of course.

For several long minutes she stayed seated, without moving, her hands on her face.

She looked to the right, then to the left, as though she needed air. Then she said:

'Listen to me. Don't say anything. You know if you do they'll charge you with involuntary manslaughter, and you'll go to jail.'

'Yes.'

'And then? And then? What will that change? Even more lives fucked up, and how does that make it any better?'

She was crying.

'Well, there you have it. My life's already fucked.'

She was shouting.

'Well, yours maybe, but not the kids'! So don't you say a thing!'

I didn't have the strength to shout.

'Let's talk about the kids. Look at that one. Take a good look at him.'

And I held out the newspaper, on the page that showed a little boy in tears on the A13.

A little boy walking away from an unrecognisable car.

A photo in the paper.

In the section 'Lead Story.'

'. . . He's the same age as Camille.'

'For God's sake, stop that!' My wife was shrieking, grabbing me by the shirt collar. . . . 'Stop that shit! You shut up, now! Let me ask you a question. Just one. What good does it do for a guy like you to go to jail? Huh? Tell me, what good will it do?!'

'It might make them feel better.'

She walked away, crushed.

I heard her shut herself in the bathroom.

When I saw her this morning, I nodded. But now,

tonight, in my silent house with just the background noise of the dishwasher . . .

I'm lost.

I'm going to go downstairs. I'm going to drink a glass of water and I'm going to smoke a cigarette in the garden. Then I'm going to come back up here and reread everything from start to finish. Maybe that will help.

But I don't think so.

Catgut

In the beginning, none of it was supposed to work out this way. I'd answered an ad in *Veterinary Week* to fill in for someone for two months, August and September. And then the guy who'd hired me was killed on the road on his way back from holiday. Fortunately, no one else was in the car.

So I stayed on and took over the practice. It has a good clientele. People in Normandy have a hard time paying, but eventually they pay.

People up there are like all rustics – once an idea gets ingrained . . . And a woman for the animals – that can't be good. To feed them, okay, and to milk them and clean up their shit, fine. But when it comes to things like shots, calving, colic, and metritis, they'll have to see. . . .

They saw. They spent several months checking me out before anyone finally invited me for a drink.

Of course, in the mornings, it's no big deal – that's when I do consultations at the office. Mostly people bring in cats and dogs. I have all kinds of cases. Sometimes they'll bring one in for me to put down, because the father can't bring himself to do it and the animal's in pain . . . or they'll bring me one to treat, because 'this one's a really good hunter' . . . and every now and then they'll bring one in for vaccinations – but in that case, the owner's always Parisian.

The hard part, at first, was the afternoons. The house calls. The cowsheds. The silences. *Hafta see 'er at work, then we'll see.* Nothing but mistrust – and, I can imagine, nothing but ridicule behind my back. I must have really given them something to laugh about at the cafés, what with my lab work and my sterile gloves. Plus, my last name is Sirloine. Doctor Sirloine. What a joke.

In the end, I had to forget all the theoretical stuff we'd learned in college. I'd stand there silently in front of the livestock, waiting for the owner to spit out some scraps of information to help me figure out what was going on.

And then, most important – and this is the reason I've lasted this long – I bought myself some weights.

Now, if I had to give one piece of advice to a young person who wanted to go rural (although after everything that's happened, I'd be surprised if anyone asked), here's what I'd say: Muscles. Lots of muscles – it's the most important thing. A cow weighs between five and eight hundred kilos, a horse between seven hundred kilos and a ton. That's all there is to it.

Imagine a cow who's having a hard time birthing.

Naturally it's night. It's really cold, the barn is dirty, and there's barely any light.

Okay.

The cow's in pain, and the farmer's unhappy too, because that cow is his livelihood. If the vet costs him more than the price of the meat that's about to be born, he's got to think twice. . . . You say:

'The calf is breeched. I just have to turn it around, and it will come out on its own.'

The cowshed comes to life. They pull their oldest kid out of bed, and the younger one follows. For once, there's something going on.

You get the animal tied up – nice and close. You don't want any kicking. You strip down to a T-shirt. Now it's suddenly cold. You find a tap and scrub your hands with the bit of soap sitting there. You put on your gloves, which come up to just under your armpits. Then you take your left hand and pull on the enormous vulva, and in you go.

You go looking for the sixty- or seventy-kilo calf in the far reaches of the uterus, and you turn it around – with one hand.

It takes a while, but you manage. Later, back inside, you drink a little brandy to warm yourself up, and you think about your weights.

Another time, the calf won't come out. You have to open up, and that costs more. The farmer watches you, and his decision is based on the way you look. If you look confident and make a move towards your car as if you're going to get your equipment, he'll say yes.

If you stand there looking at the other animals and shift your weight as if you're about to leave, he'll say no.

And still another time, the calf is already dead. You have to be careful not to ruin the heifer, so you cut the calf up into little pieces and pull them out one after another, always with the glove.

When you go home later, your heart feels empty.

Years have gone by, and I'm still a long way from getting it all paid off, but everything's going well.

When old man Villemeux died, I bought his farm and did it up a little.

I met someone, and then he left. My big carpet-beater hands, I guess.

I took in two dogs. The first showed up on his own and decided he liked the place. The second had seen some rough times before I adopted him. Naturally, the second one rules the roost. There's also a handful of cats. I don't ever see them, but their bowls are always empty. And I love my garden. It's a bit of a mess, but there are some old rosebushes that have been there since before my time that don't require any care from me. They're really beautiful.

A year ago I bought some teak lawn furniture. It cost a lot, but it's meant to age well.

From time to time, I go out with Marc Pardini,

who teaches I don't know what at the local school.
We go to the movies or out to eat. He likes to play the
intellectual with me, which I find funny – because to
tell the truth, I've turned into quite a hick. He lends
me books and CDs.

From time to time, I sleep with him. It's always
good.

Late last night, I got a phone call. It was the Billebaudes
– the farm on the road to Tianville. The guy said there
was some big problem and it couldn't wait.

That phone call cost me, to put it mildly. I'd had to
work the weekend before, and that made thirteen days
straight that I'd been working. I talked to my dogs for a
while – nothing in particular, I just wanted to hear the
sound of my voice – and I made myself a cup of coffee,
black as ink.

The minute I pulled my key out of the ignition, I
knew something was wrong. The house was dark and
the cowshed silent.

I kicked up a hell of a racket, banging on the
corrugated steel door as if to wake the dead, but it was
too late.

He said, 'My cow's cunt is all better, but how's
yers? You even go' one? 'Round here they say you
ain't a woman, you got balls. That's what they say, ya
know. So we told 'em we'd see fer oursel's.'

★

And everything he said made the other two laugh.

I stared at their fingernails, chewed down to the flesh. You think they'd have taken me on a bale of straw? No, they were too drunk to bend down without falling over. They pinned me up against an icy tank in the dairy barn. There was a length of bent pipe grinding into my back. It was pitiful to see them struggling with their flies.

The whole thing was pitiful.

They hurt me really badly. Put like that, it doesn't mean much, but I'll say it again for those who might not have got it the first time: they hurt me really badly.

Ejaculation sobered up the Billebaude boy all of a sudden.

'Hey, uh, doctor, we was just havin' a lil fun, right? We don't get much chance to have no fun out here, ya know, an' my brother-in-law there, it's his stag party, ain't that right, Manu?'

Manu was already sleeping, and Manu's friend was starting to booze it up again.

I said, 'Of course, of course.' I even joked with him a little, until he handed me the bottle. It was plum brandy.

The alcohol had rendered them harmless, but I gave them each a dose of Ketamine. I didn't want them twitching around. Then I saw to my own comfort.

I put on my sterile gloves and washed everything thoroughly with Betadine.

Next, I pulled the skin of the scrotum tight. With my scalpel blade I made a small incision. I pulled out the testicles. I cut. I ligated the epididymis and the vessel with catgut No. 3.5. I put it back in the sac and made a continuous suture. Good, clean work.

The one who'd been on the phone had been the most brutal, since this was his home. I grafted his balls just above his Adam's apple.

It was nearly six in the morning when I stopped by my neighbour's. Madame Brudet was seventy-two years old, and had been on her feet for a good while – all shrivelled up, but brave.

'I'm afraid I'm going to have to go away for a while, Madame Brudet. I need someone to look after my dogs, and the cats too.'

'Nothing serious, I hope?'

'I don't know.'

'I'll be happy to keep an eye on the cats, although I still say it's not a good idea to fatten them up like that. All they have to do is hunt field mice. The dogs . . . that's a little harder because they're so big, but if it's not for too long, I'll keep them here.'

'I'll write you a cheque for the food.'

'That's fine. Just put it behind the TV. Nothing serious, I hope?'

'Tttttt tttttt,' I said with a smile.

Now, I'm sitting at my kitchen table. I've made some more coffee and I'm smoking a cigarette. I'm waiting for the police car.

I only hope they don't use the siren.

Junior

His name is Alexander Devermont. He's a young man, all pink and blond.

Raised in a vacuum. One hundred per cent pure soap and fluoride Colgate, with short-sleeved check shirts and a dimple on his chin. Cute. Clean. A real little suckling pig.

He's almost twenty – that discouraging age where you still think anything's possible. So many prospects and so many illusions. So many knocks to take, too.

But not for this rosy young man. Life has never done him any harm. No one's ever pulled his ears till it really hurt. He's a good kid.

His mum's a social climber – she farts higher than her arse. She says, 'Hello, this is Elisabeth De-vermont . . .', separating out the first syllable. As if she still hoped to fool someone. . . . Tut tut tut. . . . You can pay to have a lot of things these days, but for the particle – those two little letters that mean your ancestors were nobles – no way.

You can't buy that sort of pride anymore. It's like

Obélix, who fell into a pot of magic potion when he was a baby and ended up invincible: you have to luck into it when you're little. That doesn't stop Junior's mum from wearing a signet ring engraved with a coat of arms.

What coat of arms? I wonder. A crown and some fleurs-de-lis jumbled together on a heraldic shield. The Association of Pork Butchers and Delicatessens of France uses the same one on its syndicate letterhead, but she doesn't know that. Phew.

His dad took over the family business – a company that makes white resin lawn furniture, known as Rofitex.

Guaranteed ten years against yellowing in any climate.

Of course, resin kind of makes you think of camping trips and picnics in the back garden. It would have been more chic to make stuff out of teak – classy benches that would pick up a nice patina over time, and some lichen, under the hundred-year oak that great-grandpa planted in the middle of the grounds. . . . But, oh well – you have to take what they leave you, huh?

Speaking of furniture, I was exaggerating a little when I said earlier that life had never dealt Junior any harsh blows. Of course it had. One day, while he was dancing with a young lady from a good family, flat and pedigreed like a true English setter, he had his share of angst.

It was during one of those elegant little get-togethers that the mums organise at exorbitant cost to keep their progeny from venturing one day between the breasts of some Leïla or Hannah or some other girl who reeks of heresy or harissa.

So there he was, with his neck bent and his hands sweaty. He was dancing with this girl, being extra careful not to let his fly brush against her belly. He was trying to sway his hips a little and beating time with the heels of his Westons. Like that, you know, kind of laid-back. The way young people do.

And then the babe asked:

'So what does your father do?' (It's a question that girls ask at this sort of affair.)

He pretended to be distracted, spinning her around as he answered:

'He's the CEO at Rofitex – I dunno if you've heard of it. . . . Two hundred empl – '

She didn't give him time to finish. She stopped dancing at once and opened her setter's eyes wide:

'Hold on . . . Rofitex? . . . You mean the . . . the . . . the condoms, Rofitex?'

Now that, that was the best.

'No, the lawn furniture,' he answered, but really, he'd been ready for anything but that. But really, what an airhead this girl was. What an airhead. Fortunately, the music had stopped and he could head for the buffet to drink a little champagne and digest it all. Really.

Turns out she wasn't even one of the society girls — she'd infiltrated herself.

Twenty years old. My God.

It took young Devermont two tries to pass his baccalaureat, but not his driving test. That was all right. He just passed it, and on the first try.

Not like his brother, who had to retake it three times.

At dinner, everyone is in a good mood. It wasn't in the bag, because the local examiner is a real arsehole. A drunk, too. It's the country here.

Like his brother and his cousins before him, Alexander got his licence over the summer holiday, out at his grandmother's place, because the fees in the provinces are a lot less than in Paris: nearly a hundred and fifty euros difference for the driver's course.

But finally, the drunk was more or less sober and put his scrawl on the pink slip without being too clever about it.

Alexander's allowed to use his mother's Golf as long as she doesn't need it. Otherwise, he's supposed to take the old Peugeot that's in the barn. Same as all the kids.

It's still in good condition, but it smells like chicken shit.

It's the end of the holidays. Soon he'll have to go back to the big apartment on Avenue Mozart and get into the private business school on Avenue de Saxe. A school that's not yet accredited, but whose name is complicated, with lots of initials: the IHERP or the IRPHE or the IHEMA or something like that. (The Institute of Higher Education My Arse.)

Our little suckling pig has changed a lot over the summer. He's been dissolute – he's even started smoking.

Marlboro Lights.

It's because of the new company he's keeping: he's grown chummy with the son of a big local farmer, Franck Mingeaut. This kid is a piece of work – filthy rich, flashy, rowdy, and loud. Says 'hello' politely to Alexander's grandmother and checks out his younger cousins at the same time. Tut-tut.

Franck Mingeaut is happy to know Junior. Thanks to him, he can enter society, go to parties where the girls are slender and pretty and where they serve the families' own champagne instead of cheap Valstar beer. Instinct tells him that this is the way to go if he wants to land himself a nice cushy set-up. The back rooms of cafés, unsophisticated Marylines, pool tables, county fairs – none of that stuff lasts. Whereas an evening with the Widget girl in her home at Chateau Widgetière . . . now there's energy well spent.

★

Junior Devermont is happy with his *nouveau riche* friend. Thanks to him, he skids through gravel courtyards in a sports convertible, he charges down the back roads of Touraine, giving peasants the finger to get them to move their old Renaults out of the way, and he treats his father like crap. He leaves an extra shirt button open, and he's even started wearing his baptismal pendant again, like a tough guy still tender at heart. The girls eat it up.

Tonight is *the* party of the summer. The count and countess of La Rochepoucaut are receiving in honour of their youngest daughter, Éléonore. All the upper crust will be there – from Mayenne down to the far end of Berry, from the Society Pages, you name it. It will be raining young virgin heiresses.

Money. Not the flashiness of money; the smell of it. Low necklines, creamy complexions, pearl necklaces, ultra-light cigarettes, and nervous laughter. For Franck-of-the-bracelet and Alexander-of-the-fine-chain, this is the big night.

No way they're going to miss this.

To those people, a rich farmer will always be a peasant, and a well-brought-up industrialist will always be a tradesman. All the more reason to drink their champagne and jump their daughters in the bushes. The young ladies aren't all antisocial. They're direct descendents of the crusader Godefroy de Bouillon, and they have no problem pushing the last crusade a little further.

Franck doesn't have an invitation, but Junior knows the guy at the door – no problem, you slip him twenty euros and he'll let you in. He'll even bark out your name like they do at the Automobile Club shows if you want.

The big hitch is the car. The car makes all the difference if you want to clinch the deal with the ones who don't like prickly bushes.

If some pretty young thing doesn't want to leave too early, she'll bid her daddy good night and find an escort to take her home. If you haven't got a car out here, where everyone lives miles apart, you're either hopeless or a virgin.

And right now the situation is critical. Franck doesn't have his chick magnet – it's in for a service – and Alexander doesn't have his mother's car. She took it back to Paris.

What else is there? The sky-blue Peugeot with the chicken droppings on the seats and along the doors. There's even straw on the floor and a 'Hunting Is Natural' bumper sticker on the back. God, it's disgusting.

'What about your father? Where's he?'

'Out of town.'

'And his car?'

'Uh . . . it's here. Why?'

'Why's it here?'

'Because Jean-Raymond has to give it a clean.'

(Jean-Raymond's their groundsman.)

'That's brilliant! We'll borrow his car for the night and bring it straight back. There you go – what he doesn't know won't hurt him.'

'Uh-uh, Franck, that's not an option. Not an option.'

'Why not?'

'Listen, if anything should happen, I'm dead. Uh-uh, it's not an option. . . .'

'But what do you think's going to happen, arse-wipe? Huh? Just what do you think's going to happen?'

'Uh-uh . . .'

'Holy shit! Knock it off with that "uh-uh" – what the hell does that mean? It's fifteen kilometres there and fifteen back. The road is perfectly straight and there won't be a soul out at that hour, so just tell me, what's the problem?'

'If we should get into any shit at all . . .'

'*But what* kind of shit? Huh? *What* kind of shit? I've had my licence for three years and I've never had one single problem, do you hear me? Not one.'

He flicks his front tooth with his thumb as if to yank it loose.

'Uh-uh – no way. Not my dad's Jag.'

'Fuck, this can't be for real, are you really this stupid? This cannot be for real!'

106

'. . .'

'So what are we going do then? We show up at La Roche-my-balls in your shitty henhouse on wheels?'

'Well, yeah. . . .'

'Hold on — weren't we supposed to pick up your cousin and her girlfriend at Saint-Chinan?'

'Well, yeah. . . .'

'And you think they're going to put their pretty little arses on your shit-covered seats?!'

'Well, no. . . .'

'Well, what, then? . . . We borrow your dad's wheels, we ride in style, and in a few hours we put it ever-so-gently back where it came from. And that's that.'

'Uh-uh, not the Jag . . .' (silence) '. . . not the Jag.'

'Listen, I'm going to find someone else to take me. You're too fucking stupid — it's the party of the summer, and you want us to show up in your cattle truck. Out of the question. Does it even run?'

'Yeah, it runs.'

'Fuuuck, this can't be for real. . . .'

He pulls on the skin of his cheeks.

'Anyway, without me, you can't get in.'

'Yeah, well, between not going at all or going in your dustbin, I don't know which is worse. . . . Hey, watch out there aren't still chickens in it!'

On the road home. Five in the morning. Two drunk, tired boys who smell of cigarettes and sweat but not of fornication. (Nice party, luck of the draw . . . it happens.)

Two silent boys on the D49 between Bonneuil and Cissé-le-Duc in Indre-et-Loire.

'Well, see . . . We didn't crash it. . . . Hey, you see . . . It wasn't worth pissing me off with all your uh-uhs. Big ol' Jean-Raymond can polish your daddy's car tomorrow. . . .'

'Pfff. . . . Lot of good it did us. . . . We might as well have taken the other one. . . .'

'You're right on that front. No joy. . . .'

He touches his crotch.

'. . . Not a lot of action for you, huh? . . . Anyway . . . I'm hooking up with a blonde with big tits tomorrow, to play tennis. . . .'

'Which one?'

'You know, the one that – '

He never finished his sentence because a wild boar, a pig of at least a hundred and fifty kilos, crossed the road just at that moment, but without looking either right or left, the brute.

A wild boar in a great big hurry who was maybe on his way home from a party and afraid his parents were going to yell at him.

First they heard the screeching of tyres, and then an enormous *thunk* up front. Alexander Devermont said:

'Oh, shit.'

They stopped the car. They left their doors open and went to check – the stiff, dead pig and the stiff, dead front end of the car: no more bumper, no more radiator, no more headlights, and no more bodywork. Even the little Jaguar on the bonnet had taken a hit. Alexander Devermont said again:

'Oh, shit.'

He was too tipsy and too tired to say anything more. Still, at that precise moment, he was already clearly conscious of the immense expanse of shit that was waiting for him. He was *clearly* conscious of it.

Franck gave the boar a kick in the paunch and said:

'Well, we're not leaving it here. At least if we bring it back, we can have a barbecue. . . .'

Alexander started to laugh very quietly:

'Yeah, that's good stuff, roast boar. . . .'

It wasn't at all funny – actually, the situation was somewhat tragic – but they got the giggles. Doubtless because they were so tired and nervous.

'Your mum's going to be so happy. . . .'

'Oh, yeah – she's going to be thrilled!'

And those two little jackasses laughed so hard their stomachs hurt.

'Okay, then. . . . Shove it in the boot? . . .'

'Yeah.'

★

'Shit!'

'What now?!'

'It's full of stuff. . . .'

'Huh?'

'I'm telling you, it's full! . . . Your dad's got his golf bag in there, and cases of wine. . . .'

'Shit. . . .'

'What do we do?'

'We'll put it in the back, on the floor. . . .'

'You think?'

'Yeah, hold on. I'll put something down to protect the seats. . . . Look at the back of the boot – see if you can't find a throw. . . .'

'A what?'

'A throw.'

'What's that?'

'. . . That thing with the green and blue squares, right at the back. . . .'

'Oh, the rug! . . . A fancy-schmancy Parisian one. . . .'

'Yeah, whatever. . . . Come on, hurry up.'

'Hold on, I'll help you. No point staining his leather seats, too. . . .'

'Got that right.'

'Fuck, he's heavy! . . .'

'No shit.'

'He stinks, too.'

'Hey, Alex . . . it's the country. . . .'

'Screw the country.'

★

They got back in the car. No problem getting it started again – at least nothing had happened to the engine. That's something, anyway.

And then a few miles farther on: a big, big fright. It started with some noises and groans behind them.

Franck said:

'Fuck – he's not dead, the bastard!'

Alexander didn't answer. Enough was enough, already.

The pig started to get back up and turn every which way.

Franck slammed on the brakes and yelled:

'Let's get out of here!'

He was all white.

They slammed the doors shut and moved away from the car. Inside, it was total shit.

Total Shit.

The cream-coloured leather seats, destroyed. The steering wheel, destroyed. The elm-veneered gear lever, destroyed; the headrests, destroyed. The whole interior of the car, destroyed, destroyed, destroyed.

Devermont Junior, devastated.

The animal's eyes were popping out of their sockets, and there was a white foam around his big curving teeth. It was a horrible sight.

They decided to hide behind the door, pull it open, and then climb up and take refuge on the roof. It might have been a good plan, but they never would find out, because in the meantime the pig had stomped on the automatic lock and locked himself inside.

And the key was still in the dash.

Oh, that . . . you could say, when it all goes to hell, it all goes to hell.

Franck Mingeaut pulled his mobile out from the pocket of his chic dinner jacket and dialed 999, totally embarrassed.

When the firemen arrived, the beast had calmed down a little. Barely. Let's just say there was nothing left to destroy.

The fire chief walked around the car. Really, he was impressed. He couldn't help saying:

'Such a beautiful car – that's got to hurt.'

This next part is unbearable for those people who like nice things. . . .

One of the men went to get an enormous shotgun, a sort of bazooka. He moved away from the rest of the group and took aim. The pig and the window exploded at the same time.

The interior of the car was freshly painted: red.

Blood everywhere – even at the back of the glove compartment, even between the buttons on the carphone.

Alexander Devermont was in a daze. You'd have thought he wasn't thinking anymore. At all. About anything. Or only about burying himself alive or turning the fireman's bazooka on himself.

But no, he was thinking about the local gossips and about what a windfall this was going to be for the ecologists. . . .

It must be said that not only did his father have a magnificent Jaguar, but he'd also set his tenacious political sights on fighting the Greens.

The Greens wanted to outlaw hunting and create a Nature Park and whatever else besides, just when it would be a real pain for the big landowners.

It was a battle that he enjoyed enormously and that he'd nearly won up to this point. Just last night at the dinner table, while he was carving the duck, he'd said:

'Look! Here's one that Grolet and his bunch of arseholes won't be seeing in their binoculars anymore! Ha, ha, ha!'

But this . . . the wild boar exploding into a thousand pieces in the future regional councillor's Jaguar Sovereign – that's got to chafe a little. Surely a little, doesn't it?

There's even fur stuck to the windows.

The firemen leave; the cops leave. Tomorrow a tow truck will come and take care of the . . . that . . . well . . . the metallic grey thing blocking the road.

Our two friends walk down the road, dinner jackets tossed over their shoulders. There's nothing to say. Anyway, at the point things are at, it's not even worth thinking about it anymore, either.

Franck says:

'You want a cigarette?'

Junior answers:

'Yeah, I'd really like one.'

They walk like that for a while. The sun is coming up over the fields. The sky is pink and some stars are still lingering. There's not the slightest noise – only the rustling of rabbits running through the grass in the ditch.

And then Alexander Devermont turns to his friend and says:

'So? . . . This blonde, now, that you were telling me about . . . the one with the big tits. . . . Who is this girl?'

And his friend smiles at him.

For Years

For years I believed that this woman was outside my life – not very far maybe, but *outside*.

That she didn't exist anymore, that she lived far away, that she had never been all that beautiful, that she belonged to the world of the past. The world back when I was young and romantic, when I believed that love lasted forever and that there wasn't anything greater than my love for her. All that foolishness.

I was twenty-six years old, and I was on the platform at a train station. I couldn't understand why she was crying so much, and held her in my arms and buried my face in her neck. I thought she was sad because I was leaving, and she was letting me see her distress. And then a few weeks later, after I'd walked all over my pride like a fool on the phone and whined on and on in letters that were too long, I finally understood.

That she'd broken down that last day because she knew she was looking at my face for the last time. That she was crying over me – over my mortal remains. And that she wasn't happy to see me that way.

★

For months, I bumped into everything.

I couldn't focus on anything and I bumped into everything. The worse I felt, the more I bumped into things.

I was an absolute wreck, but I pulled it off pretty well. Day after empty day, I managed to put a good face on it. I'd get up, work 'til I was ready to drop, eat like I was supposed to, drink beer with the guys I worked with, and have a good laugh with my brothers. But that whole time, if any of them had so much as flicked his finger against my skin, it would've broken me clean in half.

But I'm not being entirely honest with myself. It wasn't courage. It was stupidity – because I thought she'd come back. I really believed she would.

I hadn't seen anything coming, and my heart had completely come apart on a train platform one Sunday night. I couldn't come to terms with it, and I kept bumping into anything and everything.

The years that followed had no effect on me. Some days I'd be surprised to think:

'You know? . . . That's strange . . . I don't think I thought about her yesterday. . . .' But instead of congratulating myself, I'd wonder how that could have happened – how I'd managed to go a whole day without thinking of her. I was especially obsessed with her name. That and two or three very precise images of her – always the same ones.

It's true. Every morning I put my feet on the ground, ate, showered, got dressed, and went to work.

Every now and then I'd see a girl naked. Every now and then, but without any tenderness.

Emotions: nil.

And then at last, in spite of all that, I got another chance – although by then I really didn't care.

Another woman met me. A very different woman, with a different name. She fell in love with me and decided to make me a whole man. Without asking my opinion, she set me back on my feet and married me, less than a year after our first kiss, exchanged in a lift during a conference.

An unhoped-for woman. I have to admit: I was petrified. I no longer believe in any of it, and I must have frequently hurt her. I'd caress her stomach, and my mind would wander. I'd lift her hair and hope to find another scent there. She never said a word. She knew my phantom life wouldn't last long. Not when I had her laughter, not when I had her skin, not when I had this whole jumble of basic, unconditional love that she was ready to give me. She was right: My phantom life let me live in peace.

She's in the next room right now. She is sleeping.

On a professional level, I never could have guessed I'd be this successful. Maybe it pays to be hard, maybe I was in the right place at the right time, maybe I made some good decisions . . . I don't know.

At any rate, I see clearly in the eyes of my old classmates, as much surprised as suspicious, that it all disconcerts them: the pretty wife, the fancy business card, the shirts tailor-made to fit . . . especially since I started out with so little. It's perplexing.

Back then, above all, I was the guy who thought of nothing but girls . . . well, of nothing but *this* girl. I was the guy who wrote letters every day during lectures and who didn't look at the arses or breasts or eyes or anything else on the café terraces. The guy who took the first train to Paris every Friday and who came back sad on Monday mornings, with circles under his eyes, cursing the distance and the conductor's zeal. More harlequin than golden boy, it's true.

Since I loved her, I neglected my studies. And since I was blowing off my studies, and vacillating on other things, she dumped me. She must have thought the future was too . . . uncertain with a guy like me.

When I read my bank statements today, I see very well that life is quite a joker.

So I went on with my life as if nothing had happened.

Of course, just for fun, every now and then my wife and I would talk about our student days, either on our own or with friends. We'd talk about the movies and books that had shaped us, and *the loves of our youth* – faces we'd forgotten over time, which some little

118

coincidence happened to make us think of. The price of a cup of coffee and all that sort of nostalgia. . . . It was like that part of our lives was sitting on a shelf. We'd dust it off from time to time, but I never dwelled on it. Oh, no.

For a while, I remember, every day I passed a sign that had the name of the town where I knew she lived, with the number of kilometres.

Every morning on my way to my office and every night on the way back, I'd glance at the sign. I glanced at it — that's all. I never followed it. I thought about it, but even the idea of flipping on my indicator seemed like spitting on my wife.

Still, I did glance at it, it's true.

And then I changed jobs. No more sign.

But there were always other reasons, other pretexts. Always. How many times did I turn around on the street, my heart in a tailspin because I thought I'd caught sight of a silhouette that . . . or a voice that . . . or a head of hair like . . . ?

How many times?

I thought I didn't think about her anymore, but all it took was to be alone for just one minute in a more or less quiet place, and she'd come back to me.

On the terrace of a restaurant one day — it was less than six months ago — when the client I'd invited didn't show up, I went looking for her in my memories. I loosened my collar and sent the waiter to buy me a packet of cigarettes – the strong, acrid ones I used to smoke way back when. I stretched out my legs and refused to let the waiter clear off the place setting across from me. I ordered a good wine, a Gruaud-Larose, I think . . . and as I smoked, eyes half closed, savouring a little ray of sun, I watched her coming towards me.

I watched and watched. I couldn't stop thinking about her – and about what we'd done when we were together and slept in the same bed.

I never once asked myself whether I still loved her or what my exact feelings toward her were. That would serve no purpose. But I loved to find her at the detour of a moment of solitude. I must say it, because it's the truth.

Fortunately for me, my life didn't leave me many moments of solitude. Honestly, the only time it ever happened was if some client forgot me completely or if I was alone in my car at night, with nothing else to worry about. In other words, almost never.

And even if I wanted to let myself indulge in a good dose of blues, of nostalgia – to assume a joking tone, for example, and try to find her phone number on the Internet or some other nonsense of the sort – I know now that it's out of the question, because for the past several years I've had some real safeguards.

The fiercest kind: my kids.

I'm crazy about my kids. I've got three: a big girl, Marie, who's seven; another who'll soon be four, Josephine; and Yvan, the baby of the family, who's not quite two. Besides, I'm the one who begged my wife to give me a third. I remember her talking about fatigue and the future . . . but I love babies so much, their gibberish and their wet kisses. 'Go ahead,' I told her, 'make me another baby.' She didn't hold out for long – and for that alone, I know that she's my only friend and that I'll never leave her. Even if I do brush shoulders with a tenacious shadow.

My kids are the best thing that ever happened to me.

An old love story doesn't count for anything next to that. Nothing at all.

So that's more or less how I've lived . . . and then last week, she said her name on the phone:

'It's Hélèna.'

'Hélèna?'

'I'm not interrupting?'

My little boy was on my knees, trying to grab the phone and squealing.

'Well . . .'

'Is that your kid?'

'Yes.'

'How old is he?'

'. . . Why are you calling me like this?'

'How old is he?'

'Twenty months.'

'I'm calling because I'd like to see you.'

'You want to see me?'

'Yes.'

'What is this shit?'

'. . .'

'Just like that. You said to yourself, "Hey! . . . I think I'd like to see him again. . . ."'

'Almost like that.'

'Why? . . . I mean, why now? . . . After all these ye –'

'Twelve years. It's been twelve years.'

'Okay. So? . . . What happened? It just hit you? What do you want? You want to know how old my kids are or if I've lost my hair or . . . or see what effect you'd have on me or . . . or just like that, to talk about the good old days?!'

'Listen, I didn't think you'd take it like this – I'm going to let you go. I'm sorry. I . . .'

'How did you get my number?'

'From your father.'

'What!'

'I called your father earlier and asked him for your number, that's all.'

'Did he remember you?'

'No. Well . . . I didn't tell him who I was.'

★

I put my son down and he went to join his sisters in their bedroom. My wife wasn't at home.

'Hold on, don't hang up. . . . Marie! Can you put his booties back on, please? . . . Hello? Are you there?'

'Yes.'

'Well? . . .'

'Well, what? . . .'

'You want to get together sometime?'

'Yes. Well, not for long. Just to have a drink or walk around for a little while, you know. . . .'

'Why? What for?'

'I just want to see you again – to talk to you for a little while.'

'Hélèna?'

'Yes.'

'Why are you doing this?'

'Why?'

'Yes, why are you calling me? Why so late? Why now? You didn't even ask yourself whether you might be throwing shit into my life. . . . You just dial my number and you – '

'Listen, Pierre. I'm going to die.'

'. . .'

'I'm calling you now because I'm going to die. I don't know when exactly, but before very long.'

I pulled the phone away from my face as though to get a little air. I tried to stand up, but without success.

'That can't be true.'

'Yes, it's true.'

'What's the matter?'

'Oh . . . it's complicated. To cut a long story short, you could say that my blood is . . . Well, I don't even know anymore just what it is now because the diagnoses are confusing. But in the end, it's pretty serious.'

I said:

'You're sure?'

'What? What do you think? You think I'd make up some over-the-top sob story just to have a reason to call you?!'

'I'm sorry.'

'Okay.'

'Maybe they made a mistake.'

'Yes . . . maybe.'

'You don't think so?'

'No. I don't think so.'

'How is this possible?'

'I don't know.'

'Are you in pain?'

'Not really.'

'Are you in pain?'

'Well, a little.'

'And you want to see me again *one last time*?'

'Yes. You could put it that way.'

'. . .'

'. . .'

'You're not worried that I'll disappoint you? You

wouldn't rather hold on to a . . . good impression?'

'An impression from when you were young and handsome?'

I could hear her smile.

'Exactly. When I was young and handsome and didn't have grey hair yet. . . .'

'You have grey hair?!'

'I have five, I think.'

'Ah! Okay, then – you had me worried! You're right. I don't know if it's a good idea, but I've been thinking about it for a while . . . and I told myself that it was one thing that would really make me happy. . . . So since there aren't many things that make me happy anymore . . . I . . . I called you.'

'How long have you been thinking about this?'

'For twelve years! No . . . I'm kidding. I've been thinking about it for several months. Since my last stay in the hospital, to be exact.'

'You really want to see me again, you think?'

'Yes.'

'When?'

'Whenever you want. Whenever you can.'

'Where do you live?'

'Same place. A hundred kilometres from you, I think.'

'Hélèna?'

'Yes.'

'No, never mind.'

'You're right. Never mind. That's how it is, that's

125

life. I'm not calling you to unravel the past or to build castles in the sky, you know. I . . .

'I'm calling you because I want to see your face again. That's all. It's like when people go back to the village where they spent their childhood or to their parents' house . . . or to whatever place touched their life.'

'Like some kind of pilgrimage.'

I realised that my voice sounded different.

'Yes, exactly – it's like a pilgrimage. I guess your face is a place that touched my life.'

'Pilgrimages are always so sad.'

'Why do you say that?! Have you ever made one!?'

'No. Yes. To Lourdes. . . .'

'Oh, well, okay, then . . . okay, then, Lourdes, of course. . . .'

She forced herself to use a mocking tone.

I could hear the kids squabbling, and I didn't feel like talking anymore. I wanted to hang up. I ended up saying:

'When?'

'You tell me.'

'Tomorrow?'

'If you like.'

'Where?'

'Halfway between our two towns – in Sully, for example. . . .'

'Are you able to drive?'

'Yes. I can drive.'

'What's in Sully?'

'Well, not much, I would guess. . . . We'll see. We can just meet in front of the town hall. . . .'

'At lunchtime?'

'Oh, no. I'm not much fun to eat with, you know. . . .'

She forced out another laugh.

'. . . After lunch would be better.'

He couldn't fall asleep that night. He stared at the ceiling, eyes open wide. He wanted to keep them good and dry. Not to cry.

It wasn't because of his wife. He was afraid of deceiving himself, of making a mistake – of crying more because of the death of his inner life than because of her death. He knew that if he got started, he wouldn't be able to stop.

Mustn't open the floodgates. Absolutely not. Because for so many years now he'd been a show-off, grumbling about people's weaknesses. Other people's. People who didn't know what they wanted, who dragged all their mediocrity along behind them.

For so many years he'd looked back on his youth with such fucking tenderness. Whenever he thought of her, he always got philosophical. He always pretended to smile over it or to understand something from it – whereas in reality he'd never understood a thing.

He knows perfectly well that he's never loved

127

anyone but her and that he's never been loved by anyone but her. That she was his only love and that nothing will ever be able to change that. That she dropped him like a cumbersome, useless thing. That she never reached out a hand to him, never dropped him a line to encourage him to get back on his feet – to confess that she wasn't really doing all that great. That he was wrong. That he deserved better than her. Or even that she'd made the mistake of her life and that she'd regretted it in secret. He knew how proud she was – to tell him that for twelve years she'd been suffering, too, and that now she was going to die. . . .

He didn't want to cry. He told himself all sorts of things to keep the tears back – all sorts of things. Then his wife rolled over, putting her hand on his stomach, and immediately he regretted his delusions. Of course he'd loved and been loved by another – of course. He looks at this face next to him, and he takes her hand and kisses it. She smiles in her sleep.

No, he has nothing to complain about. He has no reason to lie to himself. Romantic passion, hey, ho, that only lasts a moment. And now enough of that, huh? Plus, tomorrow afternoon doesn't work out too well, because he's got an appointment with the guys from Sygma II. He's going to have to put Marcheron in charge, and that's another problem altogether, because with Marcheron. . . .

★

He hadn't been able to fall asleep that night. He thought about all sorts of things.

That's how he'd explain his insomnia. But his lamp doesn't cast much light, and he can't see a thing. And, just as back in the days of his great sorrows, he bumps into everything.

She couldn't fall asleep that night, either, but she is used to it. She almost never sleeps anymore. It's because she doesn't tire herself out enough during the day – that's the doctor's theory. Her sons are at their father's, and all she does is cry.

Cry. Cry. Cry.

She's breaking up – dropping the ballast and letting herself go under. She doesn't care. She thinks that everything's fine now. It's time to move on to something else and clear the stage. It's all very well for the doctor to say she's not tiring herself out – he doesn't know a thing about it, with his neat white coat and his complicated words. To tell the truth, she's exhausted. Exhausted.

She cries because, finally, she called Pierre. She always managed to keep track of his phone number, and several times she went so far as to dial the ten numbers that separated her from him. She would hear his voice and hang up right away. One time, she even followed him for a whole day. She wanted to know where he lived, what kind of car he drove, where he worked, how he dressed, and whether he seemed worried. She followed his wife, too. She had had to admit that his wife was cheerful and pretty, and that she had had kids with him.

She cries because her heart started beating again today, and for some time now she had no longer thought that was possible. She's had a harder life than she could have imagined. She has mostly known solitude. She thought it was too late now to feel anything – that her good days were over. Especially since *they* got all worked up one day over a blood test, a routine check-up that she happened to have done because she felt a little out of sorts. Everyone, from the little doctors to the great professors, had an opinion about her condition – but not much to say when it came to getting rid of it.

She cries for so many reasons that she doesn't want to think about it. Her whole life comes flying back in her face. So, to protect herself a little, she tells herself that she's crying for the sake of crying and that's all there is to it.

She was already there when I arrived. She smiled and said, 'This must be the first time I haven't kept you waiting! See – there was no need to lose hope.' I told her I hadn't lost hope.

We didn't hug. I said, 'You haven't changed.' It's a

dumb thing to say, but it's what I thought, except that I thought she was more beautiful than ever. She was very pale, and you could see all the little blue veins around her eyes, on her eyelids, and at her temples. She'd got thin, and the hollows in her face were deeper than before. She seemed more resigned, whereas I remember the air of vivacity she used to exude. She never stopped looking at me. She wanted me to talk to her; she wanted me to be quiet. She smiled the whole time. She'd wanted to see me again. For my part, I didn't know how to move my hands, or if I could smoke or touch her arm.

It was a creepy town. We walked as far as the public garden a little farther on.

We told each other the stories of our lives. It was somewhat disjointed. We each kept our secrets. She had trouble finding the right words. At one point, she asked me the difference between helplessness and idleness. I couldn't remember. She made a gesture to show that, anyhow, it didn't really matter. She said that it had all made her too bitter, or too hard – in any case, too different from what she'd been before.

We barely touched on the subject of her illness, except when she talked about her kids: she said it was no life for them. Not long ago, she'd wanted to cook them some noodles, but she hadn't even been able to manage that, because the pot of water was too heavy

for her to lift. And really, that was no life. They'd had
more than their share of sadness up to now.

She made me talk about my wife and kids and work.
And even about Marcheron. She wanted to know
everything, but I could tell that most of the time she
wasn't listening.

We were sitting on a peeling bench, across from a
fountain that must not have spit any water since the
day of its inauguration. Everything was ugly. Sad and
ugly. A light mist was beginning to fall, and we sort of
shrank into ourselves to keep warm.

Finally, she got up. It was time for her to go.

She said, 'I have just one favour I'd like to ask, just
one. I want to smell you.' And when I didn't respond,
she confessed that through all these years she'd wanted
to breathe in my scent. I kept my hands right down at
the bottom of my coat pockets, because otherwise . . .

She went behind me and leaned over my hair. She
stayed like that for a long time, and I felt terrible.
Next, she moved her nose to the hollow at the nape of
my neck and all around my head, taking her time, and
then she went down the length of my neck to my
collar. She breathed in. She kept her hands behind her
back, too. Next, she loosened my tie and opened the
first two buttons of my shirt. I felt the tip of her
nostrils all cold against the base of my collarbone, and
I . . . I . . .

I shifted somewhat abruptly. She stood back up behind me and put both hands flat on my shoulders. She said, 'I'm going to go. I want you not to move and not to turn around. Please – I'm begging you. I'm begging you.'

I didn't move. I didn't want to, anyway, because I didn't want her to see me with my eyes swollen and my face all contorted.

I waited a while, then headed to my car.

Clic-Clac

For five and a half months now I've wanted Sarah Briot, director of sales.

Would it not be better for me to say: for five and a half months now I've been *in love* with Sarah Briot, director of sales? I don't know.

During all this time, I haven't been able to think of her without getting a massive erection, and since it's the first time this has happened to me, I'm not sure what to call it, this sentiment.

Sarah Briot knows something's up. No, she hasn't ever bumped up against my trousers or anything, but she knows.

Of course, she doesn't realise that it'll be five and a half months on Tuesday, because she doesn't pay as much attention to numbers as I do. (I'm an account auditor, so it's only natural. . . .) But I know she knows, because she's sharp.

She speaks to men in a way that shocked me before and that now drives me to despair. She speaks to them as if she's got special glasses, the Superman X-ray kind, that let her see the exact size of the sexual organ of whatever guy she's talking to.

The size at rest, I mean. So, obviously, that makes for some entertaining interactions at work. . . . You can imagine.

She'll shake your hand, answer your questions, smile at you, even have coffee with you in the cafeteria, from a plastic cup . . . and you, like a fucking idiot, all you can think about is pressing your knees together or crossing your legs. It's sheer hell.

The worst of it is that the whole time, she never stops looking you in the eye – and only in the eye.

Sarah Briot isn't beautiful. She's cute, and that's not the same thing.

She's not very tall. She's blonde, but it doesn't take a genius to see that it's not her real colour – those are highlights.

Like most girls, she wears trousers often, and even more often, jeans. Which is too bad.

Sarah Briot is just a tiny little hair overweight. I often hear her discussing different diets on the phone with her girlfriends. (Since she talks loud and I'm in the office next door, I hear everything.)

She says she's got to lose 4 kilos to get down to 50. I think about that every day, because I jotted it down on my desk blotter while she was talking: '54!!!'

That's also how I found out that she'd already tried the Montignac Method and that she'd have been 'better off keeping the fifteen euros' . . . that she'd ripped out the centre section from the April issue of *Biba*, with all Estelle Hallyday's *special weight loss* recipes . . . that she had a giant poster in her tiny kitchen showing calorie counts for every food . . . and that she'd even bought a little pair of kitchen scales to weigh everything, like they do at Weight Watchers.

She talks about it a lot with her friend Marie, who's tall and thin, from what I gather.

(Between you and me, it's stupid, because I don't see what her girlfriend could have to say to her about it. . . .)

At this point in my story, any moron's probably wondering, 'So what exactly does he see in this girl?'

Hold on . . . I'll put a stop to that!

The other day I heard Sarah Briot laughing gleefully as she told someone (Marie maybe?) how she'd ended up palming the scales off on her mother so she could make Sarah 'lovely cakes on Sundays'. She got a big kick out of telling that story.

Besides, Sarah Briot isn't vulgar . . . she's alluring. Everything about her inspires caresses. And that's not the same thing, either.

So shut up.

The week before Mother's Day, I was strolling through the lingerie department at the Galeries Lafayette one day during my lunch break. All the

saleswomen – a red rose in the topmost buttonhole –
were on full alert, on the lookout for indecisive dads.

I'd tucked my briefcase under my arm and was
playing if-I-were-married-to-Sarah-Briot-what-would-
I-buy-her? . . .

Lou, Passionata, Simone Pérèle, Lejaby, Aubade
. . . My head was spinning.

Some things seemed too naughty – it was Mother's
Day, after all. Others, I didn't like the colour or the
saleswoman. (I like foundation just fine, but still, there
are limits.)

Not to mention all the styles I didn't understand.

I had a hard time seeing myself unfastening all those
tiny little microscopic buttons in the heat of the action,
and I couldn't figure out how the suspender belt
worked. (To do it right, do you leave it on or take it
off?)

I felt hot.

I finally found, for the future mother of my children, a
Christian Dior bra-and-pants set in a very pale grey
silk. Classy.

'What size bra does madaaame wear?'

I set my briefcase down between my feet.

'About like this . . . ,' I said, curving my hands
about six inches in front of my chest.

'You have no idea?' asked the saleswoman, a little
dryly. 'What are her measurements?'

'Um, she comes up to about here on me . . . ,' I answered, indicating my shoulder.

'I see. . . .' She pursed her lips in consternation. 'I'll tell you what, I'll give you a 34C – it might be too big, but she can exchange it without a problem. Be sure to keep the receipt, okay?'

'Thank you. That's fine,' I said, trying to sound like the kind of guy who takes his kids out to the woods every Sunday, without forgetting the water bottles and rain jackets.

'And for the pants? Do you want the classic style or the tanga? I also have it in a thong, but I don't think that's what you're looking for. . . .'

What do you know about it, Madame Micheline of the Galeries Lafayette?

Obviously you don't know *the* Sarah Briot of Chopard & Minont's. The one who always lets the tip of her belly button show and who walks into other people's offices without knocking.

But when she showed it to me, I lost my nerve. No, it wasn't really possible that someone could wear a thing like that. Seriously, it was practically an instrument of torture. I got the 'tanga', which '. . . has all the Brazilian touches but is less cut away over the hips this year, as you can see for yourself. Shall I gift wrap it for you, monsieur?'

A tanga.

Whew.

I shoved the little pink package between my Paris map and a couple of files, and I went back to my computer screen.

Talk about a lunch break.

At least when there are kids, it'll be easier to choose things. I'll have to tell them: 'No, kids, not a waffle iron. . . . Let's see. . . .'

It was Sittier, my colleague from exports, who said to me one day:

'You like her, huh?'

We were at Mario's splitting the lunch bill, and this jerk wanted to act like we were old pals and go ahead, tell me everything so I can cuff you in the ribs.

'No shit. . . . You've got good taste, huh!'

I didn't feel like talking to him – not in the least.

'I guess she's quite a sexpot, huh. . . .' (Big wink.)

I shook my head disapprovingly.

'Dujoignot told me . . .'

'Dujoignot went out with her!'

I was lost in my accounts.

'Nah, but he heard a thing or two from Movard, because Movard had her, and from what I hear . . .'

He sat there, jerking his hand in the air like he was trying to shake it dry, making the little O of mOron with his mouth.

'. . . Yeah, that Briot's hot, all right. . . . Not exactly

inhibited, huh. . . . She'll do stuff, I can't even begin to tell you. . . .'

'So don't. Who's this Movard?'

'He used to be in advertising, but he left before you got here. Our little pond was too small for him, you know how it goes. . . .'

'I see.'

Poor Sittier. He doesn't finish his thought. He must be picturing a whole slew of sexual positions.

Poor Sittier. You know, my sisters call you Shittier, and they still giggle whenever they think about your Ford Mondeo.

Poor Sittier, who tried to come on to Myriam even though he wears a gold signet ring engraved with his initials.

Poor Sittier. Who still thinks he's got a chance with smart girls, and who goes on first dates with his mobile phone in a plastic cover attached to his belt, and his car radio under his arm.

Poor Sittier. If you only knew how my sisters talk about you . . . when they talk about you at all.

You never know what's going to happen – how things are going to unfold, or when the simplest things are suddenly going to take on demented proportions. Take me, for example. My whole life turned upside down because of five ounces of grey silk.

For five years and not quite eight months I've lived with my sisters in a one-hundred-and-ten-square-metre apartment near the Convention metro station.

In the beginning, it was just me and my sister Fanny. She's four years younger than I and a med student at René Descartes University. It was our parents' idea, to be economical and to make sure the little one wouldn't get lost in Paris. She'd never known anything but our home town, Tulle, its high school, its cafés, its reconditioned mopeds.

I get on well with Fanny: She doesn't talk much, and she's always okay with anything.

For example, if it's her week to do the cooking and I bring home, say, sole, because that's what I happen to be in the mood for, she's not the kind of person to whine that I'm upsetting all her plans. She adapts.

It's not exactly the same with Myriam.

Myriam is the oldest. We're not even a year apart, but if you saw us, you wouldn't even imagine that we were brother and sister. She talks nonstop. Sometimes I think she's a little off her rocker, but that's to be expected, I guess – she's the artist in the family. . . .

After she finished her studies at art college, she did photography, collages with hemp and steel wool, video clips with paint stains on the lenses, stuff with her body, creations of spaces with Loulou de La Rochette (?), demos, sculpture, dance, and I forget what else.

These days she's painting stuff I have trouble

understanding, no matter how much I scrunch up my eyes. Myriam says that on the day they handed out artistic ability, I stayed at home. She says I don't know how to see what's beautiful. Whatever.

The last time we got into it was when we went to the Boltanski exhibition together. (But whose idea was it to take me to see that . . . seriously. Can you imagine what a fucking idiot I looked trying to figure out which way you were supposed to walk through the exhibition?)

Myriam's a real artichoke heart – she's always falling in love. Every six months since the age of fifteen (which must make it about thirty-eight times, if I'm not mistaken), she's brought us the man of her life. Mr. Good, Mr. Right, Mr. White-Wedding, Mr. Okay-This-Time-It's-For-Real, Mr. Last-One, Mr. Sure-Thing, Mr. Last-of-the-Last-Ones.

All of Europe, just for her: Yoann was Swedish; Giuseppe, Italian; Erick, Dutch; Kiko, Spanish; and Laurent, from Saint-Quentin-en-Yvelines. Obviously, there are thirty-three others. . . . At the moment, their names don't come back to me.

When I left my studio to move in with Fanny, Myriam was with Kiko. A brilliant future director.

At first, we didn't see much of her. Every now and then the two of them would invite themselves to dinner, and Kiko would bring the wine. It was always very good. (Just as well, since that's the only thing he had to do all day long – choose the wine.)

I liked Kiko. He'd give my sister a doleful look and then pour himself some more to drink, shaking his head. Kiko smoked some bizarre shit, and I always had to spray honeysuckle deodoriser the next day to make the smell go away.

Months went by. Myriam came over more and more often, and almost always alone. She and Fanny would shut themselves in the bedroom, and I'd hear them giggling until the small hours. One night when I went in to ask if they wanted some herbal tea or anything, I found them both stretched out on the floor listening to an old Jean-Jacques Goldman cassette: 'Siiiince you're leaeaeavviiing . . . and nyanyanya.'

Pathetic.

Sometimes Myriam went away again. Sometimes not.

There was an extra toothbrush in the Duralex glass in the bathroom, and the sofa bed was often unfolded at night.

And then one day, she said:

'If it's Kiko, say I'm not here . . .' pointing to the phone.

And then, and then, and then . . . One morning, she asked me:

'Would you mind if I crash with you guys for a while? . . . I'll chip in toward expenses, of course. . . .'

I was being careful not to break my biscotti – because if there's one thing I hate, it's to break my biscottis. I told her:

'No problem.'

'Cool. Thanks.'

'Just one thing . . .'

'What's that?'

'Do you think you could go out on the balcony when you smoke? . . .'

She smiled, got up, and gave me a big artist's smack.

Of course, my biscotti broke and I said to myself, 'And so it begins . . .', stirring my hot cocoa to retrieve the little pieces. But even so, I was happy.

Still, it bothered me all day, and so that night I laid it all out. 'We'll share the rent, as much as possible, and we'll divvy up the shopping, cooking, and cleaning. Okay, girls? Look at the refrigerator door, I've posted a rota with our weeks: Fanny, you're in pink highlighter, Myriam, you're in blue, and I'm in yellow. . . . Please let the rest of us know if you're eating out or if you're having guests, and speaking of guests, if you bring home guys you plan to sleep with,

please work it out between the two of you for who
gets the bedroom when. And . . .'

'All right, enough . . . enough. . . . Don't get
worked up . . . ,' said Myriam.

'No kidding . . . ,' her sister answered.

'And what about you? When you bring home some
little chick, be nice and give us fair warning, too, okay!
So we can get rid of our fishnet stockings and our old
condoms. . . .'

And they sniggered even harder.

Damn.

Our little arrangement worked out pretty well, for the
most part. I'll admit I didn't really think it would, but I
was wrong. . . . When girls want something to work
out, it works out. It's just that simple.

When I look back on it now, I realise just how much
it meant to Fanny to have Myriam here.

Fanny's the total opposite of her sister. She's
romantic and faithful – and sensitive.

She's always falling in love with some inaccessible
guy who lives in Bumblefuck. Ever since she was
fifteen, she's waited impatiently for the post every
morning and jumped every time the phone rang.

That's no way to live.

First there was Fabrice, who lived in Lille. (From
Tulle, you can see the difficulty. . . .) He drowned her

under a flood of passionate letters in which he only talked about himself. Four years of frustrated, juvenile love.

Next, there was Paul, who went off to somewhere in Burkina Faso with Médecins Sans Frontières, leaving her with the beginnings of a vocation, the energy to rail against the slowness of the post office, and all her tears to cry. . . . Five years of frustrated, exotic love.

And now the last straw: I thought I gathered from their late-night conversations and the allusions they made at the dinner table that Fanny was in love with a doctor who was already married.

I could hear them in the bathroom. Myriam, brushing her teeth, said to her:

'He'sch got kidsch?'

I imagine that Fanny was sitting on the toilet seat cover.

'No.'

'That'sch bescht becausche . . .' (she spits) '. . . with kids that'd be too much of a drama, you know. In any case, I could never do it.'

Fanny didn't answer, but I'm sure that she was chewing on her hair and looking at the bath mat or her toes.

'It's as though you go looking for them. . . .'

'. . .'

'We've had it up to here with your star-crossed lovers. Plus, doctors are all utter bores. Later he'll take up golf, and then he'll always be stuck in meetings at the Club Med in Marrakech or wherever, and you'll still be all alone. . . .'

'. . .'

'Plus, let me tell you. . . . Maybe it'll work out – it's possible – but what makes you think it will? . . . Because the Other Woman, do you really think she's going to let go of her guy just like that? 'Cause she likes getting a tan in Marrakech, so she can be one-up on the dentist's wife from the Rotary Club.'

Fanny must be smiling – you can hear it in her voice. She murmurs:

'I'm sure you're right. . . .'

'Of course I'm right!'

Six months of frustrated, adulterous love. (Maybe.)

'So come with me to the Galerie Delaunay on Saturday night. For one thing, I know the guy who's doing the catering, and it won't be bad. I'm sure Marc will be there. . . . I absolutely have to introduce you two! You'll see – he's a great guy! Plus he's got a fabulous butt.'

'Pfff, whatever. . . . What kind of show is it?'

'I don't remember. Hey, could you hand me the towel?'

Myriam often improved upon the ordinary by bringing home little dishes from Fauchon's and fine wines. I have to admit, she'd hit again on an outrageous scheme. For several weeks, she'd pored over books and magazines on Lady Di – you couldn't cross the living room without stepping on the deceased – and practised drawing her. Now, every weekend, she planted her gear on the pont de l'Alma and sketched the weepy-eyed from around the world next to their idol.

For a ludicrous amount of money ('stupidity has its price'), a Japanese tourist on one of those big group tours could ask my sister to draw her next to a laughing Diana (at a party at Harry's school) or a crying Diana (with Belfast AIDS patients) or a Diana showing sympathy (with the Liverpool AIDS patients) or a Diana sulking (at the fiftieth anniversary of the Normandy Landings).

I salute the artist and take charge of bringing the bottles to room temperature.

Yes, our arrangement was working out well. Fanny and I didn't talk much more than before, but we laughed more. Myriam didn't settle down at all, but she painted. To my sisters, I seemed like the perfect guy – although not the one they'd have wanted to marry.

I didn't give it much thought. I just shrugged my shoulders and kept an eye on the oven door.

So it took a fistful of lingerie to bowl a ten-pin strike.

It would mean the end of the evenings seated at the foot of the couch, watching my sisters and sighing. The end of Fanny's made-to-order cocktails, which unsettle your stomach and remind you of all kinds of salacious stories. The end of the squabbles:

'Well, *think* of it! Shit! It's important – was his name Lorian or Tristan?'

'I don't know. He doesn't articulate very well, this guy of yours. . . .'

'You're impossible! Are you doing this on purpose, or what? Try to remember!'

"Hello, may I speak to Myriam? It's Ltfrgzqan.' That better?'

And she disappeared into the kitchen.

'Please don't slam the refrigerator door. . . .'

Bang.

'. . . Maybe you could give him the name of a good speech therapist. . . .'

'Chmmchmpoordjit.'

'Hey, you know, it wouldn't do you any harm, either.'

Bang.

The end of making up over my famous chicken Boursin. ('Well? . . . Don't you think you're better off here with us than off with Ltfrgzqan at some cheesy idiot fest?')

The end of the highlighted rotas, the end of Saturday-morning shopping trips, the end of the *Gala* magazines sitting in the bathroom open to the horoscope pages, the end of the artists of all kinds trying to get us to understand Boltanski's rags, the end of the all-nighters, the end of helping Fanny memorise her revision sheets, the end of stress on the days results were posted, the end of the black looks for the woman who lived downstairs, the end of the Jeff Buckley songs, the end of Sundays stretched out on the carpet reading the comics, the end of the Liquorice Allsorts orgies in front of the TV, watching celebrity chat shows, the end of toothpaste tubes with the caps never on, drying out and driving me crazy.

The end of my youth.

We'd planned a dinner to celebrate the end of Fanny's exams. She was beginning to see the light at the end of the tunnel. . . .

'Whew! Only ten more years . . . ,' she said, smiling.

Around the coffee table were her intern (without his wedding ring, the coward – future golfer in Marrakech, I still say) and her girlfriends from the hospital, including the famous Laura. My sisters had cooked up an incalculable number of plans for the two of us, each more inane than the next, under the pretext that she'd spoken about me one day with a tremor in her voice. (Like the time they had me go to her house for a surprise birthday party and I found myself alone all evening with this fury, hunting for contacts in the goat-hair carpet while trying to protect my backside. . . .)

Marc was there, too. (I took advantage to see what 'a fabulous butt' is . . . so-so. . . .)

There were also some friends of Myriam's that I'd never seen before.

I wondered where she dug up such freaks – guys tattooed from head to toe and girls with legs up to here that you wouldn't believe, laughing at everything and shaking whatever it was they had instead of hair.

My sisters had said:

'Bring your friends from work if you want. . . . You know, you never introduce us to anyone. . . .'

And for good reason, I thought later, admiring the flora and the fauna eating my peanuts, sprawled out on the state-of-the-art couch that Mum gave me when I got my accountancy diploma. *And for good reason. . . .*

It was already pretty late, and we were all good and wasted, when Myriam – who'd gone to look for a scented candle in my room – came back gobbling like a turkey in heat, with Sarah Briot's bra between her thumb and forefinger.

Holy shit.

Now I was in for it.

'Hey, but what's this?! Wait, Olivier, do you know you've got sex-shop props in your room?... Something to make every guy in Paris pitch a tent! Don't tell us you didn't know!?'

And off she goes putting on a whole damn show, out of control.

She wiggles her hips, mimes a striptease, sniffs the panties, grips the halogen lamp, and falls over backwards.

Out of control.

Everyone else is dying of laughter. Even the golf champion.

'Okay. That's enough,' I said. 'Give me that.'

'Who's it for? First you have to tell us who it's for . . . doesn't he, guys?'

So all those jackasses start whistling with their fingers, clicking their teeth against their glasses, and worst of all messing up my living room!

'Plus, did you see the boobs she's got! Look, that's gotta be at least a thirty-six!' yells this moron Laura.

'You won't get bored, huh . . . ,' Fanny whispered, her mouth twisting bizarrely.

I got up. I took my keys and jacket and slammed the door.

Bang.

I slept at the Ibis hotel at La Porte de Versailles.

No, I didn't sleep. I thought.

I spent a good part of the night standing at the window, my forehead pressed against the glass, looking at the Parc des Expositions.

How ugly.

By morning, my mind was made up. I wasn't even hungover, and I put away a huge breakfast.

I went to the flea market.

I hardly ever take time for myself.

I was like a tourist in Paris. I had my hands in my pockets and I smelled good: Nina Ricci's aftershave for men, found in all the Ibis hotels around the world. I'd have loved to run into my colleague at a bend in the path:

'Oh, Olivier!'

'Oh, Sarah!'

'Oh, Olivier, you smell so good. . . .'

'Oh, Sarah!'

I sat on the terrace at the Café des Amis, a beer in front of me, drinking in the sun.

It was June 16, about noon. It was a gorgeous day and my life was beautiful.

I bought an over-ornate birdcage with lots of wrought-iron flourishes.

The guy who sold it to me assured me that it dated

from the nineteenth century and that it had belonged to a very highly esteemed family, since it had been found in a private mansion, still in one piece, and so on and so forth and how are you paying?

I felt like saying, *Don't wear yourself out, old man, I couldn't care less*.

When I got back home, it smelled like Mr. Clean from the ground floor up.

The apartment was spotless. Not a speck of dust. There was even a bouquet on the kitchen table with a little note: 'We're at the Jardin des Plantes – see you tonight. XOXO.'

I took off my watch and set it down on my bedside table. The Christian Dior package was right there next to it, as if nothing had happened.

Aaahhh!! My dears. . . .

For dinner, I'm going to make a chicken Boursin that will be un-for-get-ta-ble.

Okay, first I've got to choose the wine . . . and put out a tablecloth, of course.

And for dessert, a semolina cake with lots of rum. Fanny loves that.

I'm not saying we threw our arms around each other, squeezing each other tight and shaking our heads, the way Americans do. They just gave me a little smile as they came in, and I saw all the little flowers of the Jardin des Plantes in their faces.

For once, we weren't in any rush to clear the table. After the debauchery of the night before, no one had any plans to go out, and Mimi served us mint tea at the kitchen table.

'What's with the cage?' asked Fanny.

'I bought it at the flea market this morning from this guy who doesn't sell anything but antique cages. . . . Do you like it?'

'Yes.'

'Good, it's for the two of you.'

'Really! Thank you. What's the occasion – because we're so full of tact and sensitivity?' joked Myriam, heading for the balcony with her pack of Cravens.

'As a souvenir of me. You have only to say that the bird has flown his cage. . . .'

'Why are you saying that?!'

'I'm leaving, girls.'

'Where are you going?'

'I'm going to go live somewhere else.'

'With who?'

'On my own.'

'But why? It's because of last night. . . . Listen, I am so sorry – you know I had too much to drink, and . . .'

'No, no, don't worry about it. It's got nothing to do with you.'

★

Fanny seemed really stunned, and I had a hard time looking her in the face.

'You're tired of us?'

'No, that's not it.'

'But why, then?' You could tell the tears were coming to her eyes.

Myriam stood rooted between the table and the window, her cigarette hanging sadly from her lips.

'Olivier, hey – what's going on?'

'I'm in love.'

You couldn't just say so right away, you jerk.

And why haven't you introduced us? What! You're afraid we'll scare her off. You don't know us very well. . . . Oh? You do know us well. . . . Ah?

What's her name?

Is she pretty? Yes? Oh, shit. . . .

What? You've barely even spoken to her? Are you an idiot, or what? Yes, you are an idiot?

No, you're not.

You've barely even spoken to her, and you're moving out because of her? Don't you think you're putting the cart before the horse? You put the cart where you can. . . . Well, if you look at it that way, of course. . . .

When are you going to talk to her? Someday. Okay, I see the problem. . . . Does she have a good sense of humour? Ah, good, good.

You really love her? You don't want to answer that?

Are we annoying you?

All you have to do is say so.

You'll invite us to the wedding? Only if we promise to be good?

Who's going to make me feel better the next time my heart turns to mush?

And me? Who's going to make me study for my anatomy class?

Who's going to pamper us now?

Just how pretty is she?

Are you going to make her your chicken Boursin?

We're going to miss you, you know.

I was surprised that I had so few things to take with me. I'd rented a small van from Kiloutou's, and one trip was enough.

I didn't know if I should take that in a good way, as in, *Well, that just proves you're not too attached to the things of this world, my friend,* or really badly, as in, *Look, friend: you're almost thirty, and eleven boxes for everything you've got. . . . Doesn't amount to much, does it?*

Before I left, I sat down one last time in the kitchen.

The first couple of weeks, I slept on a mattress right on the floor. I'd read in a magazine that it's very good for your back.

After seventeen days, I went to Ikea. My back was hurting too much.

God knows I'd considered the problem from every possible angle. I even drew out floor plans on graph paper.

The saleswoman thought the same thing I did: In an apartment so modest and so poorly laid out (you'd have thought I'd rented three little hallways . . .), a sofa bed was the way to go.

And the least expensive kind is the Clic-Clac.

A Clic-Clac it is.

I also bought a kitchen set (sixty-five pieces for sixty euros, salad spinner and cheese grater included), some candles (you never know . . .), a throw (I don't know, I thought it would be chic to buy a throw), a lamp (whatever), a doormat (thinking ahead), some shelves (predictably), a green plant (we'll see . . .), and a thousand other little things. (That's how the store wants it.)

Myriam and Fanny leave regular messages on my answering machine: *Beeeep* 'How do you turn on the oven?' *beeeeep* 'We got the oven on but now we're wondering how to change a fuse because everything blew. . . .' *beeeeep* 'We're ready to do what you said but where do you keep the torch? . . .' *beeeep* 'Hey, how do we call the fire service?' *beeep* . . .

★

I think they're exaggerating a little, but – like all people who live alone – I've learned to check and even hope for the little red blinking message light when I come home in the evenings.

I don't think anyone escapes that.

And then suddenly, your life speeds up like crazy.

And when I lose control of a situation, I tend to panic. It's stupid.

So, what do I mean by 'losing control of the situation'?

Losing control of the situation is very simple. It's having Sarah Briot show up one morning in the room where you make your living by the sweat of your brow and seat herself on the edge of your desk, hitching up her skirt.

And saying:

'Your glasses are dirty, aren't they?'

And pulling a little hem of pink shirt out from under her skirt and wiping your glasses with it, as though it's nothing.

Then you pop such a glorious boner you could lift the desk with it (with a little training of course).

'So, I hear you've moved?'

'Yeah, a couple of weeks ago.'

(Fffff . . . breathe . . . Everything's going fine. . . .)

'Where are you now?'

'In the tenth arrondissement.'

'Oh! That's funny – me, too.'

'Really?!'

'That's good – now we'll be on the same metro. . . .'

(It's a start.)

'Aren't you going to have a housewarming party or something?'

'Yes – yes, of course!'

(News to me.)

'When?'

'Oh, well, I don't know yet. . . . You know, I just had the last of my furniture delivered this morning, so . . .'

'What about tonight?'

'Tonight? Oh, no, tonight won't work. The place is a mess, and . . . and then, that doesn't give people much notice, and . . .'

'You don't have to invite anyone but me. Because, you know, I don't care about the mess – it can't be any worse than my place! . . .'

'Oh . . . well . . . well, if you want. But not too early, then?!'

'Great – that way I'll have time to stop by my place to change. . . . How about nine o'clock – does that work for you?'

'Nine o'clock, great.'

'Okay, well, see you later, then? . . .'

That's what I mean by 'losing control of the situation.'

I left early, and for the first time in my life, I didn't straighten up my desk before I put out the light.

The concierge was watching for me: 'Yes, they delivered your furniture, but what a business to get that couch up six flights!'

'Thanks, Madame Rodriguez, thanks.' (I won't forget your Christmas bonus, Madame Rodriguez. . . .)

Three little corridors shaped like a battlefield. . . . It has its charms. . . .

Put the taramasalata in a cool place, heat up the coq au vin, over low heat, okay . . . open the bottles, set a makeshift table, race back down to the convenience store to get paper napkins and a bottle of mineral water, set up the coffeemaker, take a shower, put on cologne (Eau Sauvage), clean your ears, find a shirt that's not too wrinkled, turn down the lamp, unplug the phone, put on some music (Rickie Lee Jones's *Pirates* album – anything's possible with that . . . but not too loud), arrange the throw, light the candles (well, well . . .), breathe in, breathe out, don't look at yourself anymore in the mirror.

And the condoms? (In the drawer of the bedside table – isn't that too close? . . . And in the bathroom, isn't that too far? . . .)

Dring, dring.

Is it fair to say I have the situation in hand?

Sarah Briot came in. Pretty as the day.

Later in the evening, when we'd had a few good laughs, eaten well, and let some dreamy silences set in, it was clear that Sarah Briot would be spending the night in my arms.

Only I've always had trouble making certain decisions – and yet, it was *really* time to put down my glass and make a move.

As if Roger Rabbit's wife were sitting right next to you, and you were thinking about your savings plan. . . .

She was talking about I don't know what and looking at me out of the corner of her eye.

And suddenly . . . suddenly . . . I thought about this couch that we were sitting on.

I began really, intensely, steadily to wonder: How do you open up a Clic-Clac?

I thought it would be best to begin by kissing her fairly passionately and then to tilt her back deftly in order to lay her down without incident. . . .

Yes, but afterwards . . . with the Clic-Clac?

I could already see myself getting silently worked up

over some little latch while her tongue tickled my tonsils and her hands searched for my belt. . . .

Well . . . for the moment, that wasn't exactly the case. . . . She was even beginning to stifle the beginnings of a yawn. . . .

Some Don Juan. What a disgrace.

And then I thought of my sisters. I laughed inside thinking of those two harpies.

They'd have had a ball if they could have seen me just then, with Miss Universe's thigh up against mine and me with my domestic little worries about how to open a sofa bed from Ikea.

Just then, Sarah Briot turned to me and said:

'You're cute when you smile.'

And she kissed me.

And then, at that exact moment, with 54 kilos of femininity on my knees, all sweetness and caresses, I closed my eyes, threw my head back, and thought with all my might: 'Thank you, girls.'

Epilogue

'Marguerite! When are we eating?'

'Screw you.'

Since I've been writing stories, my husband's started calling me Marguerite – for Marguerite Duras – as he taps me on the bottom. He tells everyone at dinner parties that he's going to stop working soon, thanks to my royalties:

'Listen . . . as far as I'm concerned, no problem! I'm just waiting for it all to pan out, and I'll go and pick up the kids from school in my Jaguar XK8. It's all set. . . . Of course, I'll have to massage her shoulders from time to time and put up with her little crises of doubt, but hey . . . that coupé? . . . I'll take it in dragon green.'

He keeps raving about it, and people don't know how to take it.

They say to me, in the tone you'd use to talk about a sexually transmitted disease:

'Is that true – you write?'

And I just shrug my shoulders, holding out my glass to the master of the house. I grumble out a *No, whatever, almost nothing*. And Mr. Excitable, whom I married in a moment of weakness, just keeps laying it on:

'Wait. . . . Didn't she tell you? Sweetie, didn't you tell them about the prize you won at Saint-Quentin? Hey! . . . Fifteen hundred euros, you know!!! Two nights at her computer, which she bought for seventy-five euros at a charity sale, and fifteen hundred euros fall into our laps! . . . What more could you ask? And I'm not even telling you about all her other prizes . . . huh, Pumpkin, let's stay humble.'

It's true that at these moments, I really want to kill him.

But I won't.

First of all because he weighs eighty-two kilos (he says eighty – pure vanity), and then also because he's right.

He's right – and what will become of me if I start believing in it too much?

I quit my job? I finally say some nasty things to my co-worker Micheline? I buy myself a little zobi-skin notebook and I take notes *for later*? I feel so alone, so far away, so close, so *different*? I go and meditate at the tomb of Chateaubriand? I say: 'No, not tonight, please, my head's bursting'? I forget to show up at the childminder's because I have a chapter to finish?

You should see the kids at the childminder's from five-thirty on. You ring the bell, and they all rush to the door, hearts pounding. The one who opens it is inevitably disappointed to see you, since you're not there for him, but after the first second of despair (mouth twisted, shoulders drooping, and blankie trailing on the ground again), he turns to your son (just behind him) and yells:

'Louis, it's your mum!!!!!'

And so then you hear:

'Well, yeah . . . I doh.'

But Marguerite is getting tired of all these pretences.

She wants to be clear in her own mind about it. If she's going to have to go to Combourg to track down Chateaubriand's grave, she might as well find out right away.

She chose some stories (two sleepless nights), she printed them out with her antiquated machine (more than three hours to do a hundred and thirty-four pages!), she clutched her sheets of paper to her heart and took them to the copy shop over by the law school. She stood in line behind noisy students perched on high heels (she felt old and frumpy, our Marguerite).

The salesgirl asked:

'A white binder or a black binder?'

And there she was, fretting all over again. (White? That's a little too much like a goody-goody communicant, isn't it? . . . But black, that's way too

self-assured, more like a doctoral thesis, isn't it? . . .
Misery of miseries.)

Finally the young woman loses patience:

'What is it exactly?'

'Some stories . . .'

'News stories? About what?'

'No, not news stories . . . short stories, you
know? . . . It's to send to a publisher. . . .'

'. . . ??? . . . Yeah . . . well, okay, that doesn't really
tell us what colour binding . . .'

'Use whichever one you want – I'll leave it to you.'
(*Alea jacta est.*)

'Well, in that case, I'll give you the turquoise,
because at this moment it's on sale: four euros fifty
cents instead of five twenty-five . . . (A turquoise
binder on the chic desk of an elegant Left Bank
publisher . . . oops.)

'Okay, go with the turquoise.' (Don't stand in the
way of Destiny, my girl.)

The girl lifts up the cover of her big Xerox machine and
manhandles the packet like so many cheap handouts
on civil law: there you go, I'll just turn it this way and
that for you, and there you go, I'll just dog-ear the
corners for you.

The artist suffers in silence.

As the girl takes the money, she picks up the cigarette
she'd left on the cash register and asks:

'What are they about, your stories?'
'Everything.'
'Oh.'
' . . . '
' . . . '
'But mostly about love.'
'Oh?'

She buys a magnificent manilla envelope. The sturdiest, most beautiful, most expensive one, with padded corners and an unassailable flap. The Rolls-Royce of envelopes.

She goes to the post office and asks for collectors' stamps – the prettiest ones, the ones that show works of modern art. She licks them lovingly, gracefully presses them on, casts a spell on the envelope, blesses it, makes the sign of the cross over it, and utters some other incantations that must remain secret.

She goes up to the letter slot marked 'Paris and suburbs only.' She kisses her treasure one last time, turns her eyes away, and abandons it.

Opposite the post office, there's a bar. She leans her elbows on the counter, orders a calvados. She doesn't really like them, but hey, she has her status as an accursed artist to uphold now. She lights a cigarette, and from this moment on, you could say, she waits.

I didn't say anything to anyone.

'Hey – what are you doing with the key to the mailbox on a chain around your neck?'

'Nothing.'

'Hey – what are you doing holding all those Castorama fliers?'

'Nothing.'

'Hey – what are you doing with the postman's satchel?'

'Nothing, I'm telling you! . . .'

'Wait . . . are you in love with him or what?!'

No. I didn't say anything. Can you see me answering: 'I'm waiting for an answer from a publisher.' The shame.

Anyway . . . it's crazy the junk mail you get these days – it's really just whatever.

And then there's work, and then there's Micheline and her fake nails poorly attached, and then there's the geraniums to bring in, and then the Walt Disney tapes, the little electric train, and the season's first visit to the paediatrician, and then the dog moulting, and Robert McLiam Wilson's *Eureka Street* to measure the immeasurable, and then movies, and family and friends, and then still other emotions (but nothing much next to *Eureka Street*, it's true).

Our Marguerite resigned herself to hibernation.

Three months later.
Hallelujah!
Hallelujah! Hallelu-u-u-jah!

It came.
The letter.
It's a bit light.
I slide it under my sweater and call my Kiki:
'Kiiiiiiiikiiiiiii!!!'

I go to read it all alone, in the silence and meditation of the little wooded area next door, which serves as a toilet for all the dogs in the neighbourhood. (Note that even in moments like this, I remain lucid.)

'*Madame* blablabla, *it is with great interest that* blablabla *and that's why* blablabla *I would like to meet with you* blablabla, *please get in touch with my secretary* blablabla *I'm looking forward to* blablabla *dear madame* blablabla. . . .'

I savour it.
I savour it.
I savour it.
The vengeance of Marguerite has struck.

'Honey?' I ask my husband, 'When are we eating?'
'??? . . . What are you asking me for? What's going on?'
'Oh, nothing – it's just that I won't have much time

for cooking anymore, what with all the fan letters I'll have to answer, not to mention the festivals, the conventions, the book fairs . . . all those trips all over France and in the overseas territories, my God. Come to think of it, I'll have to start getting regular manicures soon, because, you know . . . for the book signings, it's important to have impeccable hands. . . . It's crazy how people get hung up on that. . . .'

'What are you raving about?'

Marguerite lets the letter from the elegant Left Bank publisher 'escape' onto the potbellied stomach of her husband, who's reading the classifieds in *Auto Plus*.

'Hold on . . . hey! What is this?!'

'Nothing – I haven't had it for long. It's just something I have to tell Micheline. Go and make yourself handsome: I'm taking you to the Aigle Noir tonight. . . .'

'The Aigle Noir!?'

'Yes. That's where Marguerite would have taken her Yann, I suppose. . . .'

'Who's Yann?'

'Pfffff, forget it. . . . You don't know the first *thing* about the literary world.'

So I got in contact with the secretary. A very good contact, I think, because the young woman was more than charming.

Maybe she had a fluorescent pink Post-it stuck in front of her eyes: 'If A.G. calls, be *very* charming!' underlined twice.

Maybe . . .

The poor dears, they must think I sent my stories to others. . . . They're afraid someone's going to beat them to it. Another publisher, even more elegant, situated on an even more chic street on the Left Bank, with a secretary who's even more charming on the phone and who has an even cuter arse.

Oh, no, that would be too unfair.

You see the disaster if I hit the big time under another imprint just because what's-her-name didn't have a fluorescent pink Post-it in front of her eyes?

I don't dare think about it.

The appointment was set for one week later. (We've all wasted enough time.)

The initial pragmatic concerns were soon out of the way: taking an afternoon off ('Micheline, I won't be in tomorrow!'); making arrangements for the kids – but not just anywhere, in a place where they'll be happy; informing my love:

'I'm going into Paris tomorrow.'

'Why?'

'On business.'

'Is it a romantic tryst?'

'Same difference.'

'Who is it?'

'The postman.'

'Ah! I should have known. . . .'

. . . Leaving the one truly important problem: what am I going to wear?

Something that says true future writer, devoid of elegance because the *real* life is somewhere else. Don't love me for my big breasts; love me for my substantive marrow.

Something that says true future bestseller-writing machine, with a perm, because the real life is right here. Don't love me for my talent; love me for my tabloid potential.

Something that says woman-who-eats-up-elegant-men-from-the-Left-Bank, get it while it's hot, because the real life is on your desk. Don't love me for my manuscript; love me for my stunning marrow.

Hey, Atala, calm down.

In the end, the stress is too much for me – you know, this really isn't the time to be thinking about playing footsie and losing a stocking on the rug. This is undoubtedly the most momentous day of my tiny existence, and I'm not going to jeopardise the whole thing with some outfit that's undeniably irresistible but totally cumbersome.

(Well, yeah! A mini miniskirt is cumbersome.)

I'll wear jeans. Nothing more, nothing less. My trusty 501s, ten years old, barrel-aged, stonewashed, with copper rivets and the reddish label on the right buttock. The pair that have taken my shape and my scent. My friend.

Even so, I get nervous when I think about this elegant, brilliant man who juggles my future in his slender hands. (Publish her? Don't publish her?) . . . Jeans are pushing it a little, I have to admit.

Oh . . . nothing but worries, nothing but worries.

Okay, I've made up my mind. Jeans, but with lingerie to knock your socks off.

But he won't even see that, you tell me. . . . Don't tut-tut-tut me – you don't get to the Very High Post of Publisher without having a special gift for detecting the most improbable, fine lingerie.

No, these men know.

They know if the woman seated across from them is wearing some cotton thing that comes up to her belly button, or cheap pink pants from Monoprix, all stretched out of shape, or one of those extravagant little things that make women redden (the price they pay for them) and men turn pink (the price they're going to have to pay).

Of course they know.

And this time, let me tell you, I spared no expense (payable in two instalments). I got a matching bra-and-pants set – something out of this world.

God . . .

Super nice stuff, super material, super cut – all in ivory silk with Calais lace, hand-knitted by little old French ladies, if you please. Soft, pretty, refined, tender, unforgettable. The sort of thing that melts in your mouth and not in your hand.

Destiny, here I am.

Looking at myself in the mirror at the shop (the fiends, they've got special lighting that makes you look thin and tanned – the same halogens they use over the dead fish in the gourmet supermarkets), I told myself for the first time since Marguerite has existed:

'Well, then, I don't regret all that time I spent biting my nails, and getting eczema in front of my tiny computer screen. Oh, no! All that, all those times I wore myself out arm-wrestling the fear and the lack of self-confidence, all those scraps in my head and all those things I lost or forgot because I was thinking about "Clic-Clac", for example – well, I don't regret them. . . .'

I can't tell you exactly how much I spent, what with being politically correct – my husband's dental bridge, car insurance, the rising welfare tax, and all that – I'd risk shocking you. But know that it's something staggering; and, given what it weighs, let's not talk about the price per kilo.

After all, nothing comes from nothing, you can't catch

flies with vinegar, and you can't get yourself published without giving a little of yourself, don't you think?

Here we are: the sixth arrondissement of Paris.

The district where you find as many writers as metre maids. At the heart of life.

I'm losing my nerve.

My stomach hurts, my chest hurts, my legs hurt, I'm sweating buckets, and my ***-euro knickers are riding up.

Pretty picture.

I get lost, the street name isn't indicated anywhere, there are galleries of African art in every direction, and nothing looks more like an African mask than another African mask. I'm beginning to hate African art.

Finally, I find my way.

They make me wait.

I think I'm going to pass out. I breathe like they taught us for having a baby. Okay . . . now . . . calm . . . down. . . .

Sit up straight. Watch. You can always learn something. Breathe in. Breathe out.

'Are you feeling all right?'

'Uh . . . yes, yes . . . I'm fine.'

'*He*'s in a meeting, but *He* won't be much longer.

He'll be here in just a little while. . . .'

'. . .'

'Would you like a cup of coffee?'

'No. Thank you.' (Hey, what's-your-name, can't you see I want to throw up? Help me – a slap, a bucket, a bowl, a Rennies, a glass of nice cold cola . . . something. I'm begging you.)

A smile. She gives me a smile.

In fact, it was curiosity. Neither more nor less.

He wanted to see me. He wanted to see what I looked like. He wanted to see what sort of person would write this stuff.

That's all.

I'm not going to tell you about the interview. At the moment, I'm treating my eczema with nearly pure tar, and it's really not worth aggravating it, given the colour of my bathtub. So I won't tell you about it.

Well, okay . . . maybe just a little bit: After a while, the cat (for further details, see 'Lucifer' in *Cinderella*), who was watching the mouse gesticulating in every direction between his clawed paws . . . the cat, who was having fun ('isn't she unsophisticated, after all') . . . the cat, who was taking his time, finished by saying:

'Listen, I'll be honest with you: Your manuscript

does some interesting things, and you do have a *certain* style, but' (next come more than a few reflections on people who write in general and the hard job of a publisher in particular) '. . . The way things are now, and for reasons I'm sure you'll understand, we can't publish your manuscript. On the other hand, I'd like to follow your work very closely – and I want you to know that I'll always give it my utmost attention. There.'

There.

Jackass.

I stay seated, stunned. There's no other word for it.

He gets up (with sweeping, magnificent gestures), heads towards me, and makes as if to shake my hand. . . . Not seeing any reaction on my part, he makes as if to offer me his hand. . . . Not seeing any reaction on my part, he makes as if to take my hand. . . . Not seeing any . . .

'What's going on? Come on . . . don't be so downhearted – you know, it's extremely rare to get a first manuscript published. You know, I have confidence in you. I can tell we're going to do great things together. In fact, I'll be honest with you: I'm *counting* on you.'

Stop the chariots, Ben-Hur. Can't you tell I'm stuck?

'Listen, I'm sorry. I don't know what's happened, but I can't get up. It's as though all my strength's gone. It's stupid.'

'Does this happen often?'

'No. It's the first time.'

'Does it hurt?'

'No. Well, a little, but that's something else.'

'Wiggle your fingers, just to see.'

'I can't.'

'You're sure?'

'Well . . . yes.'

A long exchange of looks, like a couple of kids having a staring contest.

(irritated) 'Are you doing this on purpose or what?'

(very irritated) 'Well, of course not, for heaven's sake!!'

'Do you want me to call a doctor?'

'No, no, it'll pass.'

'Yes, well, okay, then. . . . The problem is, I've got other meetings. . . . You can't stay here.'

' . . . '

'Try again. . . .'

'Nothing.'

'What is this business?'

'I don't know. . . . What do you want me to say? . . . Maybe it's an arthritis attack or something, triggered by overwhelming emotions.'

'If I tell you, "Okay, fine, I'll publish you" . . . will you get up?'

'Of course not. What do you take me for? Do I really seem that moronic?'

'No, but I mean if I really do publish you? . . .'

'First of all, I wouldn't believe you. . . . Hey, wait, I'm not here to beg your charity – I'm paralysed. Can't you understand the difference?'

(rubbing his face in his slender hands) 'And it had to happen to me. . . . Good God . . .'

'. . .'

(looking at his watch) 'Listen, for the moment, I'm going to move you, because I really need my office now. . . .'

So then he pushes me down the hall as if I were in a wheelchair, except that I'm not in a wheelchair – and for him, that must make a hell of a difference. . . . I make myself comfortable.

Suffer, my friend. Suffer.

'Would you like a cup of coffee now?'

'Yes, I'd love one. That's nice of you.'

'Are you sure you don't want me to call a doctor?'

'No, no. Thank you. It'll go away just the way it came on.'

'You're too tense.'

'I know.'

What's-her-name never had a pink Post-it stuck on her phone. She was charming to me the other day because she's a girl who *is* charming.

Today won't have been a total waste.

It's true. You don't often get the chance to watch a girl like her for hours on end.

I love her voice.

From time to time, she makes little signs to me so I'll feel less alone.

And then the computers were shut down, the answering machines were set up, the lights were turned off, and the office was emptied.

I saw them all leave, one after another, and they all thought I was there because I had an appointment. Whatever.

Finally Blue-Beard came out of the lair where he makes the little wannabee writer cry.

'You're still here!!'

'. . .'

'What am I going to do with you?'

'I don't know.'

'Well, I do. I'm going to call the ambulance or the fire service and they're going to get you out of here in the next five minutes! You don't plan on sleeping here, do you?!'

'No, don't call anyone, please. . . . It's going to come unstuck, I can feel it. . . .'

'Sure, but I've got to lock up – you can understand that, can't you?'

'Then take me down to the pavement.'

You might have guessed, he's not the one who took me down. He hailed a couple of messenger boys nearby. Two tall, handsome guys – tattooed footmen for my sedan chair.

They each took an armrest and deposited me gently at the foot of the building.

Too cute.

My ex–future publisher, this tactful man who's *counting* on me in the future, said his good-byes with lots of panache.

He walked away, turning back several times and shaking his head as though he were trying to wake up from a bad dream – no, truly, he really couldn't believe it.

At least he'll have something to talk about at dinner.

It's his wife who'll be happy. For once he won't talk her ear off about the crisis in publishing.

For the first time all day, I felt good.

I watched the waiters at the restaurant across the street fussing around their damask tablecloths. They were very stylish (like my stories, I thought, sniggering) – especially one, whom I watched closely.

Exactly the sort of French *garçon de café* who upsets the hormonal systems of fat American women in Reeboks.

I smoked an exceptionally good cigarette, expelling the smoke slowly and watching the passers-by.

I was almost happy – aside from a few details, like the presence of a parking metre on my right that smelled of dog piss.

How long did I stay there, contemplating my disaster?

I don't know.

The restaurant was in full swing, and you could see couples seated on the terrace, laughing as they drank glasses of rosé.

I couldn't stop myself from thinking:

. . . In another life, maybe, my publisher would have taken me to lunch there 'because it's so convenient'. He'd have made me laugh, too, and suggested a much better wine than that Côteaux de Provence. . . . He'd have pressed me to finish my novel, 'surprisingly mature for a young woman your age . . .', and then he'd have taken my arm and escorted me to a taxi stand. He would have romanced me a little. . . .

. . . In another life. Surely.

Well, okay. . . . It's not everything, Marguerite. I've got ironing waiting for me. . . .

I got up with a bound, pulling at my jeans, and headed toward a gorgeous young woman sitting on the base of a statue of Auguste Comte.

Look at her.

Beautiful, sensual, full-blooded, with flawless legs and very fine ankles, her turned-up nose, her forehead rounded, her allure fierce and warlike.

Wearing some string and tattoos.

Lips and nails painted black.

An incredible girl.

She threw regular, irritated looks in the direction of the adjacent street. I think her lover must have been late.

I handed her my manuscript.

'Take it,' I said, 'it's a gift. To help pass the time.'

I think she thanked me, but I'm not sure – because she wasn't French! . . . Distressed by this little detail, I nearly took back my magnificent gift, and then . . . What for? I said to myself. And as I walked away, I was even rather content.

From here on, my manuscript was in the hands of the most beautiful girl in the world.

That consoled me.

A little.

Someone I Loved

For Constance

'What did you say?'

'I said I'm going to take them. It will do them good to get away for a while.'

'But when?' my mother-in-law asked.

'Now.'

'Now? You're not thinking . . .'

'Yes, I am.'

'What are you talking about? It's nearly eleven! Pierre, you – '

'Suzanne, I'm talking to Chloé. Chloé, listen to me. I want to take you away from here. What do you say?'

I say nothing.

'Do you think it's a bad idea?'

'I don't know.'

'Go and get your things. We'll leave when you get back here.'

'I don't want to stop at my place first.'

'Then don't. We'll sort everything out when we're there.'

'But you don't – '

'Chloé, Chloé, please. Trust me.'

★

My mother-in-law continued to protest:

'But − ! You're not really going to wake up the children! The house isn't even heated, and there's nothing to eat! Nothing for the girls! They − '

He stood up.

...

Marion is sleeping in her car seat, her thumb touching the edge of her lips. Lucie is beside her, rolled in a ball.

I look at my father-in-law. He sits upright. His hands grip the steering wheel. He hasn't said a word since we left. I see his profile in the headlights of oncoming cars. I think that he is as unhappy as I am. That he's tired. Disappointed.

He feels my gaze:

'Why don't you get some sleep? You should get some rest, you know − lean your seat back and go to sleep. We've got a long way to go . . .'

'I can't,' I tell him. 'I'm watching over you.'

He smiles at me. It's barely a smile.

'No . . . it's the other way around.'

We return to our private thoughts.
I cry behind my hands.

We're parked at a service station. I take advantage of his absence to check my mobile.

No messages.

Of course.

What a fool I am.

What a fool . . .

I turn the radio on, then off.

He returns.

'Do you want to go in? Do you want something?'

I give in.

I press the wrong button; my cup fills with a nauseating liquid that I throw away at once.

In the store, I buy a pack of nappies for Lucie and a toothbrush for myself.

He refuses to start the car until I have leaned my seat back.

· · ·

I opened my eyes as he switched off the engine.

'Don't move. Stay here with the girls while it's still warm. I'll go and turn on the radiators in your room. Then I'll come and get you.'

I pleaded with my phone.
At four in the morning . . .
I'm such a fool.

No way to go back to sleep.

The three of us are lying in Adrien's grandmother's bed, the one that creaks so horribly. It was our bed.

We would try to make love with as little movement as possible.

The whole house would hear if you moved an arm or a leg. I remember Christine's insinuations when we came down to breakfast the first morning. We blushed into our coffee and held hands under the table.

We learned our lesson. After that, we made love as quietly as anyone possibly could.

I know that he will return to this bed with someone else, and that with her, too, he will pick up this big mattress and throw it on the floor when they can't stand it any longer.

It's Marion who wakes us up. She is making her doll run along the quilt, and telling a story about flying lollipops. Lucie touches my eyelashes: 'Your eyes are all stuck together.'

We dress under the covers, because the room is too cold.

The creaking bed makes them laugh.

My father-in-law has lit a fire in the kitchen. I see him at the end of the garden, looking for logs in the woodshed.

This is the first time I've been alone with him.

I've never felt comfortable in his presence. Too distant. Too silent. And with everything Adrien told me about how hard it was growing up beneath his gaze, his harshness, his rages, the dramas about school.

It was the same with Suzanne. I never saw them be affectionate with each other. 'Pierre is not very demonstrative, but I know what he feels for me,' she told me one day when we were talking about love while snapping the ends off green beans.

194

I nodded, but I didn't understand. I didn't understand this man who minimised and controlled his passions. To show nothing for fear of appearing weak – I could never understand that. In my family, touching and kissing are like breathing.

I remember a stormy evening in this kitchen . . . Christine, my sister-in-law, was complaining about her children's teachers, calling them incompetent and small-minded. From there, the conversation drifted into education in general, then hers in particular. And then the winds changed. Menacingly. The kitchen was transformed into a courtroom, with Adrien and his sister as the prosecutors, and in the dock – their father. It was horrible . . . If only the lid had finally blown off, but no. All the bitterness was pushed down again, and they avoided a big explosion by making do with a few deadly jabs.

As usual.

What would have been possible, anyway? My father-in-law refused to take the bait. He listened to his children's bitter words without a word of response. 'Your criticisms roll off me like water off a duck's back,' he always said, smiling, before leaving the room.

This time, though, the argument had been fiercer.

I can still see his strained face, his hands gripping the water jug as though he had wanted to smash it before our eyes.

I imagined all those words that he would never say and I tried to understand. What possessed him? What did he think about when he was alone? And what was he like – intimately?

In despair, Christine turned to me:

'And you, Chloé, what do you make of all this?'

I was tired, I wanted the evening to be over. I had had it up to here with their family drama.

'Me?' I said thoughtfully. 'I think that Pierre doesn't live among us, I mean not really. He's a kind of Martian lost in the Dippel family . . .'

The others shrugged and turned away. But not him.

He loosened his grip on the jug. His face relaxed and he smiled at me. It was the first time I had ever seen him smile in that way. Maybe the last time, too. I think we developed some sort of understanding that evening . . . something subtle. I had tried to defend him as best I could, my odd, grey-haired Martian, who was now walking toward the kitchen door pushing a wheelbarrow full of wood.

. . .

'Is everything all right? You're not cold?'

'Yes, yes, everything's fine, thanks.'

'And the girls?'

'They're watching cartoons.'

'There are cartoons on at this hour?'

'They're on every morning during the school holidays.'

'Oh . . . great. You found the coffee?'

'Yes, thanks.'

'And what about you, Chloé? Speaking of holidays, shouldn't you – '

'Call the office?'

'Well, I just thought – '

'Yes, yes, I'm going to do it, I . . .'

I started to cry again.

My father-in-law lowered his gaze. He took off his gloves.

'I'm sorry, I'm interfering with something that's none of my business.'

'No, it's not that. It's just that . . . I feel lost. I'm completely lost . . . I . . . you're right, I'll call my boss.'

'Who is your boss?'

'A friend. At least, I think she's a friend. We'll see . . .'

I pulled my hair back with an old hairband of Lucie's that was in my pocket.

'Just tell her you're taking a few days off to take care of your cantankerous old father-in-law,' he suggested.

'All right . . . I'll say cantankerous *and* impotent. That makes it sound more serious.'

He smiled as he blew on his coffee cup.

★

Laure wasn't in. I mumbled a few words to her assistant, who had a call on another line.

I also called home. Punched in the answering machine code. Nothing important.

What did I expect?

And once again, the tears came. My father-in-law entered and quickly left.

Go on, I told myself, you need to have a good healthy cry. Dry your tears, squeeze out the sponge, wring out your big, sad body and turn the page. Think about something else. One foot in front of the other and start again.

That's what everyone keeps saying. Just think about something else. Life goes on. Think of your daughters. You can't just let yourself go. Get a grip.

Yes, I know, I know, but: I just can't.

What does 'to live' mean, anyway? What does it really mean?

My children, what do I have to offer them? A messed-up mother? An upside-down world?

I really do want to get up in the morning, get dressed, feed myself, dress them, feed them, hang on until evening and then put them to bed and kiss them good night. I've done that, anybody can. But not anymore.

For God's sake.

Not anymore.

★

'Mum!'

'Yes?' I answered, wiping my nose on my sleeve.

'Mum!'

'I'm here, I'm here . . .'

Lucie stood in front of me, wearing her coat over her nightdress. She was swinging her Barbie doll around by the hair.

'You know what Grandpa said?'

'No.'

'He said we're going to go eat at McDonald's.'

'I don't believe you,' I answered.

'But it's true! He told us himself.'

'When?'

'A little while ago.'

'I thought he hated McDonald's . . .'

'Nope, he doesn't hate it. He said we're going shopping, and afterwards we're going to McDonald's – even you, even Marion, even me, and even him!'

She took my hand as we climbed the stairs.

'I don't have many clothes here, you know. We forgot them all in Paris.'

'That's true,' I said. 'We forgot everything.'

'And you know what Grandpa said?'

'No.'

'He told me and Marion that he's going to buy us clothes when we go shopping. And we can choose them ourselves.'

'Oh, really?'

I changed Marion's nappy, tickling her tummy as I did so.

All this time, Lucie sat on the edge of the bed and kept on talking.

'And then he said okay . . .'

'Okay to what?'

'To everything I asked for . . .'

Oh no . . .

'What did you ask for?'

'Barbie clothes.'

'For your Barbie?'

'For my Barbie and for me. The same for both!'

'Not those horrendous sparkly T-shirts?'

'Yes, and everything that goes with them: pink jeans, pink sneakers with Barbie on them, and socks with the little bow . . . You know . . . right there . . . the little bow at the back . . .'

She pointed at her ankle.

I laid Marion down.

'Beeeeoooootiful,' I told her, 'you're going to look just beeeooooootiful!'

Her mouth twisted.

'Anyway, you think everything that's nice is *ugly*.'

I laughed; I kissed her adorable little frown.

She put on her dress, dreaming all the while.

★

'I'm going to look beautiful, huh?'

'You're already beautiful, my sweet. You're already very, very beautiful.'

'Yes, but even more . . .'

'You think that's possible?'

She thought for a second.

'Yes, I think so.'

'Come on, turn around.'

What a wonderful invention little girls are, I thought as I combed her hair. What a wonderful invention.

As we queued at the checkout, my father-in-law admitted he hadn't set foot in a supermarket in more than ten years.

I thought about Suzanne.

Always alone, behind her shopping trolley.

Always alone everywhere.

After their chicken nuggets, the girls played in a sort of cage filled with coloured balls. A young man told them to take off their shoes, and I kept Lucie's awful 'You're a Barbie girl!' sneakers on my lap.

The worst thing was that they had a sort of transparent wedge heel. . . .

'How could you have bought such hideous things?'

'It made her so happy . . . I'm trying not to make the same mistakes with the next generation. You see, it's like this place . . . Even if it had been possible, I would never have brought Christine and Adrien here thirty years ago. Never! And why, I ask myself now – why would I have deprived them of this type of pleasure? In the end, what would it have cost me? A miserable fifteen minutes? What's a miserable fifteen minutes compared with the shining faces of your kids?'

'I've done everything wrong,' he said, shaking his head. 'Even this bloody sandwich, I'm holding it the wrong way up, aren't I?'

His trousers were covered with mayonnaise.

'Chloé?'

'Yes.'

'I want you to eat. I'm sorry I'm talking to you as if you were Suzanne, but you haven't eaten anything since yesterday.'

'I can't seem to do it.'

He backed off.

'You're right – how could you eat something like this, anyway? Who could? Nobody!'

I tried to smile.

'All right, you can stay on a diet for now, but tonight, it's over! Tonight I'm making dinner, and you're going to have to make an effort, all right?'

'All right.'

'And this? How do you eat this astronaut thing, anyway?'

He held up an improbable salad sealed in a plastic shaker.

•••

We spent the rest of the afternoon in the garden. The

girls fluttered around their grandfather, who had got it into his head to mend the old swing. I watched them from a distance, sitting on the steps. It was cold but clear. The sun shone in their hair, and I thought they were lovely.

I thought about Adrien. What was he doing?

Where was he at this exact moment?

And with whom?

And our life, what was it going to look like?

Every thought drew me closer to the bottom. I was so tired. I shut my eyes. I dreamed that he had arrived. There was the sound of an engine in the courtyard, he sat down next to me, he kissed me and put his finger to my lips in order to surprise the girls. I can still feel his tender touch on my neck, his voice, his warmth, the smell of his skin, it's all there.

It's all there . . .

All I have to do is think about it.

How long does it take to forget the smell of someone who loved you? How long until you stop loving?

If only someone would give me an hourglass.

●●●

The last time we were in each other's arms, I was the one who kissed him. It was in the lift in the Rue de Flandre.

He didn't resist.

Why? Why did he let himself be kissed by a woman he no longer loved? Why did he give me his lips? His arms?

It doesn't make any sense.

The swing is fixed. Pierre shoots me a glance. I turn my head. I don't want to meet his gaze. I'm cold, my nose is running, and I have to go and heat the bathroom.

'What can I do to help?'

He had tied a dish towel around his waist.

'Lucie and Marion are in bed?'

'Yes.'

'They won't be cold?'

'No, no, they're fine. Tell me what I can do.'

'You can cry without embarrassing me for once . . .
It would do me good to see you cry for no reason.
Here, cut these up,' he added, handing me three
onions.

'You think I cry too much?'

'Yes.'

Silence.

I picked up the wooden cutting board near the
sink and sat down across from him. His face was
tight once again. The only sounds came from the
fireplace.

• • •

'That's not what I meant to say . . .'

'I'm sorry?'

'I didn't mean to say that. I don't think you cry too much, I'm just overwhelmed. You're so pretty when you smile . . .'

'Would you like a drink?'
I nodded.

'Let's let it warm up a bit, it would be a shame otherwise . . . Do you want a Bushmills while we're waiting?'
'No, thanks.'
'Why not?'
'I don't like whiskey.'
'What a shame! This isn't just whiskey. Here, taste this.'

I put the glass to my lips; it tasted like lighter fluid. I hadn't eaten for days, and suddenly I was drunk. My knife slipped on the onion skins, and my head rolled on my neck. I thought I was going to chop off a finger. I felt just fine.

'It's good, isn't it? Patrick Frendall gave it to me for my sixtieth birthday. Do you remember Patrick Frendall?'
'Uh . . . no.'
'Yes, you do. You met him here, don't you remember? A big fellow with huge arms.'
'The one who tossed Lucie in the air until she was about to throw up?'

'That's the one,' Pierre said, pouring me another drink.

'Yes, I remember.'

'I really like him; I think about him a lot. It's odd, I consider him to be one of my best friends and I hardly know him.'

'Do you have best friends?'

'Why do you ask that?'

'Just to ask, I . . . I don't know. I've never heard you talk about them.'

My father-in-law threw himself into cutting carrot rounds. It's always amusing to watch a man cook for the first time in his life. That way of following a recipe to the letter, as if Delia Smith were looking over his shoulder.

'It says "cut the carrots in medium-sized rounds". Do you think these will do like that?'

'Perfect!'

I laughed. With a rubber neck, my head lolled on my shoulders.

'Thanks. So, where was I? Oh yes, my friends . . . I've had three in my life. I met Patrick on a trip to Rome, some sort of pious nonsense organised by the local church. My first trip without my parents . . . I was fifteen. I didn't understand a word this Irishman, twice my size, was saying to me, but we got along immediately. He had been brought up in the most Catholic family in the world, and I was just getting out from under my suffocating family . . . Two young hounds unleashed in the Eternal City . . . What a pilgrimage that was!'

It still gave him a thrill.

He heated the onions and carrots in a casserole with bits of smoked ham. It smelled wonderful.

'And then there's Jean Théron, whom you know, and my brother, Paul, who you never met because he died in '56.'

'You considered your brother to be your best friend?'

'He was even more than that. Chloé, from what I know of you, you would have adored him. He was sensitive, funny, attentive to everyone, always in a good mood. He painted . . . I'll show you his water-colours tomorrow, they're in my study. He knew all the bird calls. He liked to tease people, but never harmed a soul. He was charming, really charming. Everyone loved him . . .'

'What did he die of?'

My father-in-law turned away.

'He went to Indochina. He came back sick and half-mad. He died of tuberculosis on Bastille Day, 1956.'

I said nothing.

'I don't need to tell you that after that, my parents never watched a single parade again for the rest of their lives. Celebrations, fireworks, that was the end of that.'

*

He added pieces of meat and turned them over, browning them on all sides.

'You see, the worst part was that he had volunteered. He was still at school at the time. He was dazzling. He wanted to work at the National Forestry Office. He loved trees and birds. He should never have gone over there. He had no reason to go. None. He was gentle, a pacifist. He quoted Giono, and he – '

'So why did he go?'

'Because of a girl. Your typical unhappy love affair. It was ridiculous; she wasn't even a woman, just a young girl. It was absurd. Even as I'm telling you this – and every time I think about it – I'm just floored by the inanity of our lives. A good boy goes off to war because of a sulky young lady . . . it's grotesque. It's something you read in bad novels. It's like a soap opera, a story like that.'

'She didn't love him?'

'No. But Paul was crazy about her. He adored her. He had known her since she was twelve; he wrote her letters she probably didn't even understand. He went swaggering off to war. So she could see what a man he was! And the night before he left, the ass, he told everyone: "When she asks you, don't give her my address right away. I want to be the first to write." Three months later, she got engaged to the son of the butcher on the Rue de Passy.'

★

He shook a dozen different spices into the pot, whatever he could find in the cupboards.

I shuddered to think what Delia would have said.

'A big pale boy who spent his days boning cuts of meat in the back of his father's shop. You can imagine what a shock it was for us. She ditched our Paul for this big lump. He was over there, halfway around the world, he was probably thinking about her, writing poetry for her, the fool, and she, all she could think about was going out with an oaf who was allowed to borrow his father's car on Saturday night. A sky-blue Renault Frégate, as I recall . . . Of course, she was free not to love him, but Paul was too impetuous, he never could do anything without bravura, without . . . without flair. What a waste . . .'

'And then?'

'And then nothing. Paul came home and my mother switched butchers. He spent a lot of time in this house, which he hardly ever left. He drew, read, complained that he couldn't sleep. He suffered a great deal, coughed constantly, and then he died. At twenty-one.'

'You've never spoken of him.'

'No.'

'Why?'

'I always liked talking about him with people who had known him; it was easier . . .'

★

I pushed my chair back from the table.

'I'll set the table. Where do you want to eat?'
    'Here in the kitchen is fine.'

He switched off the overhead light, and we sat down, facing each other.
    'It's delicious.'
    'Do you really think so? It seems a bit overcooked, don't you think?'
    'No, no, really, it's perfect.'
    'You're too good.'
    'It's your wine that's good. Tell me about Rome.'
    'About the city?'
    'No, about this pilgrimage . . . What were you like when you were fifteen?'
    'Oh . . . what was I like? I was the stupidest boy in the world. I tried to keep up with Frendall's big strides. I talked incessantly, told him about Paris, the Moulin Rouge, said anything that came into my head, and lied shamelessly. He laughed and said things that I didn't understand either, which made me laugh in turn. We spent our time stealing coins from the fountains and smirked every time we met someone of the opposite sex. We were completely pathetic, when I think of it now. I don't remember the goal of the pilgrimage anymore. There was no doubt a good cause, an occasion for prayer, as they say. I don't remember anymore. For me, it was a huge breath of

fresh air. Those few days changed my life. I discovered the taste of freedom. It was like . . . would you like some more?'

'Yes, please.'

'You have to understand the context. We were all pretending we had just won a war. There was so much ill-will in the air. We couldn't mention anyone's name, a neighbour, a shopkeeper, a friend's parents, without my father immediately pigeonholing them – this one's an informer, that one was denounced, a coward, a good-for-nothing. It was horrible. It's perhaps hard to imagine it now, but believe me, it was horrible for us children. We hardly spoke to him, or very little. Probably just the strict minimum. But one day, I asked him, "If you think humanity is so awful, then why did you go and fight for it?"'

'What did he answer?'

'Nothing . . . just dismissed it.'

'Stop, stop, that's plenty!'

'I was living on the second floor of a building that was completely grey, buried in the sixteenth arrondissement. It was such a sad . . . My parents couldn't afford to live there, but the address was prestigious, you see. The sixteenth! We were squeezed into a grim apartment that never got any sun, and where my mother forbade us to open the windows because there was a bus depot just underneath. She was mortally afraid that the curtains would . . . would become soiled . . . oh, this nice little Bordeaux has me speaking like her . . . I was terribly bored. I was too young to interest my father and my mother just fluttered around.

'She went out a lot. "Time spent helping in the parish," she would say, rolling her eyes. She overdid it, acted shocked at the behaviour of certain church ladies whom she had made up out of thin air. She would take off her gloves and toss them on the hall table as if she were throwing in her notice, then sigh, prance around, chatter, lie, sometimes tripping herself up. We just let her talk. Paul called her Sarah Bernhardt, and after she left the room my father would resume reading *Le Figaro* without a word . . . Some potatoes?'

'No, thanks.'

'I was a half-boarder at the Lycée Janson–de–Sailly. I was as grey as my building. I read Catholic comics and the adventures of Flash Gordon. I played tennis with the Mortellier boys every Thursday. I . . . I was a very good, very dull boy. I dreamed of taking the lift to the sixth floor just to have a look . . . Talk about an adventure! Going up to the sixth floor! I was soft in the head, I swear.

'I was waiting for Patrick Frendall.

'I was waiting for the Pope!'

He got up to stoke the fire.

'Anyway, the trip wasn't a revolution . . . a bit of a lark at most. I always thought I would . . . how shall I say . . . throw off the yoke one day. But no. Never. I kept on being that very good, very dull boy. But why am I telling you all this? Why am I so talkative all of a sudden?'

'It was me that asked the question.'

'Well, that's still no reason! I'm not boring you to death with my trip down memory lane?'

'No, no, on the contrary. I really like it.'

...

The following morning, I found a note on the kitchen table: *Gone to office. Back later.*

There was hot coffee, and an enormous log on the fire.

Why didn't he tell me he was going?

What a strange man . . . Like a fish, always twisting away from you, slipping out of your hands.

I poured myself a large cup of coffee and drank it standing up, leaning against the kitchen window. I looked at the robins swarming around the block of lard that the girls had put out on the bench the previous day.

The sun had almost risen above the hedge.

I was waiting for them to wake up. The house was too quiet.

I wanted a cigarette. It was stupid, I hadn't smoked in years. But that's what life is like . . . You show what incredible willpower you have, and then one winter morning you decide to walk four kilometres in the cold to buy a pack of cigarettes. You love a man, you have two children with him, and one winter morning, you learn that he has left because he loves someone else. Adding that he doesn't know what to say, that he made a mistake.

Like calling a wrong number: 'I'm sorry, it was a mistake.'

Why, think nothing of it . . .

Like a soap bubble.

It's windy. I go out to put the lard out of the way.

I watch television with the girls. I'm horrified: the characters in the cartoons seem so stupid and spoiled. Lucie gets annoyed, shakes her head, begs me to be quiet. I want to tell her about Candy.

When I was little, I was hooked on Candy.

Candy never talked about money, only about love. And then I shut up. That will teach me to act like little miss Candy . . .

The wind blows harder and harder. I give up the idea of walking to the village.

We spend the afternoon in the attic. The girls play

dressing-up. Lucie waves a fan in her sister's face:

'Are you too hot, Countess?'

The Countess can't move. She has too many hats on her head.

We bring down an old cradle. Lucie says that it needs a new coat of paint.

'Pink?' I ask her.

'How did you guess?'

'I'm very clever.'

The telephone rings. Lucie answers.

At the end, I hear her ask:

'Do you want to talk to Mummy now?'

She hangs up shortly after. Doesn't come back and join us.

I continue to strip the cradle with Marion.

I find her when I go down to the kitchen, her chin on the table. I sit down next to her.

We look at each other.

'One day, will you and Papa be in love again?'

'No.'

'Are you sure?'

'Yes.'

'I already knew it, anyway . . .'

She got up and added:

'You know what else?'

'No, what?'

'The birds have already eaten everything . . .'

'Really? Are you sure?'

'Yes, come see.'

She came around the table and took my hand.

We were in front of the window. There was my little blonde girl next to me. She was wearing an old dress-shirt and a moth-eaten skirt. Her 'You're a Barbie girl!' sneakers fitted right into her great-grandmother's button-up shoes. Her mother's large hand fitted completely around hers. We watched the trees in the garden bending in the wind, and probably thought the same thing . . .

The bathroom was so cold that I couldn't lift my shoulders out of the water. Lucie shampooed our hair and gave us all sorts of wild hairdos. 'Look, Mum! You've got horns on your head!'

I knew it already.

It wasn't very funny, but it made me laugh.

'Why are you laughing?'

'Because I'm stupid.'

'Why are you stupid?'

We danced about to dry ourselves off.

Nightdresses, socks, shoes, sweaters, dressing gowns, and more sweaters.

My two little Michelin men went down to have their soup.

There was a power cut just as Babar was playing with the lift in a big department store, under the angry gaze of the operator. Marion started to cry.

'Wait here, I'll go and turn the lights back on.'

'Waah! Waaaaahhhh!'

'Stop that, Barbie Girl, you've made your sister cry.'

'Don't call me Barbie Girl!'

'So stop.'

It wasn't the circuit breaker or a fuse. The shutters banged, the doors creaked, and the whole house was plunged into darkness.

Brontë sisters, pray for us.

I wondered when Pierre was going to return.

I brought the girls' mattress down into the kitchen. Without an electric radiator, it was impossible to let them sleep up there. They were as excited as could be. We pushed back the table and laid their makeshift bed next to the fireplace.

I lay down between them.

'And Babar? You didn't finish . . .'

'Hush, Marion, hush. Look right in front of you. Look at the fire. That's what will tell you stories . . .'

'Yes, but . . .'

'Shhhh.'

They fell asleep immediately.

...

I listened to the sounds of the house. My nose itched, and I rubbed my eyes to keep from crying.

My life is like this bed, I kept thinking. Fragile. Uncertain. Suspended.

I lay there waiting for the house to blow away.

I was thinking that I had been cast off.

It's funny how expressions are not just expressions. You have to have experienced real fear to understand the meaning of 'cold sweat', or been very anxious to know exactly what 'my stomach was in knots' means, right?

It's the same with 'cast off'. What a marvellous expression. I wonder who thought it up.

Cast off the mooring lines.

Untie the wife.

Take to the sea, spread your albatross wings, and go and fuck on some other horizon.

No, really, what better way to put it?

I'm starting to sound bitter; that's a good sign. Another few weeks and I'll be really nasty.

The trap really lies in thinking that you are moored. You make decisions, take out loans, sign agreements, and even take a few risks. You buy houses, put the children in rooms all painted pink, and sleep entwined every night. You marvel at this . . . What is it called? This *intimacy*. Yes, that's what it was called, when you were happy. And even when you were less happy . . .

The trap lies in thinking that we have the right to be happy.

How ridiculous we are. Naïve enough to think that for even a second we have control over our lives.

Our lives slip through our fingers, but it's not serious. It's not that important . . .

The best thing would be to know it earlier.

When exactly 'earlier'?

Earlier.

Before repainting the bedrooms in pink, for example . . .

Pierre is right, why show your weakness?

Just to be hurt?

My grandmother often said that nice home cooking was the best way to keep a good man. I'm certainly a long way off, Grandma, a long way. First, I don't know how to cook, and then, I never wanted to keep anyone.

Well, then, you've succeeded, Granddaughter!

I pour myself a little cognac to celebrate.

One little tear and then bedtime.

The following day seemed very long.

We went for a walk. We gave bread to the horses at the riding school and spent a lot of time with them. Marion sat on the back of a pony. Lucie didn't want to.

I felt as if I were carrying a very heavy backpack.

In the evening it was showtime. Lucky me – every night there's a show at my house. On this evening's programme: 'The Little Gurl Who Dident Wanta Leev.' They took great pains to distract me.

I didn't sleep well.

The next morning, my heart wasn't in it. It was too cold.

...

The girls whined endlessly.

I tried to amuse them by pretending to be a prehistoric cavewoman.

'Now look, this is how the cavemen used to make their Nesquik . . . They put a pan of milk on the fire, yes, just like that . . . and to make toast? Simple as can be, they put a piece of bread on a grill and voilà, they held it over the flames . . . Careful! Not too long, or it will burn to a crisp. Okay, who wants to play cavewoman with me?'

They didn't care, they weren't hungry. All they cared about was their stupid television shows.

I burned myself. Marion started to cry when she heard me yell, and Lucie spilled her cocoa on the couch.

I sat down and put my head in my hands.

I dreamed of being able to unscrew my head, put it on the ground in front of me, and kick it hard enough to send it flying as far as possible.

So far that no one would ever find it again.

But I don't even know how to kick.

I wouldn't shoot straight, that's for sure.

At that moment, Pierre arrived.

He was sorry, explained that he couldn't get in touch earlier because the line was down, and shook a bag of warm croissants under the girls' noses.

They laughed. Marion took his hand and Lucie offered him a prehistoric coffee.

'A prehistoric coffee? With pleasure, my little Cro-Magnon beauty!'

I had tears in my eyes.

He placed a hand on my knee.

'Chloé . . . Are you all right?'

I wanted to tell him no, that I was not in the least bit all right, but I was so happy to see him that I answered the opposite.

'The bakery has lights, so it's not a local power cut. I'll go and find out what's happened . . . Girls, look outside, the weather is beautiful! Go and get dressed – we're going mushroom hunting. With all the rain last night, we're going to find plenty!'

The 'girls' included me . . . We climbed the stairs giggling.

How nice to be eight years old.

We walked all the way to the Devil's Mill, a sinister old building that has delighted several generations of small children.

Pierre told the girls stories about the holes in the walls:

'Here's where his horn struck . . . and there, those are the marks of his hooves . . .'

'Why did he kick the wall with his hooves?'

'Oh, that's a long story . . . It was because he was very cross that day.'

'Why was he very cross that day?'

'Because his prisoner had escaped.'

225

'Who was his prisoner?'

'The girl at the bakery.'

'Madame Pécaut's daughter?'

'No, no, not her daughter! Her great-great-grandmother!'

'Really?'

I showed the girls how to have a miniature tea party with acorn caps. We found an empty bird's nest, pebbles, and pine cones. We picked cowslips and broke hazelnut branches. Lucie brought back moss for her dolls and Marion stayed on her grandfather's shoulders the whole time.

We brought back two mushrooms, both of them looked suspect!

On the way back, we heard a blackbird singing, and a little girl asking in a curious voice:

'But why did the devil capture Madame Pécaut's grandmother?'

'Can't you guess?'

'No.'

'Because he was very greedy, that's why!'

She thrashed at the underbrush with a stick to chase away the devil.

And what about me? I thought. What can I chase away with a stick?

...

'Chloé?'

'Yes.'

'I want to tell you . . . I hope . . . Or rather, I'd like . . . Yes, that's it, I'd like . . . I'd like you to feel you're still welcome at the house because . . . I know how much you love it. You've done so many things here. In the bedrooms, the garden . . . Until you came, there was no garden, you know? Promise me that you'll come back. With or without the girls . . .'

I turned toward him.

'No, Pierre. You know very well that I can't.'

'What about your rosebush? What is it called, anyway? That rosebush you planted last year?'

'Maiden's Blush.'

'Yes, that's it. You loved it so . . .'

'No, it's the name I loved. Listen, this is hard enough as it is . . .'

'I'm sorry, I'm sorry.'

'What about you? Can't you look after it?'

'Of course! Maiden's Blush, you say . . . How could I not?'

He was overdoing it a little.

On the way back, we ran into old Marcel, who was returning from the village. His bicycle was weaving dangerously across the road. How he managed to stop in front of us without falling off, I'll never know. He put Lucie on the seat and invited us for a quick drink.

*

Madame Marcel smothered the girls with kisses and planted them in front of the television with a bag of sweets on their knees. 'Mummy, she has a satellite dish! Guess what! A channel with nothing but cartoons!'

Thank God.

Go to the ends of the earth, clamber over thickets, hedges, ditches, get a stuffy nose, cross old Marcel's courtyard, and watch Teletoons while eating strawberry-flavoured marshmallows.

Sometimes, life is wonderful . . .

The storm, mad cow disease, Europe, hunting, the dead and the dying . . . At one point in the discussion, Pierre asked:

'Marcel, tell me, do you remember my brother?'

'Who, Paul? I should say I do, that little monkey . . . He drove me crazy with that little whistling of his. Made me think there were all kinds of things to hunt! Made me think there were birds we don't have in these parts! That little rascal! And the dogs went crazy! Oh, I remember him all right! Such a great kid . . . He often headed off into the forest with the priest. He wanted to see and know about everything . . . My word, the questions that boy would ask! He always said he wanted to study so he could work in the forest. I remember how the priest would answer, "But my boy, you don't need to go to school! What could you learn that I couldn't teach you?" Paul didn't answer, he said he wanted to visit all the forests in the world, to see other countries, travel through Africa and Russia, and then come back here and tell us all about it.'

Pierre listened to him, gently nodding his head to encourage the old man to keep talking.

Madame Marcel stood up. She returned and held out a sketchbook to us.

'Here's what little Paul – well, I call him little Paul, but he wasn't so little at the time – gave me one day to thank me for my special deep-fried acacia flowers. Look, that was my dog.'

As she turned the pages, you could see the tricks of a little fox terrier who looked spoiled to death and a real show-off.

'What was his name?' I asked.

'He didn't have a name, but we always called him Where'd-He-Go, because he was always running off. That's how he died, actually . . . Oh . . . We just loved that dog . . . We just loved him . . . Too much, too much. This is the first time I've looked at these drawings in a long time. Normally, I try not to poke around in here, it's too many deaths at once . . .'

The drawings were marvellous. Where'd-He-Go was a brown fox terrier with long black whiskers and bushy eyebrows.

'He was shot . . . He was poaching from poachers, the little imbecile . . .'

*

I got up. We had to leave before it got completely dark.

...

'My brother died because of the rain. Because he was stationed out in the rain too long, can you imagine?'

I didn't answer; I was too busy watching my step, trying to avoid the puddles.

The girls went to bed without supper. Too many sweets.

Babar left the Old Lady. She was alone. She cried. She asked herself, 'When will I see my little Babar again?'

Pierre was also unhappy. He stayed in his study a long time, supposedly looking for his brother's drawings. I made dinner. Spaghetti with bits of Suzanne's home-made *gésiers confits*.

We had decided to leave the next day before noon. This was going to be the last time I would cook in this kitchen.

I really loved this kitchen. I threw the pasta into boiling water, cursing myself for being so sentimental. *I really loved this kitchen . . .* Hey, get a grip, old girl, you'll find other kitchens . . .

I bullied myself, even though my eyes were filled with tears. It was stupid.

He put a small watercolour on the table. A woman, reading, seen from behind.

She was sitting on a garden bench. Her head was slightly tilted. Perhaps she wasn't reading. Perhaps she was sleeping or daydreaming.

I recognised the house. The front steps, the rounded shutters, and the white wisteria.

'It's my mother.'

'What was her name?'

'Alice.'

I said nothing.

'It's for you.'

I started to protest, but he made an angry face and put a finger to his lips. Pierre Dippel was someone who didn't like to be contradicted.

'You always have to be obeyed, don't you?'

He wasn't listening to me.

'Didn't anyone ever dare to contradict you?' I added, placing Paul's drawing on the mantelpiece.

'Not one person. My entire life.'

I burned my tongue.

•••

He pushed himself up from the table.

'Bah. What would you like to drink, Chloé?'

'Something that cheers you up.'

•••

He came back up from the cellar, cradling two bottles as if they were newborn babies.

'Château Chasse-Spleen . . . appropriately enough. Just exactly what we need. I took two, one for you and one for me.'
'But you're crazy! You should wait for a better occasion . . .'
'A better occasion than what?'
He pulled his chair closer to the fire.
'Than . . . I don't know . . . than me . . . than us . . . than tonight.'
He had his arms wrapped around himself to keep his spirits up.
'But Chloé, we're a great occasion. We're the best occasion in the world. I've been coming to this house since I was a boy, I've eaten thousands of meals in this kitchen, and believe me, I know a great occasion when I see one!'

There was a little self-important tone in his voice. What a shame.

• • •

He turned his back and stared at the fire, motionless.

'Chloé, I don't want you to go . . .'

★

233

I tossed the noodles into the strainer and a dish towel on top.

'Look, I'm sorry, but this is too much. You're talking nonsense. You're only thinking about yourself, and it's a bit tiresome. "I don't want you to go." How can you say something so stupid? It wasn't me who left, okay? You have a son, remember him? Well, he was the one who left. It was him, didn't you know? It's a good story. It goes like this – it's a killer. So, it was . . . When was it, anyway? Doesn't matter. The other day, Adrien, the wonderful Adrien, packed his bags. Try and put yourself in my place – I was shocked. Oh right, I forgot to mention, it turns out I'm this boy's wife. You know, a wife, that practical thing you drag around everywhere, and that smiles when you kiss it. So, I was a bit surprised, as you can imagine . . . there he was with our suitcases standing in front of the lift, already groaning, looking at his watch. He was complaining because he was stressed out, the poor dear! The lift, the suitcases, the missus, and the plane, what a dilemma! Oh, yes! It seems he couldn't miss his plane because his mistress was on board! You know, a mistress, that young impatient thing that gets on your nerves a little. No time for a scene, you're thinking . . . And then, domestic quarrels are so tiresome . . . You never learn that at the Dippels', do you? Yelling, making scenes, moodiness, all so vulgar, don't you think? That's it, vulgar. With the Dippels, it's "never complain, never explain", and then on to the next thing. Now that's class.'

'Chloé, stop that at once!'

I was crying.

'Don't you hear yourself? Do you hear the way you talk to me? I'm not a dog, Pierre. I'm not your goddamned dog! I let him leave without ripping his eyes out, I quietly shut the door, and now I'm here, in front of you, in front of my children. I'm holding on. I'm just about holding on, do you understand? Do you understand what that means? Who heard me howl in despair? Who? So don't try to make me feel sorry for you now with your little problems. You don't want me to go . . . Oh, Pierre . . . I am unfortunately obliged to disobey you . . . It's with great regret . . . It's . . .'

He had grabbed hold of my wrists and was squeezing them as hard as he could. He held my arms immobile.

'Let me go! You're hurting me! This entire family is hurting me! Pierre, let me go.'

He barely had time to loosen his grip before my head fell on his shoulder.

'You're all hurting me . . .'

. . .

I cried into his neck, forgetting how uncomfortable it must have made him. Pierre, who never touched anyone. I cried, thinking occasionally about how the spaghetti was going to be inedible if I didn't add some oil. He said, 'Now, now . . .' He said, 'Please forgive me.' And he said, 'I'm just as sad as you . . .' He didn't know what to do with his hands anymore.

Finally, he moved aside to lay the table.

'To you, Chloé.'

I clinked my glass against his.

'Yes, to me,' I repeated with a crooked smile.

'You're a wonderful girl.'

'Yes, wonderful. And then there's dependable, courageous . . . What did I leave out?'

'Funny.'

'Oh, right, I was forgetting. Funny.'

'But unfair.'

I said nothing.

'You are being a bit unfair, don't you think?'

Silence.

'You think that I only love myself?'

'Yes.'

'Well, then, you're not only unfair, you're being stupid.'

I held out my glass.

'Oh, that, I knew that already . . . Pour me some more of that marvellous nectar.'

'You think that I'm an old bastard, don't you?'

'Yes.'

I nodded my head. I wasn't being mean, I was unhappy.

He sighed.

'Why am I an old bastard?'

'Because you don't love anyone. You never let yourself go. You're never there, never really with us. Never joining in our conversations and foolishness, never participating in dull dinner-table talk. Because you're never tender, because you never talk, and because your silence looks like disdain. Because – '

'Stop, stop. That will do, thanks.'

'Excuse me, I was answering your question. You ask me why you're an old bastard, and I'm telling you. That being said, you're not as old as all that . . .'

'You're too kind.'

'Don't mention it.'

I grinned at him tenderly, baring my teeth.

'But if I'm the way you describe, why would I bring you here? Why would I spend so much time with you, and – '

'You know very well why.'

'Why?'

'Because of your sense of honour. That high-mindedness of good families. For seven years I've tagged along after you, and this is the first time you've taken any notice of me. I'll tell you what I think. I don't find you either benevolent or charitable. I can see exactly what's going on. Your son has done something stupid and you – you come along behind, you clean up and repair the damage. You're going to plaster over the cracks as best you can. Because you don't like cracks, do you, Pierre? Oh, no! You don't like them one bit . . .

'Let me tell you something. I think you brought me here for the sake of appearances. The boy has messed up, well, let's grit our teeth and sort things out without making a fuss. In the past, you'd buy off the locals when the little shit's sports car made a mess of their beet fields, and today you're distracting the daughter-in-law. I'm just waiting for the moment when you put on your sorrowful act to tell me that I can count on you. Financially, I mean. *You're in a bit of a difficult spot, aren't you?* But a big girl like me is harder to buy off than a field of beets . . .'

He got up. 'So yes . . . It's true. You are stupid. What a terrible thing to discover . . . Here, give me your plate.'

He was behind my back.

'You can't imagine how much that hurts. More than that, you've wounded me deeply. But I don't hold it against you – I blame it on the pain you are feeling . . .'

He set a steaming plate in front of me.

'But there is one thing you can't get away with saying, just one thing . . .'

'What's that?' I asked, lifting my gaze.

'Whatever you do, don't drag beets into this. You'd be hard-pressed to find a single beet field for miles around . . .'

He was smugly pleased with himself.

'Mmm, this is good . . . You're going to miss my cooking, aren't you?'

'Your cooking, yes. As for the rest, thanks but no thanks . . . You've taken away my appetite . . .'

'Really?'

'No.'

'You had me worried there!'

'It would take more than that to keep me away from this marvellous pasta . . .'

He dug into his plate and lifted up a forkful of sticky spaghetti.

'Mmm, what do they call this? *Al dente* . . .'

I laughed.

'I love it when you laugh.'

      . . .

For a long moment we didn't speak.

'Are you angry?'

'No, not angry. Confused, really . . .'

'I'm sorry.'

'You see, I feel as if I'm facing something

240

impenetrable. A sort of enormous knot . . .'

'I'd like – '

'Hold on, hold on. Let me speak. I have to sort it out now, it's very important. I don't know if you'll understand, but you must listen to me. I need to follow a thread, but which one? I don't know, I don't know how or where to begin. Oh God, it's so complicated . . . If I choose the wrong thread or pull too hard, it might tighten the knot even more. It might become so badly knotted that nothing could be done, and I'll leave you overwhelmed. You see, Chloé, my life, my whole life is like this closed fist. Here I am before you in this kitchen. I'm sixty-five years old. I'm not much to look at. I'm just an old bastard you were shaking a while ago. I have understood nothing, and I never went up to the sixth floor. I was afraid of my own shadow, and here I am, facing the idea of my own death and . . . No, please, don't interrupt me . . . Not now. Let me open this fist. Just a little bit.'

I refilled our glasses.

'I'll start with what's most unfair, most cruel . . . That is, with you . . .'

He let himself fall back against the back of his chair.

. . .

'The first time I saw you, you were completely blue. I remember how impressed I was. I can still see you

standing in that doorway . . . Adrien was holding you
up, and you held out a hand that was completely stiff
with cold. You couldn't greet me, you couldn't speak,
so I squeezed your arm in a sign of welcome, and I can
still see the white marks that my fingers left on your
wrist. Suzanne was panicking, but Adrien told her,
laughing, "I've brought you a Smurfette!" Then he
took you upstairs and plunged you into a scalding-hot
bath. How long did you stay there? I don't remember;
I just remember Adrien repeating to his mother, "Take
it easy, Mum, take it easy! As soon as she's cooked, we
can eat." It's true, we were hungry. I was hungry,
anyway. And you know me, you know how old
bastards are when they get hungry . . . I was just about
to say that we should start eating without you, when
you came in, with wet hair and a shy smile, wearing
one of Suzanne's old nightdresses.

'This time, your cheeks were red, red, red . . .

'During dinner, you told us that you had met in the
queue for the cinema, which was showing *A Sunday in
the Country,* and that there were no more seats and that
Adrien, the show-off – it runs in the family – offered
you a real Sunday in the country, standing there in
front of his motorcycle. It was a take-it-or-leave-it
offer, and you took it, which explained your advanced
state of frostbite because you had left Paris wearing
only a T-shirt under your raincoat. Adrien was eating
you up with his eyes, which was difficult for him since
you kept looking down at the table. I could see a

dimple when he spoke about you, and we imagined that you would smile at us . . . I also remember those incredible sneakers you wore . . .'

'Yellow Converses, oh God!'

'Right. That's why you have no right to criticise the ones I bought for Lucie the other day . . . That reminds me, I have to tell her . . . "Don't listen to her, sweetie; when I met your mother, she was wearing yellow sneakers with red laces . . ."'

'You even remember the laces?'

'I remember everything, Chloé, everything. The red laces, the book you read underneath the cherry tree while Adrien fixed his engine . . .'

'Which was what?'

'*The World According to Garp,* right?'

'Exactly right.'

'I also remember how you volunteered to Suzanne to clear away the brush from the little stairway that led down to the old cellar. I remember the loving glances she threw you as she watched you wear yourself out over the thorns. You could read "Daughter-in-law? Daughter-in-law?" in big, flashing neon lights in front of her eyes. I drove you to the Saint-Amand market, you bought goat cheeses, and then we drank martinis in a café on the square. You read an article, about Andy Warhol I think, while Adrien and I played table soccer . . .'

'It's unbelievable, how is it possible that you can remember all that?'

'Uhh . . . I don't deserve much credit . . . It's one of the few things that we share . . .'

'You mean with Adrien?'

'Yes . . .'

'Yes.'

I got up to get the cheese.

'No, no, don't change the plates, it's not worth it.'

'Of course it is! I know how you hate to eat your cheese from the same plate.'

'I hate that? Oh . . . It's true . . . Another thing old bastards do, right?'

'Ummm . . . Yes, that's right.'

He grimaced as he held out his plate.

'The hell with you.'

A dimple showed.

'Of course, I also remember your wedding day . . . You took my arm and you were so beautiful. You played with your hair. We were crossing that same square at Saint-Amand when you whispered in my ear: "You should kidnap me; I'd throw these horrible shoes out the window of your car and we'd go to Chez Yvette and eat seafood . . ." Your little joke made my head spin. I tightened my gloves. Here, serve yourself first . . .'

'No, no, you first.'

'What else can I tell you? I remember one day, we had arranged to meet in the café downstairs from my office so I could take back a ladle or some other such thing that Suzanne had lent you. I must have seemed disagreeable to you that day, I was in a hurry, preoccupied . . . I left before you had finished your tea. I asked you questions about your job and probably didn't pay attention to the answers. That night at dinner, when Suzanne asked me, "What's new?" without really believing it, I answered, "Chloé is pregnant." "She told you?" "No, and I'm not sure that she knows it herself." Suzanne shrugged her shoulders and rolled her eyes, but I was right. A few weeks later, you told us the good news . . .'

'How did you guess?'

'I don't know . . . It seemed to me that your complexion had changed, that your fatigue was caused by something else . . .'

I said nothing.

'I could go on and on like this. You see, you're not being fair – what were you just saying? That all this time, all these years, I never took an interest in you. Oh, Chloé, I hope you feel ashamed of yourself.'

Jokingly, he gave me a stern look.

'On the other hand, I am egotistical, you're right there. I told you I don't want you to go because I don't want you to go. I'm thinking of myself. You are closer to me than my own daughter. My daughter would never tell me that I'm an old bastard, she would just think to herself that I'm an idiot, period!'

He got up to get the salt.

'Hey now . . . what's the matter?'

'Nothing. It's nothing.'

'Yes, it is. You're crying.'

'No, I'm not crying. Look, I'm not crying.'

'Yes, you are. You're crying! Do you want a glass of water?'

'Yes.'

'Oh, Chloé . . . I don't want you to cry. It makes me unhappy.'

'There, you see! It's about you! You're just impossible . . .'

I tried for a playful tone, but bubbles of mucus came out of my nose. It was pitiful.

I laughed. I cried. This wine wasn't cheering me up at all.

'I should never have talked to you about all that . . .'

'No, it's okay. They're my memories, too . . . I just have to get used to all this. It might be hard for you to understand, but this is totally new for me. Two weeks ago, I was still your garden-variety wife and mother. I flipped through my diary on the Métro, planning dinner parties, and I filed my nails while thinking about holidays. I asked myself, "Should we take the girls, or go away just the two of us?" That kind of thing . . .

'I also said to myself, "We should find another apartment; this one is nice, but it's too dark . . ." I was waiting for Adrien to feel better, because I could see that he hadn't been himself recently . . . Irritable, touchy, tired . . . I was worried about him; I thought, "They're killing him at work, what's with the impossible hours?"'

He turned to face the fire.

'Garden variety, but not very sharp, right? I waited to have dinner with him. I waited for hours. Sometimes I even fell asleep waiting for him . . . He would finally come home, wearing a long face, with his tail between his legs. I would yawn and stretch and guide him to the kitchen, bustling about. He wasn't hungry, of course, he had the decency to not have any appetite. Or maybe they had already eaten? Most likely . . .

'It must have been hell for him to sit across from me! What a trial I must have been with my cheerful nature and my soap opera stories about the goings-on of Firmin-Gédon Square. Torture for him, when I think of it . . . Lucie lost a tooth, my mother's not doing well, the Polish au pair girl who looks after little Arthur is going out with the neighbour's son, I finished my sculpture this morning, Marion cut her hair and it looks terrible, the teacher needs egg-boxes, you look tired, take a day off, give me your hand, do you want some more spinach? Poor thing . . . a form of torture for an unfaithful but scrupulous husband. What torture . . . But I didn't suspect a thing. I didn't see it coming, do you understand? How could I have been so blind? How? Either I was completely stupid or completely trusting. It amounts to the same thing, really . . .'

I leaned my chair back.

'Oh, Pierre . . . What a bad joke life is . . .'

'It's good, isn't it?'

'Very. Too bad it doesn't keep any of its promises . . .'

'It's the first time I've drunk it.'

'Me too.'

'It's like your rosebush; I bought it for the label . . .'

'Mm. A bad joke . . . What stupidity.'

'But you're still young . . .'

'No, I'm old, I feel old. I'm all used up. I feel like I'm going to become wary. I'll watch my life through a peephole. I won't open the door. "Step back. Let me see your hands. That's good, now the other. Don't scuff the parquet. Stay in the hallway. Don't move."'

'No, you'll never become that kind of woman. As much as you might want to, you can't. People will keep walking into your life, you will continue to suffer and it's better that way. I'm not worried about you.'

'No, of course not.'

'What do you mean?'

'Of course you're not worried about me. You don't worry about people, ever . . .'

'That's true, you're right. It's hard for me to care.'

'Why?'

'I don't know. Because other people don't interest me, I suppose . . .'

'. . . except Adrien.'

'What do you mean, Adrien?'

'I think about him.'

'You worry about Adrien?'

'Yes, I think so . . . Yes.

'At any rate, he's the one I worry about the most.'

'Why?'

'Because he's unhappy.'

I was completely taken aback.

'Well, now I've heard everything! He's not unhappy at all . . . On the contrary, he's very happy! He's traded in his boring, used wife for a brand-new, amusing model. His life is a lot more fun today, you know.'

I looked at my wrist.

'Let's see, what time is it? A quarter to ten. Where is our martyr now? Where could he be? At the movies, or the theatre perhaps? Or maybe they're having dinner somewhere. They must have finished their starter by now . . . He caresses her palm while dreaming about later. Careful, here comes the main course, she pulls her hand back and gives him a smile. Or perhaps they're in bed . . . That's most likely, isn't it? In the beginning one makes love a lot, if I remember correctly . . .'

'You're being cynical.'

'I'm protecting myself.'

'Whatever he's doing, he's unhappy.'

'Because of me, you mean? I'm spoiling his fun? Oh, that ungrateful woman . . .'

'No. Not because of you, because of him. Because of this life, which never does what you want it to. Our efforts are so laughable . . .'

'You're right, the poor thing . . .'

'You're not listening to me.'

'No.'

'Why aren't you listening to me?'

I bit into a piece of bread.

'Because you're a bulldozer, you flatten everything in your path . . . For you, my sorrow is . . . what? . . . a burden, and soon it will start to get on your nerves. And then this thing about blood ties . . . This stupid notion . . . You didn't give a damn about taking your children in your arms, about telling them that you loved them even once, but despite this, I know that you'll always leap to their defence. No matter what they say or do, they will always be right in contrast to the rest of us barbarians – the ones who don't have the same name as you.

'Your children haven't given you a whole lot of reasons to be happy, but you're the only one who can criticise them. The only one! Adrien takes off and leaves me here with the girls. All right, that bothers you, but I've given up hope of hearing you speak a few harsh words against him. A few harsh words . . . it wouldn't change anything, but it would give me a bit of pleasure. So much pleasure, if you only knew . . . Yes, it's hopeless. I'm hopeless. But just a couple of heartfelt words, really bitter words, the ones you know so well how to say . . . Why not for him? I deserve that, after all. I'm waiting for the condemnation of the patriarch seated at the head of the table. All these years I've listened to you divide up the world. The good and the bad, those who have earned your respect and those who haven't. All these years I've run up against your speeches, your authority, your commander-in-chief expressions, your silences . . . So much arrogance. So much arrogance . . . While all along being a pain in the arse, Pierre . . .

'You see, I'm not that complicated a person and I need to hear you say, "My son is a bastard, and I ask for your forgiveness." I need that, do you understand?'

'Don't count on it.'

I cleared the plates.

'I wouldn't count on it.'

'Would you like dessert?'

'No.'

'You don't want anything?'

'So it's ruined . . . I must have pulled on the wrong thread . . .'

I wasn't listening anymore.

'The knot is tightened, and here we are, further

251

apart than ever. So I'm an old bastard . . . A monster . . . And what else?'

I was looking for the sponge.

'And what else?'

I looked him right in the eyes.

'Listen to me, Pierre; for years I lived with a man who couldn't stand up straight because his father hadn't given him the support he needed. When I met Adrien, he didn't dare do anything for fear of disappointing you. And everything he did disappointed me because he never did it for himself, he did it for you. To amaze you or to irritate you. To provoke you or to please you. It was pathetic. I was barely twenty years old and I gave up my life for him. To listen to him and stroke his neck when he finally opened up. I don't regret it, I couldn't do anything else, anyway. It made me sick to see someone abase himself like that. We spent whole nights unravelling things and putting them in perspective. I gave him a shaking-up. I told him a thousand times that he was taking the easy way out. The easy way out! We made resolutions and then we broke them, we made others, and then finally I quit my studies so that he could pick his up again. I rolled up my sleeves and for three years I dropped him off at the university before going off to waste time in the basement of the Louvre. It was our deal: I wouldn't complain as long as he didn't talk about you. I'm not special. I never said he was the best. I just loved him. Loved. Him. Do you know what I'm talking about?'

He said nothing.

'So, you can see why I'm a little unhappy today . . .'

I wiped the sponge around his hands that were placed on the table.

'He got his confidence back; the prodigal son is a new man. He can sail his boat like a big boy, and here he is, discarding his old self, right under the nose of his big, bad father. You have to admit, it's a little rough, no?'

Silence.

'You have nothing to say?'

'No. I'm going to bed.'

I set the machine going.

'That's it, good night.'

...

I bit my cheeks.

I kept some dreadful things to myself.

I took my glass and went to sit on the couch. I took off my shoes and sank into the cushions. I got up to get the bottle from the table. I poked the fire, turned out the light, and buried myself there.

I regretted not being drunk yet.

I regretted being there.

I regretted . . . I regretted so many things.

So many things . . .

I laid my head on the armrest and closed my eyes.

'Are you asleep?'

'No.'

He went to pour himself a glass of wine and sat down in an armchair next to the sofa.

The wind continued to blow. We sat in the dark. We watched the fire.

From time to time, one of us took a drink and then the other followed suit.

We were neither happy nor sad. We were tired.

After a very long moment he said:

'You know, I wouldn't be the person you said I was if I had had more courage . . .'

'I'm sorry?'

I already regretted having answered him. I didn't want to talk about this shit anymore. I just wanted to be left in peace.

'Everyone always talks about the sorrow of those left behind, but did you ever consider the sorrow of the ones who leave?'

Here we go again, I thought to myself, what kind of crazy idea is he going to try and put over on me now, the old fool?

I looked around for my shoes.

'We'll talk about it tomorrow, Pierre, I'm going . . . I'm fed up with this.'

'The sorrow of those who cause unhappiness . . . We pity the ones who stay, we comfort them, but what about those who leave?'

'What else do they want?' I exploded. 'A medal? Words of encouragement?'

He wasn't listening to me.

'The courage of those who look in the mirror one morning and say to themselves: "Do I have the right to make a mistake?" Just those few words . . . The courage to look their lives in the face and see nothing settled or harmonious there. The courage to destroy everything, to smash it out of . . . out of selfishness? Out of pure selfishness? No, not that . . . So what is it? Survival instinct? A moment of lucidity? Fear of death?

'The courage to confront yourself just once in your life. Confront yourself. By yourself. Finally.

' "The right to make a mistake", it's just a little expression, one tiny little phrase, but who gives you that right?

'Who, if not yourself?'

His hands were trembling.

★

'I never gave it to myself . . . I never gave myself any right. Only duty. And look what I've become: an old bastard. An old bastard in the eyes of one of the precious few people for whom I have a bit of respect. What a fiasco . . .

'I've made lots of enemies. I'm not bragging, and I'm not complaining either. I just don't give a damn. But friends, those I wanted to please? There are so few, so few . . . and you're one of them. You, Chloé, because you have such a gift for life. You grab hold of it with both hands. You move, you dance, you know how to make the rain and the sunshine in a home. You have this incredible gift for making the people around you happy. You're so at ease, so at ease on this little planet . . .'

'I have the feeling we're not talking about the same person . . .'

He hadn't heard me.

He sat straight in his chair. He had stopped speaking. He hadn't crossed his legs, and his glass rested between his thighs.

I couldn't see his face.

His face was in the shadow of the armchair.

'I loved a woman . . . I'm not talking about Suzanne, I'm talking about another woman.'

I opened my eyes.

★

'I loved her more than anything. More than anything . . . I didn't know that someone could love that much. Or me, at any rate, I thought that I wasn't . . . *programmed* to love like that . . . Declarations, insomnia, the ravages of passion, all that was for other people. Besides, just the word "passion" made me snigger. Passion, passion! I filed that somewhere between "hypnosis" and "superstition" . . . The way I said it, it was practically a four-letter word. And then, it hit me at the moment when I least expected it. I . . . I loved a woman.

'I fell in love like you catch a cold. Without wanting to, without believing in it, against my will and with no way to defend myself, and then . . .'

He cleared his throat.

'And then I lost her. In the same way.'

• • •

I couldn't move. An anvil had just fallen on my head.

'Her name was Mathilde. Her name is still Mathilde, by the way. Mathilde Courbet. Like the painter . . .

'I was forty-two years old and I thought I was already old. I've always thought I was old. It's Paul who was young. Paul will always be young and handsome.

'I'm Pierre. Pierre the plodder, Pierre the hard worker.

'When I was ten years old, I already had the face I have today. The same haircut, the same glasses, the same gestures, the same little tics. At ten, I already changed my plate for the cheese course, I imagine . . .'

In the dark, I smiled at him.

'Forty-two years old . . . What can you expect from life at forty-two?

'Me, nothing. I expected nothing. I worked. More and more and always more. It was like camouflage for me, my armour and my alibi. My alibi for not living. Because I didn't like living all that much. I thought I didn't have a gift for it.

'I invented hardships for myself, mountains to climb. Very high ones, very steep. Then I rolled up my sleeves, climbed them, and then invented others. And yet, I wasn't ambitious, I just had no imagination.'

He took a sip of wine.

. . .

'I . . . I didn't know anything about this, you know . . . It was Mathilde who taught me. Oh, Chloé . . . How I loved her . . . How I loved her . . . Are you still there?'

'Yes.'
'Are you listening to me?'
'Yes.'
'Am I boring you?'
'No.'
'Are you going to fall asleep?'
'No.'

He got up and put another log on the fire. He stayed crouched in front of the fireplace.

'You know what she complained about? That I was too talkative. Can you believe that? Me . . . too talkative! Incredible, isn't it? But it was true . . . I put my head on her stomach and I talked. I talked for hours, for whole days, even. I heard the sound of my voice grow deep beneath her skin and I loved it. I was a word machine . . . I made her head spin. I inundated her with words. She laughed. She told me, "*Shhh, don't talk so much,* I can't listen to you anymore. Why do you go on like that?"

'I had forty-two years of silence to catch up on. Forty-two years of not speaking, of keeping everything to myself. What did you say a while ago? That my silence looks like disdain, wasn't that it? That hurt, but I can understand, I understand why people criticise me. I understand, but I have no interest in defending myself. That's the problem, really . . . But disdain, I don't think so. As strange as it may seem, my silence is more like shyness. I don't like myself enough to attach the least importance to what I say. Think twice, speak once, as the old saying goes. I always think one too many times. People find me pretty discouraging . . . I didn't like myself before Mathilde and I like myself even less since. I suppose I'm hard because of that . . .'

He sat back down.

'I'm tough at work, but that's just because I'm playing a role, you see? I have to be tough, I have to make them think I'm a tyrant. Can you imagine if they discovered my secret? If they figured out that I'm shy? That I have to work three times harder than the others for the same result? That I have a bad memory? That I'm slow to understand? If they knew that, they'd eat me alive!

'Plus, I don't know how to make myself liked . . . I have no charisma, as they say. If I give someone a rise, I do it in a curt voice; when someone thanks me, I don't answer. When I want to do something nice for someone, I stop myself, and if I have good news to announce, I let my secretary Françoise do it. When it comes to management, or human resources as they say, I'm a disaster, a complete disaster.

'It was Françoise who signed me up against my will for a sort of training course for hopeless bosses. What a lot of nonsense . . . Shut up for two days at the Concorde Lafayette Hotel at Porte Maillot, being force-fed popular drivel by a shrink and an overexcited American. He sold his book at the end. *Work, Love, and Be the Best* it was called. My God, what a joke, now that I look back on it . . .

'At the end of the course, as I recall, they handed out diplomas for kind, understanding bosses. I gave it to Françoise, who pinned it up in the closet where we keep the cleaning products and toilet paper.

'"How was it?" she asked me.

'"It was pathetic."

'She smiled.

'"Listen, Françoise," I told her, "you're like God Almighty around here. Tell anyone who's interested that I'm not nice, but that they'll never lose their job because I'm very good at making the numbers work."

'"Amen," she murmured, bowing her head.

'And it was true. In twenty-five years of being a tyrant, I never had a strike and I never laid anyone off. Even when things were so bad in the early '90s, I never laid off a soul. Not one, do you understand?'

'And Suzanne?'

He was silent.

'Why are you so hard with her?'

'You think I'm hard?'

'Yes.'

'Hard in what way?'

'Hard.'

He rested his head on the armchair again.

★

'When Suzanne figured out that I had been unfaithful to her, it had already been over for a long time. I had . . . I'll tell you that later . . . In those years, we lived on Rue de la Convention. I didn't like the apartment. I didn't like the way she had decorated it. It was suffocating: too much furniture, too many knick-knacks, too many photos of us, too much of every-thing. I'm telling you this, but it's not important. I went back to that apartment to sleep and because my family lived there, period. One evening, she asked me to take her out to dinner. We went to a place just down the street, a horrible pizzeria. The neon lights made her look awful, and since she was already wearing the face of an outraged wife, they didn't help. It was cruel, but I hadn't done it on purpose, you see. I opened the door of the first cheap place I saw . . . I knew what was coming, and I had no desire to be far from my bed. And, as it turns out, it didn't take her long to get started. She had barely laid down the menu when she broke down sobbing.

'She knew everything. That it was a younger woman. She knew how long it had lasted and under-stood why I was always away from home now. She couldn't take it any longer. I was a monster. Did she deserve this much contempt? Did she deserve to be treated this way? Like a scullery maid? At first, she had looked the other way. She suspected something, but she trusted me. She thought it was just one of those things, a thrill, the need to seduce. Something to bolster my virility. And then there was my job. My work, so exhausting, so hard. And she – she had been occupied with setting up the new house. She couldn't manage everything at once. She couldn't fight every fire! She had trusted me! And then I had fallen ill and she had looked the other way. But now, now she couldn't take it anymore. No, she couldn't take me anymore. My egotism, my contempt, the way in which – At that exact moment, the waiter interrupted her and, within a split second, she had switched masks. With a smile, she asked him a question about the tortellini something-or-other. I was fascinated. When he turned to me, I managed to stammer out, "The . . . the same as Madame." I hadn't given the damn menu a single thought, you see. Not for a second . . .'

'That was when I took the full measure of Suzanne's strength. Her immense strength. She's like a steam-roller. That was when I knew that she was by far the sturdier of the two of us, and that nothing could really touch her. In fact, all of this was about her personal timetable. She was taking me to task because her beach house was finally finished. The last picture had been hung, the last curtain rod put up, and she finally turned in my direction and had been horrified by what she had discovered.

'I barely said a word, I defended myself half-heartedly. As I told you, I had already lost Mathilde by that point . . .'

*

'I looked across the table at my wife getting upset in a miserable pizzeria in the fifteenth arrondissement in Paris, and I turned off the sound.'

'She gesticulated, let big tears roll down her cheeks, blew her nose, and wiped her plate with a piece of bread. All the while, I twirled two or three strands of spaghetti around my fork without ever managing to raise them to my mouth. I also wanted very much to cry, but I stopped myself . . .'

'Why did you stop yourself?'

'A question of upbringing, I suppose . . . And I still felt so fragile . . . I couldn't take the risk of letting myself go. Not there. Not then. Not with her. Not in that awful place. I was . . . How can I put it . . . barely in one piece.

'Then she told me that she had gone to see a lawyer to start divorce proceedings. Suddenly I started paying attention. A lawyer? Suzanne was asking for a divorce? I never imagined that things had gone that far, that she had been hurt that much . . . She went to see a woman, the sister-in-law of one of her friends. She had hesitated but on the way back from a weekend here, she had made up her mind. She had decided in the car, when I hadn't spoken to her once except to ask if she had change for the motorway toll. She had invented a sort of conjugal Russian roulette: if Pierre speaks to me, I'll stay; if he doesn't, I'll divorce him.

'I was disconcerted. I never thought she was the gambling type.

'She pulled herself together and looked at me more self-confidently. Of course, she wanted to lay it all out. My trips, ever longer and more frequent, my lack of interest in family life, my neglected children, the report cards I never signed. All the lost years she had spent organising everything around me. For my well-being, for the company. The company that belonged to her family, to her, incidentally, the sacrifices she had made. How she had cared for my poor mother right up until the end. Everything really, everything she needed to say, plus everything that lawyers like to hear in order to put a price tag on the whole mess.

'But with that, I felt my old self again. We were now on familiar territory. What did she want? Money? How much? If she had given me a figure, I would have had my chequebook on the table.

'But no, she had my number, did I think I could get out of it that easily? I was so pathetic . . . She started to cry again between mouthfuls of tiramisu. Why couldn't I understand anything? Life wasn't just about power struggles. Money couldn't buy everything. Or buy everything back. Was I going to pretend that I didn't understand anything? Didn't I have a heart? I was really pathetic. Pathetic . . .

'"But why don't you ask for a divorce?" I finally blurted out, exasperated, "I'll take all the blame. All of it, you hear? Even how awful my mother was, I'll be glad to sign something and acknowledge it if that would make you happy, but please don't drag the lawyers into it, I beg you. Tell me how much you want instead."

'I had cut her to the quick.

'She lifted her head and looked me in the eye. It was the first time in years that we had looked at each other that long. I searched for something else in her face. Our youth, perhaps . . . A time when I didn't make her cry. When I didn't make any woman cry, and when the very idea of sitting at a table and hashing out one's love life seemed inconceivable.

'But there was nothing there, only the slightly sad expression of a defeated spouse who was about to make a confession. She hadn't gone back to see the lawyer because she didn't have the heart. She loved her life, her house, her children, her neighbourhood shops . . . She was ashamed to admit it, and yet it was true: she didn't have the courage to leave me.

'The courage.

'I could run after women if that pleased me, I could have affairs if that was reassuring, but she – she wasn't leaving. She didn't want to lose what she had. Her social standing. Our friends, our relations, our children's friends. And then there was her brand-new house, where we hadn't even spent one night . . . It was a risk she didn't want to take. After all, what good would it do? There were men who had cheated on their wives . . . Lots of them, even . . . She had finally told her story and had been disappointed by how banal it was. That's just how things were. The fault lay in what hangs between our legs. She just had to grin and bear it, let the storm pass. She had taken the first step, but the idea of no longer being Mrs. Pierre Dippel had drained her of her courage. That was how it was, and too bad for her. Without the children, without me, she wasn't worth much.

'I offered her my handkerchief. "It's all right," she added, forcing herself to smile. "It's all right . . . I'm staying with you because I couldn't think of a better idea. For once, I was badly organised. Me, the one who always anticipates everything. I . . . It was too much for me, I suppose." She smiled through her tears.

'I patted her hand. It was finished. I was here. I wasn't with anyone else. No one. It was over. It was over . . .'

'Over coffee we chatted about the owner's moustache and how awful the décor was.

'Two old friends covered with scars.

'We had lifted up a huge rock and had let it fall back immediately.

'It was too awful to look at what was crawling underneath.'

. . .

'That night, in the darkness, I took Suzanne chastely in my arms. I couldn't do any more than that.

'For me, it was another sleepless night. Her confession, instead of reassuring me, had left me completely shaken. I have to say, I was in a terrible way at the time. Terrible, really terrible. Everything set me on edge. I found myself in a completely depressing situation: I had lost the woman I loved and had just learned that I had hurt the other one. What a scene . . . I had lost the love of my life to stay with a woman who would never leave me because of her cheese shop and her butcher. It was impossible, everything was destroyed. Neither Mathilde nor Suzanne had deserved that. I had ruined everything. I had never felt so miserable in all my life . . .

'The medications I was taking didn't make things any easier, that's for certain, but if I had had more courage, I would have hanged myself that night.'

He tipped his head back to drain his glass.

'But Suzanne? She's not unhappy with you . . .'

'Oh, you think so? How can you say something like that? Did she say that she was happy?'

'No. Not like that. She didn't say it, but she gave me to understand . . . Anyway, she's not the type of woman to stop for a moment to ask herself if she is happy . . .'

'You're right, she isn't the type . . . That's where

her strength lies, by the way. You know, if I was so miserable that night, it was really on account of her. When I see what she has turned into . . . So bourgeois, so conventional . . . If you could have seen what a little number she was when I met her . . . I'm not happy with what I did, really, it's nothing to be proud of. I suffocated her. I wilted her. For me, she was always the one who was there. Within reach. Close to hand. On the end of the phone. With the children. In the kitchen. A sort of vestal who spent the money that I earned and made our little world go around comfortably and without complaining. I never looked any further than the end of my nose.

'Which of her secrets had I found out? None. Did I ask her about herself, about her childhood, her memories, her regrets, her weariness, our physical relations, her faded hopes, her dreams? No. Never. Nothing. I wasn't interested.'

'Don't take it too much to heart, Pierre. You can't carry all the blame. Self-flagellation has its charms, but still . . . You don't make a very convincing Saint Sebastian, you know . . .'

'I like that, you don't let me get away with anything. You're the one who keeps me straight . . . That's why I hate to lose you. Who's going to take a shot at me when you're no longer here?'

'We'll have lunch together every once in a while . . .'

'Promise?'

'Yes.'

'You say that but you'll never do it, I know . . .'

'We'll make a ritual out of it, the first Friday of the month, for example . . .'

'Why Friday?'

'Because I love a good fish dish! You'll take me to good restaurants, right?'

'The best!'

'All right, now I'm reassured . . . But it won't be for a long time . . .'

'A long time?'

'Yes.'

'How long?'

I said nothing.

'Fine. I can wait.'

I poked at a log.

'To come back to Suzanne . . . Her bourgeois side, as you say. You had nothing to do with it, and it's a good thing. There are some things that are all hers without any of your help. It's like those English products that proclaim "By appointment to Her Majesty the Queen." Suzanne became who she is without any need for your "appointment". You can be annoying, but you're not all-powerful! That Lady Bountiful routine of hers, chasing after sales and recipes, she didn't need you to create that whole show for her. It comes naturally, as they say. It's in her blood, that *I dust, I remark, I judge, and I forgive* side of her. It's exhausting; it exhausts me, anyway — the parcelling out of her good deeds, and God knows she has plenty of good deeds, right?'

'Yes. God knows . . . Would you like something to drink?'

'No, thanks.'

'Some herbal tea, perhaps?'

'No, no. I'm fine getting slowly drunk . . .'

'All right then, I'll leave you in peace.'

'Pierre?'

'Yes?'

'I can't get over it.'

'Over what?'

'What you've just told me . . .'

'I can't either.'

'And Adrien?'

'What about him?'

'Will you tell him?'

'What would I tell him?'

'Well . . . all of that . . .'

'Adrien came to see me, believe it or not.'

'When?'

'Last week, and . . . I didn't tell him about it. I mean, I didn't talk about myself, but I listened . . .'

'What did he tell you?'

'What I told you, what I already knew . . . That he was unhappy, that he didn't know where he was going anymore . . .'

'He came to confide in you?!'

'Yes.'

I began to cry again.

'Does that surprise you?'

I shook my head.

'I feel betrayed. Even you . . . You . . . I hate that. I would never do that to someone, I – '

'Calm down. You're mixing everything up. Who said anything about betrayal? Where is the treason? He showed up without warning, and as soon as I saw him I suggested that we go out. I switched off my mobile and we went down to the parking garage. As soon as I started up the car, he said to me, "I'm going to leave Chloé." I remained calm. We drove up into the open air. I didn't want to ask questions, I waited for him to speak . . . Always this problem of which thread to pull . . . I didn't want to rush things. I didn't know what to do. I was a bit shaken up, to tell you the truth. I turned on to the Paris ring road and opened the ashtray.'

'And then?' I added.

'And then nothing. He's married, he has two children. He had thought it over. He thought that it was worth – '

'Shut up, please shut up . . . I know the rest.'

I got up to get the roll of paper towels.

'You must be proud of him, eh? It's great what he did, right? There's a man for you! What courage. What sweet revenge – he really got you there! What sweet revenge . . .'

'Don't use that tone of voice.'

'I'll use any tone I want, and I'm going to tell you what I think . . . You're even worse than he is. You, you ruined everything. Oh yes, beneath your high-minded attitude, you've ruined everything and you're using him, using his sleeping around to comfort yourself. I think that's pathetic. You make me sick, both of you.'

'You're talking nonsense. You know that, don't you? You know that you're talking nonsense?'

He spoke to me very gently.

'If it was just a question of sleeping around, as you say, we wouldn't be here, and you know it . . .

'Chloé, talk to me.'

'I'm a royal bitch . . . No, don't contradict me for once. It would make me very happy for you to not contradict me.'

'Can I make a confession? A very difficult confession?'

'Go ahead, given the state I'm in . . .'

'I think that it's a good thing.'

'That what's a good thing?'

'What's happened to you . . .'

'Becoming a royal bitch?'

'No, that Adrien left. I think that you deserve better . . . Better than this forced happiness . . . Better than filing your nails in the Métro while flipping through your diary, better than Firmin-Gédon Square, better than what the two of you had become. It's shocking that I'm telling you this, isn't it? And what business is it of mine, anyway? It's shocking, but too bad. I'm not going to pretend, I care about you too much. I don't think that Adrien was in your class. He was a little out of his league with you. That's what I think . . .

'I know, it's shocking because he's my son and I shouldn't talk about him that way. But there you are, I'm an old bastard and I don't give a damn about appearances. I'm telling you this because I believe in you. You . . . You weren't really properly loved. And if you could be as honest as I am right this minute, you'd act offended, but you'd think exactly the same thing.'

'You're talking nonsense.'

'And there you are. That little offended air of yours . . .'

'So now you're a psychoanalyst?'

'Haven't you ever heard that little voice inside that pokes you from time to time, to remind you that you weren't really properly loved?'

'No.'

'No?'

'No.'

'All right. I guess I'm wrong . . .'

He leaned forward, pressing on his knees.

'I think that someday you should come up out of there.'

'Out of where?'

'That basement.'

'You really do have an opinion about everything, don't you?'

'No. Not about everything. Why are you slaving away in the basement of a museum when you know what you're capable of? It's a waste of time. What is it you do? Copies? Plaster casts? You're tinkering. Who cares? And how long are you going to do it? Until you retire? Don't tell me you're happy in that hellhole stuffed with civil servants . . .'

'No, no,' I said ironically, 'I would never say that, rest assured.'

'If I were your lover, I would grab you by the scruff of the neck and drag you back up into the light. You're really talented with your hands and you know it. Accept it. Accept your gifts. Take responsibility. I would sit you down somewhere and tell you, "It's up to you now. It's your move, Chloé. Show us what you're made of."'

'And what if there's nothing?'

'Well, it would be the moment to find out. And stop biting your lip, it hurts me.'

275

Anna Gavalda

'Why is it you have so many good ideas for other people and so few for yourself?'

'I've already answered that question.'

'What is it?'

'I thought I heard Marion crying.'

'I didn't h – '

'Shhh.'

'It's okay, she's gone back to sleep.'

I sat back down and pulled the blanket over me.

'Shall I go and see?'

'No, no. Let's wait a little.'

'And what do you think I deserve, Mr. Know-It-All?'

'You deserve to be treated like what you are.'

'Which is . . . ?'

'Like a princess. A modern princess.'

'Pfff . . . That's ridiculous.'

'Yes, I'm prepared to say anything. Anything if that makes you smile . . . Smile for me, Chloé.'

'You're crazy.'

He got up.

'Ah . . . that's perfect! I like that better. You starting to say fewer stupid things . . . Yes, I am crazy, and you know what I say? I'm crazy and I'm hungry. What could I eat for dessert?'

'Look in the fridge. You'll have to finish the girls' yogurts . . .'

'Where are they?'

'Down on the bottom.'

'Those little pink things?'

'Yes.'

'It's not so bad . . .'

He licked his spoon.

'Do you see what they're called?'

'No.'

'Look, specially for you.'

'*Little Rascals* . . . That's cute.'

. . .

'We should probably go to bed, don't you think?'

'Yes.'

'Are you sleepy?'

I was upset.

'How can you expect me to sleep with everything that's been churned up? I feel like I'm stirring a huge cauldron . . .'

'I untie knots while you stir your cauldron. It's funny, the images we use . . .'

'You the mathematician and me the crone.'

'The crone? Rubbish. My princess a crone . . . The number of ridiculous things you've said tonight.'

'You're a pain in the neck, aren't you?'

'Very much so.'

'Why?'

'I don't know. Perhaps because I say what I think. It's not all that common . . . I'm no longer afraid of not being liked.'

'What about by me?'

'Oh, you; you like me, I'm not worried about that!'

'Pierre?'

'Yes?'

'What happened with Mathilde?'

He looked at me. He opened his mouth and closed it again. He crossed and uncrossed his legs. He got up. He poked the fire and stirred the embers. He lowered his head and murmured:

'Nothing. Nothing happened. Or very little. So few days, so few hours . . . Almost nothing, really.'

'You don't want to talk about it?'

'I don't know.'

'You never saw her again?'

'Yes, once. A few years ago. In the gardens of the Palais-Royal . . .'

'And then?'

'And then nothing.'

'How did you meet her?'

'You know . . . if I start, I don't know when I'll stop.'

'I told you I wasn't sleepy.'

He began to examine Paul's drawing. The words didn't come easily.

• • •

'When was it?'

'It was . . . I saw her for the first time on June 8, 1978, in Hong Kong at about eleven o'clock, local time. We met on the nineteenth floor of the Hyatt Tower in the office of a Mr. Singh, who needed me to drill somewhere in Taiwan. You find this funny?'

'Yes, because it's so precise. She worked with you?'

'She was my translator.'

'From Chinese?'

'No, from English.'

'But you speak English, don't you?'

'Not well. Not well enough to handle this type of thing; it was too subtle. When you get to that level, it's no longer language, it's like magic tricks. You miss one innuendo and you're out of your depth. What's more, I didn't know the exact terms to translate the technical jargon we were using that day, and to top it off, I could never get used to the Chinese accent. I feel like I hear "ting ting" at the end of every word. Not to mention the words that I don't even understand.'

'And so?'

'And so I was confused. I had expected to be working with an old Englishman, a local translator with whom Françoise had flirted on the phone, "You'll see, he's a real gentleman . . ."'

'My foot! There I was, under pressure, jet-lagged, anxious, tied up in knots, shaking like a leaf, and not an Englishman in sight. It was a huge deal, enough to keep the business going for two years. I don't know if you can understand . . .'

'What were you selling, exactly?'

'Storage tanks.'

'Storage tanks?'

'Yes, but wait. These weren't just ordinary storage tanks, they were – '

'No, no, I don't care! Keep going!'

'So, as I said, I was at the end of my rope. I had worked on this project for months, and I had a huge amount of money tied up in it. I had put the company in debt, and I had even invested my personal savings. With this deal, I could slow the closing of a factory near Nancy. Eighteen employees. I had Suzanne's brothers on my back; I knew they wanted to get even, and they were not going to cut me any slack, those useless – What's more, I had a ferocious case of diarrhoea. I'm sorry to be so prosaic, but . . . Anyway, I walked into that office as if I were going into battle, and when I learned that I was putting my life in the hands of . . . of . . . this creature, I nearly passed out.'

'But why?'

'The oil business is a very macho world, you see. It has changed somewhat now, but at the time, you didn't see many women.'

'And you too . . .'

'What about me?'

'You're a little macho yourself.'

He didn't say no.

'Hold on – Put yourself in my place for a moment. I was expecting to be greeted by an old phlegmatic Englishman, someone with a moustache and a rumpled suit who was well versed in the colonial ways of doing things, and there I was shaking the hand of a young woman and casting sidelong glances at her décolleté . . . No, believe me, it was too much. I didn't need that . . . I felt the ground give way under my feet. She explained that Mr. Magoo was ill, that they had sent for her yesterday evening, and then she shook my hand very hard to give me strength. Anyway, that's what she told me afterwards: that she had shaken me until my teeth rattled because she thought I looked rather pale.'

'His name was really Mr. Magoo?'

'No. I'm just making that up.'

'What happened next?'

'I whispered in her ear: "But I hope you're aware . . . I mean, of the technical data . . . It's pretty specific . . . I don't know if they alerted you . . ." And then she gave me this marvellous smile. The type of smile that more or less says, "Shhh . . . Don't try to confuse me, my dear man."

'I was devastated.

'I leaned into her lovely little neck. She smelled good. She smelled wonderfully good . . . Everything

281

was mixed up in my head. It was a catastrophe. She sat across from me, just to the right of a vigorous Chinese man who had me by the balls, if you'll pardon the expression. She rested her chin on her crossed fingers and threw me confident glances to give me strength. There was something cruel in those little half-smiles; I was completely in a daze and I was aware of it. I stopped breathing. I crossed my arms over my stomach to cover my paunch and prayed to heaven. I was at her mercy, and I was about to live the most wonderful hours of my life.'

'You tell a good story . . .'

'You're making fun of me.'

'No, no! Not at all!'

'Yes, you are. You're making fun of me. I'll stop.'

'No, please! Absolutely not. And then what happened?'

'You broke my momentum.'

'I won't say anything more.'

He was silent.

'And then?'

'And then what?'

'And then how did it go with Mr. Singh?'

'You're smiling. Why are you smiling? Tell me!'

'I'm smiling because it was incredible . . . Because she was incredible . . . Because the whole situation was completely incredible . . .'

'Stop smiling to yourself! Tell me, Pierre! Tell me!'

'Well . . . First she pulled a case from her bag, a small, plastic, imitation crocodile glasses case. She did it very self-importantly. Then she balanced a horrible pair of spectacles on her nose. You know, those severe little glasses with white metal frames. The kind that retired schoolteachers wear. And from that moment on, her face closed up. She ceased to look at me in the same way. She held my gaze and waited for me to recite my lesson.

'I talked, she translated. I was fascinated because she started her sentences before I finished mine. I don't know how she pulled it off; it was a tour de force. She listened and spoke nearly at the same time. It was simultaneous translation. It was fascinating . . . Really . . . At first, I spoke slowly, and then more and more quickly. I think that I was trying to rattle her a bit. She didn't bat an eye. On the contrary, she got a kick out of finishing my sentences before I did. She was already making me feel just how predictable I was . . .

'And then she got up to translate some charts on a board. I took advantage of the situation to look at her legs. She had a little old-world side to her, outmoded, completely anachronistic. She was wearing a plaid knee-length skirt, a dark green twinset, and – Now why are you laughing?'

'Because you used the word "twinset". It makes me laugh.'

'Really, I don't see what's so funny! What else am I supposed to say?'

'Nothing, nothing . . .'

'You're such a pain . . .'

'I'll be quiet, I'll be quiet.'

'Even her brassiere was old-fashioned. She had pushed-up breasts like the girls in my youth. They were nice, not too large, slightly spread, pointed . . . Pushed up. And I was fascinated by her stomach. A round little stomach, round like a bird's belly. An adorable little stomach that stretched the squares on her skirt and that I found . . . I could already feel it beneath my hands . . . I was trying to get a glimpse of her feet when I saw she was upset. She had stopped speaking. She was completely pink. Her forehead, her cheeks, her neck were pink. Pink as a little shrimp. She looked at me, alarmed.

"What's happening?" I asked her.

"You . . . Didn't you understand what he said?"

"Um . . . no. What did he say?"

"You didn't understand or you didn't hear?"

"I . . . I don't know . . . I didn't hear, I think . . ."

She stared at the ground. She was overcome. I imagined the worst, a disaster, a mistake, a huge blunder . . . while she straightened her hair, in my mind I was already closing down the business.

"What's happened? Is there a problem?"

Mr. Singh laughed, said something to her that I still couldn't understand. I was completely lost. I didn't understand a thing. I looked like a complete idiot!

"But what did he say? Tell me what he said!"
She stammered.

"It's hopeless, is that it?"

"No, no, I don't think so . . ."

"Then what is it?"

"Mr. Singh is wondering if it is a good idea to discuss such an important deal with you today . . ."

"But why? What is not going right?"

I turned to him to reassure him. I nodded idiotically, and tried the winning smile of a confident French businessman. I must have seemed ridiculous . . . And the big boss just kept on laughing . . . He was so pleased with himself that you couldn't see his eyes.

"Did I say something wrong?"

"No."

"Did you say something wrong?"

"Me? Of course not! All I'm doing is repeating your gobbledygook."

"Then what is it?"

I could feel sweat running down my sides.

She laughed and fanned herself. She seemed a bit nervous.

"Mr. Singh says that you are not concentrating."

"But I am, I am concentrating! I am concentrating very hard! I even said it in English. *I am very concentrated!*"

"*No, no,*" he answered in English, shaking his head.

"Mr. Singh says that you are not concentrating

because you are falling in love, and Mr. Singh does not want to do business with a Frenchman who is falling in love. He says that it is too dangerous."

It was my turn to go crimson.

"No, no . . . I said it again, in English. *I'm fine, I mean, I am calm . . . I . . . I . . .*" I was speaking a mixture of English and French.

And to her I said:

"Tell him that it is not true. That it's fine. That everything is fine. Tell him that . . . *I am okay. Yes, yes, I'm okay.*"

I fidgeted.

She smiled one of those little smiles from earlier.

"That it's not true?"

What kind of shit had I got myself into?

"No, I mean, yes, uh . . . no, I mean that's not the problem . . . I mean, that's not a problem . . . I . . . *There IS no problem, I am fine!*"

'I think they were all making fun of me. The big boss, his associates, and this young lady.

'She didn't try to make it easy on me:

"Is it true or not true?"

The bitch! Was this really the moment?

"It's not true," I lied.

"Oh, all right then! You had me worried . . ."

The bitch, I thought again to myself.

'She had me completely floored.'

'And then?'

286

'And then we got back to work. Very professionally. As though nothing had happened. I was drenched with sweat. I felt as if someone had electrocuted me and I had definitely lost my edge . . . I didn't look at her anymore. I didn't want to. I wished that she didn't exist. I couldn't turn in her direction. I wanted her to disappear down a hole and to disappear with her. And the more I ignored her, the more I fell in love with her. It was exactly like I told you a while ago, like a sickness. You know how it goes: you sneeze once, twice. You shiver, and boom. It's too late. What's done is done. It was the same thing: I was caught, I was done for. It was hopeless and when she repeated the words of old Mr. Singh, I plunged into my files headfirst. She must have had fun. This ordeal lasted nearly three hours . . . What is it? Are you cold?'

'A little, but I'm fine, I'm okay . . . Go on. What happened then?'

He leaned over to help me pull up the cover.

'After that, nothing. Afterwards . . . I told you, I had already experienced the best part . . . Afterwards I . . . It was . . . Afterwards it got sadder.'

'But not right away?'

'No, not right away. There were still some good times . . . But all the moments we shared after that meeting, it was as if I had stolen them . . .'

'Stolen them from whom?'

'From whom? From what? If only I knew . . .

'Afterwards, I gathered up my papers and put the cap back on my pen. I got up, I shook the hands of my tormentors and left the room. And in the lift, when the doors closed, I really felt as if I had fallen down a hole. I was exhausted, empty, totally wrung out and on the verge of tears. Nerves, I suppose . . . I felt so miserable, so alone . . . Alone, above all. I went back to my hotel room, ordered a whiskey and ran a bath. I didn't even know her name. I knew nothing about her. I made a list of what I did know: she spoke remarkably good English. She was intelligent . . . Very intelligent . . . Perhaps too intelligent? I was flabbergasted by her technical, scientific, and steel-making knowledge. She was a brunette. She was very pretty. She was . . . let's see . . . about five foot four. She made fun of me. She wasn't wearing a wedding ring and she gave the impression of having the cutest little stomach. She . . . what else? I began to lose hope as my bath cooled.

'That evening, I went to dinner with some of the men from Comex. I ate nothing. I agreed with every-thing, and answered yes or no without knowing what I was saying. She haunted me.

'She haunted me, do you understand?'

He knelt in front of the fire and slowly worked the bellows.

'When I returned to the hotel, the receptionist handed me a message with my key. In small hand-writing I read:

It wasn't true?

'She was sitting at the bar, watching me and smiling.

'I walked over, lightly hitting myself in the chest.

'My poor heart had stopped and I was trying to get it working again.

'I was so happy. I hadn't lost her. Not yet.

'So happy and also surprised because she had changed her outfit. Now she was wearing an old pair of blue jeans and a shapeless T-shirt.'

"You changed your clothes?"

"Um . . . yes."

"But why?"

"When you saw me earlier, I was in a sort of disguise. I dress that way when I work with old-school Chinese types. I figured out that the old-fashioned look pleased them, reassured them . . . I don't know . . . They feel more confident . . . I dress up like a maiden aunt and I become harmless."

"But you didn't look like a maiden aunt, I can assure you! You . . . You were just fine . . . You . . . I . . . I mean, it's a shame – "

"That I changed clothes?"

"Yes."

"So you like me harmless, too?"

She smiled. I melted.

"I don't think that you are any less dangerous in your little plaid skirt. I don't think so at all, not in the least little bit."

★

'We ordered Chinese beers. Her name was Mathilde, she was thirty years old, and although she had astounded me, she couldn't take all the credit: her father and her two brothers worked for Shell. She knew the jargon by heart. She had lived in every oil-producing country in the world, had gone to fifty schools, and knew how to swear in every language. She couldn't say exactly where she lived. She owned nothing, just memories. And friends. She loved her work, translating thoughts and juggling with words. She was in Hong Kong at the moment because all she had to do to find work was hold out her hand. She loved that city where the skyscrapers spring up overnight and where you can eat in some cheap joint just a few steps down the road. She loved the energy of the place. She had spent a few years in France when she was a child, and occasionally returned to see her cousins. One day she would buy a house there. It didn't really matter what kind of house or where, as long as there were cows and a fireplace. She laughed as she said that, because she was afraid of cows! She stole cigarettes from me and answered all my questions by first rolling her eyes. She asked me a few, but I ducked them. I wanted to listen to her, I wanted to hear the sound of her voice, that slight accent, her way of putting things that was hesitant and old-fashioned. I took it all in. I wanted to immerse myself in her, in her face. I already adored her neck, her hands, the shape of her nails, her slightly rounded forehead, her adorable little nose, her beauty marks, the dark circles under her eyes, those serious eyes . . . I was completely head over heels. You're smiling again.'

'I don't recognise you.'

'Are you still cold?'

'No, it's fine.'

'She fascinated me . . . I wanted the world to stop turning, for the night to never end. I didn't want to leave her. Not ever. I wanted to stay slumped in that armchair and listen to her recount her life until the end of time. I wanted the impossible. Without knowing it, I had set the tone of our relationship . . . time in suspension, unreal, impossible to hold on to, to retain. Impossible to savour, too. And then she got up. She had to be at work early in the morning. For Singh and Co. again. She really loved that old fox, but she had to get some sleep, because he was tough! I stood up at the same time. My heart failed me again. I was afraid of losing her. I mumbled something while she put on her jacket.

"Excuse me?"

"Imafrloosngou."

"What did you say?"

"I said I'm afraid of losing you."

'She smiled. She said nothing. She smiled and swung lightly back and forth, holding on to the collar of her jacket. I kissed her. Her mouth was closed. I kissed her smile. She shook her head and gently gave me a little push.

'I could have fallen over backwards.'

...

'That's all?'

'Yes.'

'You don't want to tell me the rest, is that it? It gets X-rated?'

'Not at all! Not at all, my dear . . . She left and I sat back down. I spent the rest of the night in a reverie, smoothing her little note on my thigh. Nothing very steamy, you see . . .'

'Oh! Well, anyway . . . it was your thigh . . .'

'My dear, how stupid you are.'

I giggled.

'But why did she come back, then?'

'That's exactly what I asked myself that night, and the next day, and the day after and all the other days until I saw her again . . .'

'When did you see her next?'

'Two months later. She landed in my office one evening in the middle of August. I wasn't expecting anyone. I had come back from holiday a little early to work while things were calm. The door opened and it was her. She had dropped by just like that. By chance. She had just been in Normandy, and was waiting for a friend to call to know when she would leave again.

She looked me up in the telephone directory and there she was.

'She brought back a pen I had left halfway around the world. She had forgotten to give it to me in the bar, but this time she remembered it at once and was digging around in her bag.

'She hadn't changed. I mean, I hadn't idealised her, and I asked her:

'But . . . you came just for that? Because of the pen?'

'Yes, of course. It's a beautiful pen. I thought you might be attached to it.'

'She held it out to me, smiling. It was a Bic. A red Bic biro.

'I didn't know what to do. I . . . She took me in her arms and I was overcome. The world was all mine.'

'We walked across Paris holding hands. Along the Seine, from the Trocadero all the way to the Ile de la Cité. It was a magnificent evening. It was hot, and the light was soft. The sun never seemed to set. We were like two tourists, carefree, filled with wonder, coats slung over our shoulders and fingers entwined. I played tour guide. I hadn't walked like that in years. I rediscovered my city. We ate at the Place Dauphine and spent the following days in her hotel room. I remember the first evening. Her salty taste. She must have bathed right before taking the train. I got up in the night because I was thirsty. I . . . It was marvellous.

'It was marvellous and completely false. Nothing

was real. This wasn't life. This wasn't Paris. It was the month of August. I wasn't a tourist. I wasn't single. I was lying. I was lying to myself, to her, to my family. She wasn't fooled, and when the party was over, when it was time for the telephone calls and the lies, she left.

'At the boarding gate, she told me:

"I'm going to try to live without you. I hope I'll find a way . . ."

'I didn't have the courage to kiss her.'

'That evening, I ate at the Drugstore. I was suffering. I was suffering as if part of me was missing, as though someone had cut off an arm or a leg. It was an incredible sensation. I didn't know what had happened to me. I remember that I drew two silhouettes on a paper napkin. The one on the left was her from the front, and the one on the right was her from the back. I tried to remember the exact location of her beauty marks, and when the waiter came over and saw all those little dots, he asked if I was an acupuncturist. I didn't know what had happened to me, but I knew it was something serious! For several days, I had been myself. Nothing more or less than myself. When I was with her, I had the impression that I was a good guy . . . It was as simple as that. I didn't know that I could be a good guy.

'I loved this woman. I loved this Mathilde. I loved the sound of her voice, her spirit, her laugh, her take on the world, that sort of fatalism you see in people who have been everywhere. I loved her laugh, her curiosity, her discretion, her spinal column, her slightly bulging hips, her silences, her tenderness, and . . . all the rest. Everything . . . Everything. I prayed that she wouldn't be able to live without me. I wasn't thinking about the consequences of our encounter. I had just discovered that life was much more joyful when you were happy. It took me forty-two years to find it out, and I was so dazzled that I forced myself not to ruin everything by fixing my gaze on the horizon. I was on cloud nine.'

He refilled our glasses.

'From that moment on, I became a workaholic. I spent most of my time in the office. I was the first to arrive and the last to leave. I worked on Saturdays, and couldn't wait for Sundays to be over. I invented all kinds of pretexts. I finally landed the contract with Taiwan and was able to manoeuvre more freely. I took advantage of the situation to pile on extra projects, more or less sensible. And all of it, all of those insane days and hours were for one reason: because I hoped that she would call.

'Somewhere on the planet there was a woman – perhaps around the corner, perhaps ten thousand kilometres away – and the only thing that mattered was that she would be able to reach me.

'I was confident and full of energy. I think I was fairly happy at that time in my life because even if I wasn't with her, I knew she existed. That was already incredible.

'A few days before Christmas, I heard from her. She was coming to France and asked if I would be free for lunch the following week. We decided to meet in the same little wine bar. However, it was no longer summer, and when she reached for my hand, I swiftly drew it back. "Do they know you here?" she asked, hiding a smile.

'I had hurt her. I was so unhappy. I gave her my hand back, but she didn't take it. The sky darkened, and we still hadn't found each other. I met her that same evening in another hotel room, and when I was finally able to run my fingers through her hair, I started to live again.

'I . . . I loved making love with her.'

'The following afternoon, we met in the same spot, and the day after that . . . Then it was the day before Christmas Eve, we were going to part. I wanted to ask her what her plans were, but I couldn't seem to open my mouth. I was afraid – there was something in my gut that kept me from smiling at her.

'She was sitting on the bed. I came close to her and laid my head on her thigh.

"What's going to become of us?" she asked.

I didn't say a word.

"Yesterday, when you left me here in this hotel room in the middle of the afternoon, I told myself that I would never go through this again. Never again, do you hear? Never . . . I got dressed, and I went out. I didn't know where to go. I don't want to do this again; I can't lie down with you in a hotel room and then have you walk out the door afterwards. It's too difficult."

She had a hard time getting her words out.

"I promised myself that I would never go through this again with a man who would make me suffer. I don't think I deserve it, do you understand? I don't deserve it. So that's why I'm asking you: What's going to become of us?"

I stayed silent.

"You have nothing to say? I thought so. What could you say, anyway? What could you possibly do? You have your wife and your kids. And me, what am I? I'm almost nothing in your life. I live so far away . . . so far away and so strangely . . . I don't know how to live like other people. No house, no furniture, no cat, no cookbooks, no plans. I thought I was the smart one, that I understood life better than other people. I was proud of myself for not falling into the trap. And then you came along, and I feel completely at sea.

"And now I'd like to slow down a bit because I found out that life is wonderful with you. I told you I was going to try to live without you . . . I tried and I tried, but I'm not that strong; I think about you all the time. So I'm asking you now and maybe for the last time: What do you plan to do with me?"

"Love you."

"What else?"

"I promise that I will never leave you behind in a hotel room ever again. I promise you."

And then I turned and put my head back between her thighs. She lifted me up by the hair.

"And what else?"

"I love you. I'm only happy when I'm with you. I love only you. I . . . I . . . Trust me . . ."

'She let go of my head and our conversation ended there. I took her tenderly, but she didn't let herself go, she just let it happen. It's not the same thing.'

'What happened after that?'

'After that we parted for the first time . . . I say "the first time" because we broke it off so many times . . . Then I called her . . . I begged her . . . I found an excuse to return to China. I saw her room, her landlady . . .

'I stayed for a week. While she was at work I played plumber, electrician, and mason. I worked like a fiend for Miss Li, who spent her time singing and playing with her birds. She showed me the port of Hong Kong and took me to visit an old English lady who thought I was Lord Mountbatten! I played the part, if you can imagine!'

*

298

'Can you understand what all this meant for me? For the little boy who had never dared to take the lift to the sixth floor? My entire life was spent between two arrondissements in Paris and a little country house. I never saw my parents happy, my only brother suffocated to death, and I married my first girlfriend, the sister of one of my friends, because I didn't know how to pull out in time . . .

'That was it. That was my life . . .

'Can you understand? I felt as though I had been born a second time, as though it had all started again, in her arms, on that dubious harbour, in that damp little room of Miss Li . . .'

He stopped talking.

'Was that Christine?'

'No, it was before Christine . . . That one was a miscarriage.'

'I didn't know.'

'No one knows. What is there to know? I got married to a young girl whom I loved, but in the way that you love a young girl. A pure, romantic love; the first rush of feelings . . . The wedding was a pretty sad affair. It felt like my first communion all over again.

'Suzanne also hadn't imagined that things would happen so quickly. She lost her youth and her illusions in one fell swoop. We both lost everything, while her father got the perfect son-in-law. I had just graduated from the top engineering school and he couldn't

299

imagine anything better, since his sons were studying
. . . *literature*. He could barely pronounce the word.

'Suzanne and I were not madly in love, but we
were kind to each other. At that time, the one made
up for the other.

'I'm telling you all this, but I really don't know if
you can fully understand. Things have changed so
much . . . It was forty years ago, but it seems like two
centuries. It was a time when girls got married when
they missed their periods. This must seem prehistoric
to you . . .'

He rubbed his face.

'So, where was I? Oh yes . . . I was saying that I found
myself halfway around the world with a woman who
earned her living jumping from one continent to
another and who seemed to love me for who I was,
for what was inside. A woman who loved me, I'm
tempted to say . . . tenderly. All of this was very, very
new. Very exotic. A marvellous woman who held her
breath while watching me eat cobra soup with
chrysanthemum flowers.'

'Was it good?'

'A bit gelatinous for my taste . . .'

He smiled.

'And when I got back on the plane, for the first time
in my life I was not afraid. I said to myself: let it

explode, let it fall out of the sky and crash, it doesn't matter.'

'Why did you tell yourself that?'

'Why?'

'Yes, why? I would have said just the opposite . . . I'd tell myself: "Now I know why I'm afraid, and this goddamn plane better not fall!"'

'Yes, you're right. That would have been smarter . . . But there you are, and this is the heart of the problem: I didn't say that. I was probably even hoping that it would crash . . . My life would have been so much simpler . . .'

'You had just met the woman of your life and you thought about dying?'

'I didn't say I wanted to die!'

'I didn't say that either. I said you *thought about* dying . . .'

'I probably think about dying every day, don't you?'

'No.'

. . .

'Do you think your life is worth something?'

'Uh . . . Yes . . . A little, anyway . . . And then there are the children . . .'

'That's a good reason.'

He had settled back down in the armchair and his face was once again hidden.

'Yes. I agree with you, it was absurd. But I had just

been so happy, so happy . . . I was intrigued and also a bit terrified. Was it normal to be so happy? Was it right? What price was I going to have to pay for all that?

'Because . . . Was it because of my upbringing or what the priests told me? Was it in my character? I'm not always good at seeing things clearly, but one thing is sure: I've always compared myself to a workhorse. Bit, reins, blinkers, plough, yoke, cart, and furrow . . . the whole thing. Since I was a boy, I have walked in the street with my head down, staring at the ground as though it had a crust – hard earth to be broken up.

'Marriage, family, work, the maze of social life, everything. I have always worked with lowered head and clamped jaw. Dreading everything. Mistrustful. I'm very good at squash, or I used to be, and it's not by chance – I like the feeling of being shut up in a cramped room, whacking a ball as hard as possible so that it comes back at me like a cannonball. I really liked that.

' "You like squash and I like swingball, and that explains everything . . . ," Mathilde said one evening as she was massaging my aching shoulder. She was quiet for a moment, then added, "You should think about what I just said, it's not that dumb. People who are rigid inside are always bumping into life and hurting themselves in the process, but people who are soft – no, not soft, *supple* is the word – yes, that's it, supple on the inside, well, when they take a hit they suffer less . . . I think that you should take up swingball, it's much more fun. You hit the ball and you don't know where it's going to come back, but you know it will come back because of the string, and it makes for a wonderful moment of suspense. But you see, for example, I sometimes think . . . that I'm your swingball . . ."

'I didn't react, and she kept rubbing me in silence.'

'You never thought about starting your life over again with her?'

'Of course I did. A thousand times.

'A thousand times I wanted to and a thousand times I gave it up . . . I went right to the edge of the abyss, I leaned over, and then I fled. I felt accountable to Suzanne, to the children.

'Accountable for what? There's another difficult question . . . I was committed. I had signed, I had promised, I had to fulfil my obligations. Adrien was sixteen, and nothing was going right. He changed schools all the time, scribbled *No Future* in English in the lift, and the only thing on his mind was to go to London and come back with a pet rat. Suzanne was distraught. Here was something stronger than her. Who had changed her little boy? For the first time, I watched her waver; she spent whole evenings without saying a word. I couldn't see myself making the situation worse. I told myself . . . I told myself that . . .'

'What did you tell yourself?'

'Wait a moment, it's so grotesque . . . I have to find the words I used at the time . . . I must have told myself something like: "I am an example for my children. Here they are, on the threshold of their adult lives, about to scale the wall, a time when they are thinking about making important decisions. What a horrendous example for them if I were to leave their mother now . . ." Rather lofty sentiments, don't you think? "How will they face things afterwards? What sort of chaos would I be causing? What irreparable damage? I am not a perfect father, far from it, but I am still the most obvious role model for them, and the nearest, and therefore . . . hmmm . . . I must keep myself in check."'

He grimaced.

'Wasn't that good? You have to admit it was priceless, no?'

I said nothing.

'I was especially thinking of Adrien . . . of being a model of commitment for my son, Adrien . . . You have the right to snigger with me at that one, you know. Don't hold back. It's not often you get the chance to hear a good joke.'

I shook my head.

'And yet . . . Oh, what's the use? That was all so long ago . . . so very long ago . . .'

'And yet what?'

'Well . . . There was one moment when I came very close to the abyss . . . Really very near . . . I started looking around to buy a studio. I thought about taking Christine away for a weekend. I thought about what I would say; I rehearsed certain scenes in my car. I even made an appointment with my accountant, and then one morning – you see what a tease life can be – Françoise came into my office in tears . . .'

'Françoise? Your secretary?'

'Yes.

'Her husband had just left her . . . I didn't recognise her anymore. She was always so exuberant, so imperious, this little woman who was in control of both herself and the universe – I watched her waste away day after day. In tears, losing weight, stumbling about, suffering. She suffered terribly. She took pills, lost more weight, and took the first sick leave of her career. She cried. She even cried in front of me. And what did I do, upright man that I was? I screwed up my courage and . . . went along with the crowd. *What a bastard,* I agreed, what a bastard. How could he do that to his wife? How could he be so selfish, to just close the door and wash his hands of the whole thing? Step out of his life like he was going for a walk? Why . . . why, that was too easy! Too easy!

'No, really, what a bastard. What a bastard that man was! No, sir, I'm not like you! I'm not leaving my wife, sir. I'm not leaving my wife, and I despise you . . . Yes, I despise you from the depths of my soul, sir!

'That's what I thought. I was only too happy to get out of it so easily. Only too happy to assuage my conscience and stroke my beard. Oh yes, I supported my Françoise, I spoiled her. Oh yes, I often agreed. Oh no, I kept repeating to her, what bad luck you've had. What bad luck . . .

'In fact, I secretly had to thank him, this Mr. Jarmet whom I didn't know from Adam. I was secretly grateful to him. He handed me the solution on a silver platter. Thanks to him, thanks to his disgraceful behaviour, I could return to my comfortable little situation with my head held high. Work, Family, and Country, that was me. Head high and walking tall! I prided myself on it, as you can imagine, you know me . . . I had arrived at the agreeable conclusion that . . . I wasn't like other people. I was a notch above them. Not much, but above. I wouldn't leave my wife, no, not me . . .'

'Was that when you broke it off with Mathilde?'

'What on earth for? No, not in the least. I continued to see her, but I shelved my escape plans and stopped wasting time looking at horrible little studios. Because you see, as I have just brilliantly demonstrated, that's not the stuff I was made of: I wasn't about to stir up a hornet's nest. That was for irresponsible types, all that. For a husband who cheats with his secretary.'

His voice was filled with sarcasm, and he was trembling with rage.

'No, I didn't break it off with her, I continued to tenderly screw her, promising things like *always* and *later*.'

'Really?'

'Yes.'

'You mean like in all those trashy stories?'

'Yes.'

'You asked her to be patient, and promised her all kinds of things?'

'Yes.'

'How did she stand it?'

'I don't know, really. I don't know . . .'

'Maybe because she loved you?'

'Perhaps.'

He drained his glass.

'Perhaps, yes . . . Maybe she did . . .'

'And you didn't leave because of Françoise?'

'Exactly. Because of Jean-Paul Jarmet, to be precise. Well, that's what I say now, but if it hadn't been him, I would have found some other excuse. Two-faced people are good at finding excuses. Very good.'

'It's incredible . . .'

'What is?'

'This story . . . To see what it hinges on. It's incredible.'

'No, my dear Chloé, it's not incredible . . . it's not incredible at all. It's life. It's what life is like for nearly everyone. We hedge, we make arrangements, we keep our cowardice close to us, like a pet. *C'est la vie.* There are those who are courageous and those who settle, and it's so much less tiring to settle . . . Pass me that bottle.'

'Are you going to get drunk?'

'No, I'm not going to get drunk. I've never been able to. The more I drink, the more lucid I become . . .'

'How awful!'

'As you say, how awful . . . Can I offer you some?'

'No, thanks.'

'Would you like that herbal tea now?'

'No, no. I'm . . . I don't know what I am . . . dumbstruck, maybe.'

'Dumbstruck by what?'

'By you, of course! I've never heard you speak more than two sentences at once, you never raise your voice, you never make a scene. Not once, since the first time I saw you play the Grand Inquisitor. I never caught you in the act of being tender or sensitive, and now, all of a sudden, you dump all of this on me without even yelling *Timber!* . . .'

'Do you find it shocking?'

'No, not at all! That's not it! On the contrary . . . On the contrary . . . But . . . But how have you managed to play that role all this time?'

'What role?'

'That one . . . the role of the old bastard.'

'But Chloé, I am an old bastard! I'm an old bastard

– this is what I've been trying to explain to you this whole time!'

'But no! If you're aware of it, it's because you aren't one after all. The real ones aren't aware of anything!'

'Psshhh, don't believe that one . . . It's just another one of my tricks to get out of this honourably. I'm very talented that way . . .'

He smiled at me.

'It's incredible, just incredible.'

'What?'

'All of this. Everything you've told me.'

'No, it's not incredible. On the contrary, it's all quite banal.

'Very, very banal . . . I'm telling you because it's you, because it's here, in this room, in this house, because it's night, and because Adrien has made you suffer. Because his choice makes me feel both hopeless and reassured. Because I don't like to see you unhappy. I've caused too much suffering myself . . . And because I would rather see you suffer a lot today rather than suffer a little bit for the rest of your life.

'I see people suffering a little, only a little, not much at all, just enough to ruin their lives completely . . . Yes, at my age, I see that a great deal . . . People who are still together because they're crushed under the weight of that miserable little thing – their ordinary little life. All those compromises, all of those contradictions . . . All of that to end up . . .

'Bravo! Hurray! We've managed to bury it all: our

friends, our dreams, our loves, and now, now it's our turn! Bravo, my friends, bravo!'

He applauded.

'Retirees, they call them. Retired from everything. How I hate them. I hate them, do you hear me? I hate them because I see myself in them. There they are, wallowing in self-satisfaction. *We made it, we made it!* they seem to say, without ever really having been there for each other. But my God, at what price? What price?! Regrets, remorse, cracks and compromises that don't heal over, that never heal. Never! Not even in the Hesperides. Not even posing for the photo with the great-grandchildren. Not even when you both answer the game-show question at the exact same moment.'

He said he'd never been drunk before, but . . .

He stopped talking and gesticulating. We sat like that for a long moment. In silence. Except for the muted fireworks in the chimney.

. . .

'I didn't finish telling you about Françoise . . .'

He had calmed down, and I had to strain my ears to hear him.

'A few years ago, it was in '94, I think, she became seriously ill . . . Very seriously . . . A goddamn cancer that was eating away at her abdomen. They started by removing one ovary, then the other, then her uterus . . . I don't really know much about it, really; she never confided in me, as you can imagine, but it turned out to be much more serious than they had imagined. Françoise was calculating the time she had left. She wanted to make it to Christmas. Easter was too much to hope for.

'One day, I called her at the hospital and offered to lay her off with a huge severance package so that she could travel around the world when she got out, so she could go shopping at the top designers, pick out the prettiest dresses, and then sashay along the deck of a huge ocean liner sipping Pimm's. Françoise adored Pimm's . . .

"Save your money, I'll drink it with the others at your retirement party!"

'We chatted. We were good actors – we had a lump in our throats but our exchange was upbeat. The latest prognosis was a disaster. I heard it from her daughter. Christmas looked doubtful.

' "Don't believe everything you hear, you're still not going to get your chance to replace me with some young thing," she chided me in a whisper before hanging up. I pretended to grumble and found myself in tears in the middle of the afternoon. I found out how much I cared for her as well. How much I needed her. Seventeen years we had worked together. Always, every day. Seventeen years she put up with me, helped me . . . She knew about Mathilde and never said a word. Not to me, nor to anyone else. She smiled at me when I was unhappy, and shrugged her shoulders when I was disagreeable. She was barely twenty years old when she came to work for me. She didn't know how to do anything. She was a graduate of a hotel school, and quit a job because a cook had pinched her bottom. She told me this during our first meeting. She didn't want anyone pinching her bottom, and she didn't want to go back to live with her parents in the Creuse. She would only go back when she had her own car, so she could be sure that she could leave! I hired her because of that sentence.

'She, too, was my princess.'

'I called from time to time to complain about her substitute.

'And then, a long time afterwards, I went to see her, when she finally let me. It was in the spring. She had changed hospitals. The treatment was less aggressive and her progress had encouraged her doctors, who stopped by to congratulate her on being good-natured and a real fighter. On the phone, she told me she had started to give advice about everything and to everyone. She had ideas for changing the décor, and she had started a quilting circle. She criticised their foul-ups and poor organisation. She asked to meet with someone from social services to clear up a few simple problems. I teased her, and she defended herself: "But it's common sense! Just good common sense, you see!" She was back in fighting form, and I drove to the clinic with a happy heart.

'And yet, seeing her again was a shock. She was no longer my princess; in her place was a jaundiced little bird. Her neck, her cheeks, her hands, her arms — everything had disappeared. Her skin was yellowish and somewhat coarse, and her eyes had doubled in size. What shocked me the most was her wig. She had probably put it on in a hurry, and the parting wasn't quite in the middle. I tried to fill her in on the news from the office, about Caroline's baby and the contracts under way, but I was obsessed by that wig. I was afraid it was going to slip.

'At that moment, a man knocked on the door. "Oops!" he said when he saw me before turning around. Françoise called him back. "Pierre, this is Simon, my friend. I don't believe you two have ever met . . ." I got up. No, we had never met. I didn't even know he existed. We were so discreet, Françoise and I . . . He shook my hand very firmly and there was all the kindness in the world in his eyes. Two little grey eyes, intelligent, alive, and tender. While I sat back down, he went over to Françoise to kiss her, and then do you know what he did?'

'No.'

'He took that little broken doll's face in his hands as if he wanted to kiss her enthusiastically, and he took advantage of that to straighten her wig. She cursed and told him to be careful, I was her boss after all, and he laughed before he went out, on the pretext of wanting to get the paper.

'And when he had closed the door, Françoise slowly turned towards me. Her eyes were full of tears. She murmured, "Without him, I would have come to the end by now, you know . . . If I'm putting up a fight, it's because there is so much I want to do with him. So many things . . ."'

'Her smile was frightful. Her jaw was huge, almost indecent. I had the feeling that her teeth were going to come out. That the skin on her cheeks would split. I was overcome with nausea. And the smell . . . That smell of drugs and death and Guerlain perfume all mixed together. I could barely stand it, and I had to fight to keep from putting my hand over my mouth. I thought I was going to lose it. My vision blurred. It was hardly noticeable, you know, I pretended to pinch my nose and rub my eyes as if I had a speck of dust in them. When I looked up at her again, forcing myself to smile, she asked, "Are you all right?" "Yes, yes, I'm fine," I answered. I could feel my mouth curving into a sad child's frown. "I'm fine, it's fine . . . It's just that . . . I don't think you look all that well, Françoise . . ." She closed her eyes and laid her head on her pillow. "Don't you worry about me. I'm going to beat this . . . He needs me too much, that one does . . ."'

*

'I left completely broken up. I held myself up on the walls. I took forever to remember where I had parked my car, and I got lost in the damn parking garage. What was happening to me? My God, what was happening to me? Was it seeing her like that? Was it the smell of disinfected death, or just the place itself? That pall of misery, of suffering. And my little Françoise with her ravaged arms, my angel lost in the midst of all those zombies. Lost in her minuscule bed. What had they done to my princess? Why had they mistreated her like that?

'It took forever to find my car and forever to get it started, then it took me several minutes to put it in first gear. And you know what? Do you know why I was reeling like that? It wasn't because of her, or her catheters, or her suffering. Of course it wasn't. It was . . .'

He lifted his head.

'It was despair. Yes, the boomerang had come back to hit me in the face . . .'

Silence.

• • •

I finally said:

'Pierre?'

'Yes?'

'You're going to think I'm kidding, but I think I'll have herbal tea now . . .'

315

He got up, complaining in order to hide his gratitude.

'Oh, you women never know what you want; you can be so annoying . . .'

I followed him into the kitchen and sat down on the other side of the table, while he put a pan of water on the burner. The light from the suspension lamp was harsh. I pulled it down as far as it would go while he rummaged through all the cupboards.

'Can I ask you a question?'

'If you can tell me where to find what I'm looking for.'

'Right there, in front of you, in that red box.'

'That one? We never used to put it there, it seems to me that − Oh sorry, I'm listening.'

'How many years were you together?'

'With Mathilde?'

'Yes.'

'Between Hong Kong and our final discussion, five years and seven months.'

'And did you spend a lot of time together?'

'No, I already told you. A few hours, a few days . . .'

'And was that enough?'

He said nothing.

'Was it enough for you?'

'No, of course not. Well, yes really, since I never did anything to change the situation. It's what I told myself afterward. Maybe it suited me. "Suited" − what an ugly word that is. Perhaps it suited me to have a reassuring wife on one side and a thrill on the other.

Dinner on the table every night and the feeling that I could sneak off from time to time . . . A full stomach and all the comforts of home. It was practical, and comfortable.'

'You called her when you needed her?'

'Yes, that was more or less the case . . .'

He set a mug down in front of me.

'Well, no, actually . . . It didn't happen exactly like that . . . One day, right at the beginning, she wrote me a letter. The only one she ever sent, by the way. It read:

'I've thought about it, I don't have any illusions, I love you but I don't trust you. Because what we are living is not real, it's a game. And because it's a game, we have to have rules. I don't want to see you in Paris. Not in Paris or in any other place that makes you afraid. When I'm with you, I want to hold your hand in the street and kiss you in restaurants, otherwise I'm not interested. I'm too old to play cat and mouse. Therefore, we will see each other as far away as possible, in other countries. When you know where you will be, you will write to me at this address, it's my sister's in London, she'll know where to forward it. Don't take the trouble to write a love letter, just the details. Tell me which hotel you're in and when and where. If I can join you, I'll come, otherwise too bad. Don't try to call me, or to find out where I am or how I'm living, this is no longer the issue. I've thought it over, I think it's the best solution: to do the same as you, live my own life, and be fond of you from a distance. I don't want to wait for your phone calls, I don't want to keep myself from falling in love, I want to be able to sleep with whom I want, when I want, and with no scruples. Because you're right, a life without scruples is more . . . *convenient*. That's not the way I see things, but why not? I'll give it a try. What do I have to lose, after all? A cowardly man? And what do I stand to gain? The pleasure of sleeping in your arms sometimes . . . I've thought about it, I want to give it a try. Take it or leave it . . .'

'What is it?'

'Nothing. It's amusing to see that you had found an opponent equal to you.'

'No, unfortunately I hadn't. She went through the motions and acted like a femme fatale, but she was really soft-hearted. I didn't know it when I accepted her proposal, I only found out much later. Five years and seven months later . . .

'Actually, that's a lie. I read between the lines, I guessed what those sorts of phrases must have cost her. But I wasn't going to dwell on it, because these rules suited me fine. They suited me down to the ground. All I had to do was step up the import-export department and get used to take-offs, and that was that. A letter like that is a godsend for men who want to cheat on their wives without complications. Of course, I was bothered by all that talk about sleeping around and falling in love, but we weren't at that point yet . . .'

He sat down at the end of the table, at his usual place.

'Pretty smart of me, eh? Oh, I was a smart one then . . . Especially because the whole thing helped me make a lot of money . . . I had always neglected the international side of the business a bit . . .'

'Why all the cynicism?'

'You gave a very good answer to that question yourself a little while ago . . .'

I leaned down to get the tea strainer.

'In addition, it was very romantic . . . I would get off the plane, my heart pounding, I checked into the hotel hoping that my key wouldn't be on its hook, I put my bags down in strange rooms, rummaging around to see if she had already been there, I went off to work, I came back in the evening praying to God she would be in my bed. Sometimes she was, sometimes not. She would join me in the middle of the night and we would lose ourselves in each other without exchanging a single word. We laughed under the covers, amazed to find each other there. At last. So far away, and so close. Sometimes, she would only arrive the next day, and I spent the night sitting at the bar, and listening for noises in the corridor. Sometimes she took another room, ordering me to come and join her in the early morning hours. Sometimes she didn't show and I hated her. I would return to Paris in a very bad mood. At first, I really had work to do; later, I had less and less . . . I made up any excuse to be able to leave. Sometimes I saw something of the country, and sometimes I saw nothing but my hotel room. Sometimes we never even left the airport. It was ridiculous. There was no logic to it. Sometimes we would talk nonstop, and other times we had nothing to say to each other. True to her word, Mathilde never talked about her love life, or only during pillow talk. She talked about men and situations that drove me wild, but that was only between the sheets . . . I was completely at the mercy of that woman, of the mischievous little way she had of pretending to say the wrong name in the dark. I acted annoyed, but I was devastated. I took her even more forcefully, when all I wanted to do was hold her tightly in my arms.

'When one of us joked, the other one suffered. It was completely absurd. I dreamed of catching hold of her and shaking her until all her venom was gone. Until she told me she loved me. Until she told me she loved me, damn it all. But I couldn't, it was me that was the bastard. All of this was my fault . . .'

He got up to find his glass.

'What was I thinking? That it was going to go on like that for years? For years on end? No, I didn't believe that. We would say good-bye to each other furtively, sadly, awkwardly, without ever talking about the next time. No, it was untenable . . . And the more I hesitated, the more I loved her, and the more I loved her, the less I believed it. I felt overwhelmed, powerless, caught in my own web. Immobile and resigned.'

'Resigned to what?'

'To losing her one day . . .'

'I don't understand.'

'Oh yes, you do. You understand what I'm saying . . . What could I have possibly done? Answer me that.'

'I can't.'

'No, of course you can't answer . . . You're the last person in the world who could answer that question.'

'What exactly did you promise her?'

'I don't remember now . . . not much, I imagine, or else the unimaginable. No, not very much . . . I had the decency to shut my eyes when she asked me questions, and to kiss her when she waited for me to answer. I was almost fifty and I thought I was old. I thought this was the end of the road, a bright, happy ending . . . I said to myself: "Don't rush into things, she's so young, she'll be the first to leave." And every time I saw her again, I was amazed but also surprised. What? She's still here? But why? I had a hard time seeing what she liked in me, and I told myself, "Why get into a mess, since she's going to leave me?" It was inevitable, it was sure to happen. There was no reason for her to still be there the next time, no reason at all . . . In the end, I was practically hoping that she wouldn't be there. Up to then, life had been so kind as to decide everything for me, why should that change now? Why? I had proved that I didn't have the ability to take things in hand . . . Business, yes, that was a game and I was the best, but on the home front? I preferred to suffer; I wanted to console myself by thinking that I was the one who was suffering. I wanted to dream or regret. It's so much simpler that way . . .

'My great-aunt on my father's side was Russian, and she used to tell me:

"You, you're like my father, you have nostalgia for the mountains."

"Which mountains, Mouschka?" I would ask.

"Why, the ones you've never seen, of course!"

'She told you that?'

'Yes. She said it each time I looked out the window . . .'

'And what were you looking at?'

'The bus depot!'

He laughed.

'Another character you would have liked . . . Some Friday I'll tell you about her.'

'We'll go to Chez Dominique, then . . .'

'As I told you, wherever and whenever you want to go.'

He filled my mug with tea.

'But what was she doing all that time?'

'I don't know . . . She was working. She had found a job at UNESCO, but had left it shortly after. She didn't like translating their smooth talk. She couldn't stand being cooped up day after day, mind-lessly repeating politicians' rhetoric. She preferred the business world, where the adrenaline was of a higher calibre. She travelled around, went to visit her brothers, sisters, and friends who were scattered all over the globe. She lived in Norway for a time, but she didn't like it there either, with all those blue-eyed ayatollahs, and where she was always cold . . . And when she had enough of jet lag, she stayed in London translating technical manuals. She loved her nephews.'

'But aside from work?'

'Ah, that . . . that is shrouded in mystery. God knows I tried to drag it out of her . . . She closed up, hesitated, wriggled out of my questions. "At least leave me that," she said. "Let me keep my dignity. The dignity of those who are discreet. Is that too much to ask?" Or she would give me a taste of my own medicine and torture me, laughing all the while. "In fact, didn't I tell you I got married last month? How stupid of me, I wanted to show you the pictures but I forgot them. His name is Billy; he's not very smart but he takes good care of me . . .'"

'Did that make you laugh?'

'No, not really.'

'You loved her?'

'Yes.'

'Loved her how?'

'I loved her.'

'And what do you remember from those years?'

'A life like a dotted line . . . Nothing, then something. Then nothing again. And then something. Then nothing again . . . It went by very quickly . . . When I think about it, it seems like the whole thing only lasted a season . . . Not even a season, the length of a single breath. A sort of mirage . . . We had no daily life together. That was what Mathilde suffered from the most, I think . . . I suspected it, mind you, but the proof came one evening after a long day of work.

'When I came in, she was sitting at a small desk, writing something on the hotel stationery. She had already filled a dozen pages with her small, cramped handwriting.

'Who are you writing to like that?' I asked her, bending over her neck.

'To you.'

'Me?'

She's leaving me, I thought, and at once I began to feel ill.

'What is it? You're completely pale. Are you all right?'

'Why are you writing to me?'

'Oh, I'm not really writing you a letter, I'm writing down all the things I want to do with you . . .'

There were pages everywhere. Around her, at her feet, on the bed. I picked one up at random:

. . . go for a picnic, have a nap on the bank of a river, eat peaches, shrimps, croissants, sticky rice, swim, dance, buy myself shoes, lingerie, perfume, read the paper, window-shop, take the Métro, watch time pass, push you over when you're taking up all the room, hang out the laundry, go to the opera, to Bayreuth, to Vienna, to the races, to the supermarket, have a barbecue, complain because you forgot the charcoal, brush my teeth at the same time as you, buy you underwear, cut the grass, read the paper over your shoulder, keep you from eating too many peanuts, visit the vineyards in the Loire, and those in Hunter Valley, act like an idiot, talk my head off, introduce you to Martha and Tino, pick blackberries, cook, go back to Vietnam, wear a sari, garden, wake you up because you're snoring again, go to the zoo, to the flea market, to Paris, to London, to Melrose, to Piccadilly, sing you songs, stop smoking, ask you to trim my nails, buy dishes, foolish things, things that have no purpose, eat ice cream, people-watch, beat you at chess, listen to jazz, reggae, dance the mambo and the cha-cha, get bored, throw tantrums, pout, laugh, wrap you around my little finger, look for a house among the cows, fill up huge shopping trolleys, repaint a ceiling, sew curtains, spend hours around a table talking with interesting people, grab you by the goatee, cut your hair, pull up weeds, wash the car, see the sea, watch old B-movies, call you up again, say dirty words to you, learn to knit, knit you a scarf, unravel that horrible scarf, collect cats, dogs, parrots, elephants, rent bicycles, not use them, stay in a hammock, reread my grandmother's *Winnie Winkle* adventures, look at Winnie's dresses again, drink margaritas in the shade, cheat, learn to use an iron, throw the iron out of the window, sing in the rain, run away from tourists, get drunk, tell you everything, remember that some things are better left unsaid, listen to you, give you my hand, go and find the iron, listen to the words of songs, set the alarm, forget our suitcases, stop rushing off everywhere, put out the trash, ask you if you still love me, chat with the neighbour, tell you about my childhood in Bahrain, my nanny's rings, the smell of henna and balls of amber, make toast for eggs, labels for jam jars . . .

It went on like that for pages. Page after page . . . I'm just telling you the ones that come into my head, the ones I remember. It was incredible.

"How long have you been writing that?"

"Since you left."

"But why?"

"Because I'm bored," she answered cheerfully. "I'm dying of boredom, if you can believe it!"

'I picked up the whole stack and sat down on the edge of the bed to see better. I was smiling but, to tell you the truth, I was paralysed by so much desire, so much energy. But I smiled anyway. She had a way of putting things that was so amusing, so witty, and she was watching my reactions. On one page, between "start from scratch" and "paste pictures in a photo album" she had written "a baby". Just like that, with no commentary. I continued to examine this huge list without batting an eyelid while she bit her cheeks.

"Well?" She wasn't breathing anymore. "What do you think?"

"Who are Martha and Tino?" I asked her.

'From the shape of her mouth, the way her shoulders slumped, how her hand dropped, I knew that I was going to lose her. Just by asking that stupid question, I had put my head on the block. She went into the bathroom and said, "Some nice people," before shutting the door. And instead of going to her, instead of throwing myself at her feet saying yes, anything she wanted because yes, I was put on this earth to make her happy, I went out on the balcony to smoke a cigarette.'

'And then?'

'And then nothing. The cigarette tasted terrible. We went down to dinner. Mathilde was beautiful. More beautiful than ever, it seemed to me. Lively, vivacious. Everyone looked at her. The women turned their heads and the men smiled at me. She was . . . how shall I say it . . . she was radiant . . . Her skin, her face, her smile, her hair, her gestures, everything in her captured the light and gracefully reflected it back. It was a mixture of vitality and tenderness that never ceased to amaze me. "You're beautiful," I told her. She shrugged. "In your eyes." "Yes," I agreed, "in my eyes . . ."

'When I think about her today, after all these years, that's the first image that comes to mind – her long neck, her dark eyes, and her little brown dress in that Austrian dining room, shrugging her shoulders.'

'After all, it was intentional, all of that beauty and grace. She knew very well what she was doing that evening: she was making herself unforgettable. Perhaps I'm mistaken, but I don't think so . . . It was her swan song, her farewell, her white handkerchief waving at the window. She was so perceptive, she must have known it . . . Even her skin was softer. Was she aware of it? Was she being generous or simply cruel? Both, I think . . . It was both . . .

'And that night, after the caresses and the sighing, she said:

"Can I ask you a question?"

"Yes."

"Will you give me an answer?"

"Yes."

I opened my eyes.

"Don't you think that we go well together?"

I was disappointed; I was expecting a question a bit more . . . um . . . provocative.

"Yes."

"Do you think so, too?"

"Yes."

"I think we go well together . . . I like being with you because I'm never bored. Even when we're not talking, even when we're not touching, even when we're not in the same room, I'm not bored. I'm never bored. I think it's because I have confidence in you, in your thoughts. Do you understand? I love everything I see in you, and everything I don't see. I know your faults, but as it turns out, I feel as though your faults go well with my qualities. We're not afraid of the same things. Even our inner demons go well together! You, you're worth more than you show, and I'm just the opposite. I need your gaze in order to have a bit more . . . a bit more substance? What is the word? Her French failed her. Complexity? When you want to say that someone is interesting inside?"

"Depth?"

"That's it! I'm like a kite; unless someone holds me by the string, I fly away . . . And you, it's funny . . . I often say to myself that you are strong enough to hold me and smart enough to let me go . . ."

"Why are you telling me all this?"

"Because I want you to know."

"Why now?"

"I don't know . . . Perhaps it's because it's incredible to meet someone and say: with this person, I'm happy."

"But why are you saying this to me now?"

"Because sometimes I have the feeling that you don't understand how lucky we are . . ."

"Mathilde?"

"Yes?"

"Are you going to leave me?"

"No."

"You're not happy?"

"Not very."

And then we stopped talking.

'The next day we went tramping around the mountains, and the day after, we each went our separate ways.'

•••

My tea was getting cold.

'Was that the end?'

'Nearly.'

★

'A few weeks later, she came to Paris and asked if I could spare her a few moments. I was both happy and annoyed. We walked for a long time, barely speaking, and then I took her to lunch on the Champs-Elysées.

'While I was getting up the courage to take her hands in mine, she stunned me by saying:

"Pierre, I'm pregnant."

"By whom?" I answered, growing pale.

She rose to her feet, radiant.

"No one."

She put on her coat and pushed the chair back in place. There was a magnificent smile on her face.

"Thank you, you said the words that I was expecting. I came all this way to hear you say those two words. I took a bit of risk."

I stuttered; I wanted to get up, but the table leg was . . . She made a gesture:

"Don't move."

Her eyes shone.

"I got what I wanted. I couldn't bring myself to leave you. I can't spend my life waiting for you, but I . . . Nothing. I needed to hear those two words. I needed to see your cowardice. To experience it up close, do you understand? No, don't move . . . Don't move, I tell you! Don't move! I have to go now. I'm so tired . . . If only you knew how tired I was, Pierre . . . I . . . I can't do this anymore . . ."

I stood up.

"You are going to let me leave, right? You are

going to let me? You have to let me leave now, you have to let me . . ." Her voice caught. "You're going to let me leave, aren't you?"

I nodded.

"But you know I love you, you know that, don't you?" I finally managed to say.

She moved away and turned back before opening the door. She looked at me intently and shook her head from left to right.

. . .

My father-in-law got up to kill an insect on the lamp.

He emptied the last of the bottle into his glass.

'And that was the end?'

'Yes.'

'You didn't go after her?'

'Like in the movies?'

'Yes. In slow motion . . .'

'No. I went to bed.'

'You went to bed?'

'Yes.'

'But where?'

'At home, of course!'

'Why?'

'A great weakness, a great, great weariness . . . For several months, I had been obsessed by the image of a dead tree. At all times of the day and night, I dreamed

I was climbing a dead tree and that I let myself slide down its hollow trunk. The fall was so gentle, so gentle . . . as if I were bouncing on the top of a parachute. I would bounce, fall farther, and then bounce again. I thought about it constantly. In meetings, at the dinner table, in my car, while I was trying to sleep. I climbed my tree and let myself fall.'

'Was it depression?'

'Don't use such a big word, please, no big words . . . You know how it is at the Dippels'.' He chuckled. 'You said so a while ago. No moodiness, no bile, no spleen. No, I couldn't allow myself to give in to that kind of whim. So I came down with hepatitis. It was more convenient. I woke up the next day and the whites of my eyes were lemon yellow. Everything tasted bad, my urine was dark, and the deed was done. A vicious case of hepatitis for someone who travelled a good deal, it was patently obvious.

'Christine undressed me that day.

'I couldn't move . . . For a month I stayed in bed, nauseous and exhausted. When I was thirsty, I waited until someone came in and held out a glass, and when I was cold, I didn't have the strength to pull up the coverlet. I no longer spoke. I forbade people to open the shutters. I had become an old man. Everything exhausted me: Suzanne's kindness, my powerlessness, the whispering of the children. Could someone please close the door once and for all and leave me alone with my sorrow? Would Mathilde have come if . . .

Would she . . . Oh . . . I was so tired. And all of my memories, my regrets, and my cowardice just knocked me down even more. With half-closed eyes and stomach churning, I thought about the disaster my life had been. Happiness had been mine, and I had let it slip away in order to not complicate my life. And yet it was so simple. All I had to do was hold out my hand. The rest could have been settled one way or another. Everything falls into place when you're happy, don't you think?'

'I don't know.'

'But I know. Believe me, Chloé. I don't know much, but I know this. I'm not more psychic than the next person, but I'm twice your age. Twice your age, do you realise that? Life is stronger than you are, even when you deny it, even when you neglect it, even when you refuse to admit it. Stronger than anything. People came home from the camps and had children. Men and women who had been tortured, who had watched their loved ones die and their houses burn to the ground. They came home and ran for the bus, talked about the weather, and married their daughters off. It's incredible, but that's the way it is. Life is stronger than anything. And who are we to be so self-important? We bustle about, talk in loud voices, and for what? And then what happens, afterward?

'What happened to little Sylvie, for whom Paul died in the next room? What happened to her?

'The fire is going out.'

He got up to put another log on.

And me, I thought, where do I fit into all of this?
Where am I?

He crouched in front of the fireplace.

'Do you believe me, Chloé? Do you believe me when I say that life is stronger than you?'

'Certainly . . .'

'Do you trust me?'

'That depends on the day.'

'What about today?'

'Yes.'

'Then I think that you should go to bed now.'

'You never saw her again? You never tried to find out how she was? Never called her?'

He sighed.

'Haven't you had enough?'

'No.'

'I called her sister, of course, I even went there in person, but it didn't do any good. She had flown the coop . . . To find her, I had to know in which hemisphere to start looking . . . And then, I had promised I would leave her alone. That's one of my outstanding qualities, by the way. I'm a good loser.'

'What you're saying is completely ridiculous. It's not about being a good or bad loser. That's completely stupid reasoning, stupid and childish. It wasn't a game, after all . . . or was it? Was it all a game?'

He was delighted.

'Really, I don't have to worry about you, my girl. You have no idea how much I respect you. You are everything that I'm not, you are my star and your good sense will save us all . . .'

'You're drunk, is that it?'

'You want to know something? I've never felt so good in my life!'

He lifted himself to his feet by holding on to the mantelpiece.

'Let's go to bed.'

'You haven't finished . . .'

'You want to hear me ramble on some more?'

'Yes.'

'Why?'

'Because I love a good story.'

'You think that this is a good story?'

'Yes.'

'Me too . . .'

'You saw her again, right? At the Palais-Royal?'

'How did you know that?'

'You told me yourself!'

'Oh really? Did I say that?'

I nodded.

'Well, then, this will be the last act . . .

'That day, I invited a group of clients to the Grand Véfour. Françoise had organised everything. Good vintages, flattery, excellent dishes. I pulled out all the stops. I had been doing the same thing forever, it seems . . . The lunch was utterly boring. I've always hated that sort of thing, spending hours at the table with men I don't give a damn for, being forced to listen to them go on about their work . . . And in addition, I was the killjoy of the group because of my liver. For a long time, I didn't drink a drop of alcohol and asked the waiters to tell me exactly what was in each dish. You know the type of pain in the arse I mean . . . Plus, I don't really care for the company of men. They bore me. They're the same as they were at boarding school. The braggarts are the same, and so are the brownnosers . . .'

'So, there I was at that point in my life, in front of the door of a fancy restaurant, a bit sluggish, a little weary, tapping another big cigar, dreaming of the moment when I could loosen my belt, when I caught sight of her. She was walking fast, almost running, and dragging a small, unhappy boy behind her. "Mathilde?" I murmured. I saw her turn pale, and the ground open under her feet. She didn't slow down. "Mathilde!" I said more loudly, "Mathilde!" And then I ran after her like a crazy thing. "Mathiiilde!" I nearly shouted. The little boy turned round.'

*

'I invited her for a coffee under the arcades. She didn't have the strength to refuse; she . . . She was still so beautiful. I tried to act naturally. I was a bit awkward, a bit stupid, a bit too playful. It was difficult.

'Where was she living? What was she doing here? I wanted her to tell me about herself. Tell me how you are. Do you live here? Do you live in Paris? She answered grudgingly. She was ill at ease and gnawed the end of her coffee spoon. At any rate, I wasn't listening, I had stopped listening. I was looking at this little blond boy who had collected all the leftover bread from nearby tables and was throwing crumbs to the birds. He had made two piles, one for the sparrows and one for the pigeons, and was busily organising this little world. The pigeons were not supposed to take the crumbs from the smaller birds. "*Go away, you!*" he yelled in English, giving them a kick. "Go away, you stupid bird!" When I turned back toward his mother, about to speak, she cut me short:

"Don't bother, Pierre, don't bother. He's not five years old . . . He hasn't turned five, do you understand?"

I closed my mouth.

"What's his name?"

"Tom."

"He speaks English?"

"English and French."

"Do you have other children?"

"No."

"Do you . . . Are you . . . I mean . . . do you live with someone?"

She scraped at the sugar in the bottom of her cup and smiled at me.

"I have to go now. We're expected."

"Already?"

She stood up.

"Can I drop you somewhere? I . . ."

She picked up her bag.

"Pierre, please . . ."

'And then, I broke down. I didn't expect it at all. I began to cry like a baby. I . . . That child was for me. It was for me to show him how to chase pigeons, for me to pick up his sweater and put his hat on. It was for me to do that. What's more, I knew she was lying! The boy was more than four. I wasn't blind after all! Why was she lying to me that way? Why had she lied to me? No one has the right to lie like that! No one . . . I sobbed. I wanted to say that –

She pushed back her chair.

"I'm going now. I've already cried all my tears."

'And afterwards?'

'Afterwards I left . . .'

'No, I mean with Mathilde, what happened?'

'After that it was over.'

'Really over?'

'Over.'

★

There was a long silence.

'Was she lying?'

'No. Since then I started paying more attention. I compared him with other children, with your daughters . . . no, I think that she wasn't lying. Children are so big these days . . . With all the vitamins you put in their bottles . . . I think about him sometimes. He must be around fifteen today . . . He must be huge, that boy.'

'You never tried to see her again?'

'No.'

'What about now? Maybe she – '

'Now it's finished. Now I . . . I don't even know if I would still be capable of . . .'

He folded the fire screen.

'I don't want to talk about it anymore.'

He went to lock the front door and turned out all the lights.

I hadn't moved from the couch.

'Come on, Chloé . . . Do you see what time it is? Go to bed now.'

I didn't answer.

'Do you hear me?'

'So love is just bullshit? That's it? It never works out?'

'Of course it works out. But you have to fight . . .'

'Fight how?'

'Every day you have to fight a bit. A little bit each day, with the courage to be yourself, to decide to be happ –'

'Oh, that's beautiful! You sound just like Paulo Coelho . . .'

'Go ahead and laugh, go ahead . . .'

'Being yourself, does that mean walking out on your wife and kids?'

'Who said anything about walking out on the kids?'

'Oh, stop it. You know exactly what I mean . . .'

'No, I don't.'

I started to cry again.

'Go on, leave. Leave me alone. I can't take any more of your noble sentiments. I can't take them anymore. It's too much for me, Mr. Bare-Your-Soul, it's too much . . .'

'I'm going, I'm going. Since you ask so nicely . . .'

At the door of the room, he said:

'One last story, if I may?'

I didn't want to hear it.

'One day, a long time ago, I took my little daughter to the bakery. It was rare for me to go to the bakery with my daughter. It was rare for us to hold hands, and even rarer to be alone with her. It must have been a Sunday morning, and the bakery was full of people buying fruit tarts and meringues. On the way out, she asked me for the tip of the baguette to eat. I refused. *No,* I said. *When we're at the table.* We went home and sat down to eat. A perfect little family. I was the one who cut the bread. I insisted. I wanted to keep my promise. But when I handed the bread end to my daughter, she gave it to her brother.

"But you told me you wanted it . . ."

"I wanted it back then," she said, unfolding her napkin.

"But it tastes the same," I insisted. "It's the same . . ."

She turned away.

"No thank you."

'I'm going to bed, and I'll leave you in the dark if that's what you want, but before I turn out the lights, I want to ask one question. I'm not asking you, I'm not asking myself, I'm asking the walls:

'Wouldn't that stubborn little girl have preferred living with a father who was happier?'

www.vintage-books.co.uk